J

ALISTAIR GRIM'S ODDITORIUM

[AUG 18

CH

ALSO BY GREGORY FUNARO

Alistair Grim's Odd Aquaticum

ALISTAIR GRIM'S ODDITORIUM

GREGORY FUNARO

Illustrations by
VIVIENNE TO

DISNEP • HYPERION

Los Angeles   New York

Text copyright © 2015 by Gregory Funaro
Illustrations copyright © 2015 by Vivienne To

All rights reserved. Published by Disney • Hyperion, an imprint of Disney Book Group. No part of this book may be reproduced or transmitted in any form or by any means, electronic or mechanical, including photocopying, recording, or by any information storage and retrieval system, without written permission from the publisher. For information address Disney • Hyperion, 125 West End Avenue, New York, New York 10023.

Printed in the United States of America
First Hardcover Edition, January 2015
First Paperback Edition, December 2015
10 9 8 7 6 5 4 3 2 1
FAC-025438-15258

SUSTAINABLE FORESTRY INITIATIVE
Certified Chain of Custody
Promoting Sustainable Forestry
www.sfiprogram.org
SFI-01054
The SFI label applies to the text stock

This book is set in Adobe Caslon
Designed by Whitney Manger

Library of Congress Control Number for Hardcover: 2014012826
ISBN 978-1-4847-0899-6
Visit www.DisneyBooks.com

For Jack Schneider, Grubb's first fan.
And for my daughter, who gave me the most
powerful Odditoria of them all.
—G.F.

For my mother,
who never once made me sweep chimneys
—V.T.

Table of Contents

— O N E —

Grubb with a Double *B* 1

— T W O —

The Lamb *13*

— T H R E E —

The Boy in the Trunk 35

— F O U R —

Good Evening, Mr. Grim *51*

— F I V E —

A New Friend *69*

— S I X —

Pocket Watches Can Be Trouble *83*

— S E V E N —

The Man in the Goggles *103*

— E I G H T —

Shadows Fall *129*

— N I N E —

Unexpected Guests *147*

— T E N —

The Battle in the Clouds *175*

— ELEVEN —

A Lesson in Power *195*

— TWELVE —

Nigel's Secret *215*

— THIRTEEN —

Sirens' Eggs and Banshees, Please *241*

— FOURTEEN —

The Wasp Rider *261*

— FIFTEEN —

Prisoners *289*

— SIXTEEN —

There Be Dragons *311*

— SEVENTEEN —

In the Court of Nightshade *333*

— EIGHTEEN —

The Tournament *353*

— NINETEEN —

The Mirror *385*

— TWENTY —

One Last Bit *409*

From an article in *The Times*, London. May 23, 18—

WILLIAM STOUT SENTENCED TO HANG!

In light of a guilty plea and overwhelming evidence against the accused, the trial of the ruffian William Stout for the murder of Mr. Abel Wortley and his housekeeper, Mrs. Mildred Morse, of Bloomsbury, ended yesterday in the only possible way. The unhappy man was rightly convicted and sentenced to death for as cruel and cold-blooded a deed as was ever committed.

Readers of the *Times* will recall that Wortley, an elderly philanthropist and purveyor of antiquities, and Mrs. Morse were brutally struck down last month in a trend of burglaries that have become all too common amongst London high society. Thanks, however, to the steadfast police work of Scotland Yard, William Stout, an acquaintance and sometimes coachman of Wortley's, was quickly apprehended and charged with the crime. His plea of guilt, conviction, and subsequent execution shall prove, in the opinion of the *Times,* a shining example of Her Majesty's judicial system.

It is also the opinion of the *Times* that, with more and more villains roaming the streets of London, a little pain and cares on the part of the elderly might in some cases preserve them from such dangers.

Grubb with a Double *B*

The odd was the ordinary at Alistair Grim's. The people who lived there were odd. The things they did there were odd. Even the there itself there was odd.

There, of course, was the Odditorium, which was located back then in London.

You needn't bother trying to find the Odditorium on any map. It was only there a short time and has been gone many years now. But back then, even a stranger like you would have had no trouble finding it. Just ask a bloke in the street, and no doubt he'd point you in the right direction. For back then, there wasn't a soul in London who hadn't heard of Alistair Grim's Odditorium.

On the other hand, if you were too timid to ask for directions, you could just walk around until you came upon a black, roundish building that resembled a fat spider with its legs tucked up against its sides. Or if that didn't work, you could try looking for the Odditorium's four tall chimneys poking up above the rooftops—just keep an eye on them, mind your step, and you'd get there sooner or later.

Upon your arrival at the Odditorium, the first thing you'd notice was its balcony, on top of which stood an enormous organ—its pipes twisting and stretching all the way up the front of the building like dozens of hollow-steel tree roots. *That's an odd place for a pipe organ*, you might remark. But then again, such oddities were ordinary at Alistair Grim's. And what the Odditorium looked like on the outside was nothing compared to what it looked like on the *inside*.

You'll have to take my word on that for now.

And who am I that you should do so? Why, I'm Grubb, of course. That's right, no first or last name, just Grubb. Spelled like the worm but with a double *b*, in case you plan on writing it down someday. I was Mr. Grim's apprentice—the boy who caused all the trouble.

You see, I was only twelve or thereabouts when I arrived at the Odditorium. I say "thereabouts" because I didn't know exactly how old I was back then. Mrs. Pinch said I looked "twelve or thereabouts," and, her being Mrs. Pinch, I wasn't about to quarrel with her.

Mrs. Pinch was Mr. Grim's housekeeper, and I'm afraid she didn't like me very much at first. Oftentimes I'd meet her in the halls and say, "Good day, Mrs. Pinch," but the old woman would only stare down at me over her spectacles and say, "Humph," as she passed.

That said, I suppose I can't blame her for not liking me back then. After all, it was Mrs. Pinch who found me in the trunk.

Good heavens! There I go getting ahead of myself. I suppose if I'm going to tell you about all that trunk business, I should back up even further and begin my story with Mr. Smears. Come to think of it, had it not been for Mr. Smears taking me in all those years ago, I wouldn't have a story to tell you.

All right then: Mr. Smears.

I don't remember my parents, or how I came to live with Mr. Smears, only that at some point the hulking, grumbling man with the scar on his cheek entered my memories as if he'd always been there.

Mr. Smears was a chimney sweep by trade, and oftentimes when he'd return to our small, North Country cottage, his face was so black with soot that only his eyeballs showed below his hat. The scar on his cheek ran from the corner of his mouth to the lobe of his left ear, but the soot never stuck to it. And when I was little, I used to think his face looked like a big black egg with a crack in it.

His wife, on the other hand, was quite pleasant, and my memories of her consist mainly of smiles and kisses and

stories told especially for me. All of Mrs. Smears's stories were about Gwendolyn, the Yellow Fairy, whom she said lived in the Black Forest on the outskirts of town. The Yellow Fairy loved and protected children, but hated grown-ups, and her stories always involved some bloke or another who was trying to steal her magic flying dust. But the Yellow Fairy always tricked those blokes, and in the end would gobble them up—"Chomp, chomp!" as Mrs. Smears would say.

Mrs. Smears was a frail woman with skin the color of goat's

milk, but her cheeks would flush and her eyes would twinkle when she spoke of the Yellow Fairy. Then she would kiss me good night and whisper, "Thank you, Miss Gwendolyn."

You see, it was Mrs. Smears who found me on the doorstep, and after she made such a fuss about the Yellow Fairy, her husband reluctantly agreed to take me in.

"He looks like a grub," said Mr. Smears—or so his wife told me. "All swaddled up tight in his blanket like that. A little grubworm is what he is."

"Well then, that's what we'll call him," Mrs. Smears replied. "Grub, but with a double *b*."

"A double *b*?" asked Mr. Smears. "Why a double *b*?"

"The extra *b* stands for *blessing*, for surely this boy is a blessing bestowed upon us by the Yellow Fairy."

"Watch your tongue, woman," Mr. Smears whispered, frightened. "It's bad luck to speak of her, especially when the moon is full."

"It's even worse luck to refuse a gift from her," replied Mrs. Smears. "So shut your trap and make room for him by the fire."

"Bah," said Mr. Smears, but he did as his wife told him.

Mr. and Mrs. Smears had no children of their own—an unfortunate circumstance that Mr. Smears often complained about at supper when I was old enough to understand such things.

"That grub ain't free, Grubb," Mr. Smears would say, scratching his scar. "You best remember the only reason I agreed to take you in is because the wife said you'd make a good apprentice someday. And since we got no other grubs squirming about, I suggest you be quick about getting older, or you'll find yourself picking oakum in the workhouse."

"Shut your trap," Mrs. Smears would say. "He'll find himself doing no such thing."

Upon which her husband would just shake his head and say: "Bah!"

Mrs. Smears was the only person I ever saw get away with talking to Mr. Smears like that, but she died when I was six or thereabouts. I never had the courage to ask Mr. Smears what from, but I remember how old I was because Mr. Smears was very upset.

After the funeral, he knocked me down on the cottage floor and growled:

"Six years of feeding and clothing you, and what have I got to show for it? A dead wife in the ground and a useless worm what ain't fit for nothing but the workhouse!"

The workhouse was a black, brooding building located near the coal mines on the south edge of town. It had tall iron gates that were always locked and too many windows for me to count. Worst of all were the stories Mr. Smears used to tell about the children who worked there—how they were often beaten, how they had no playtime and very little to eat. Needless to say, I didn't have to be told much else to know that the workhouse was a place from which I wanted to stay as far away as possible.

"Oh please don't send me to the workhouse!" I cried. "I'll make you a good apprentice. I swear it, Mr. Smears!"

"Bah!" was all he said, and knocked me down again. Then he threw himself on his bed and began sobbing into his shirtsleeves.

I picked myself up and, remembering how gentle he was around his wife, poured him a beer from the cupboard as I'd seen Mrs. Smears do a thousand times.

"Don't cry, Mr. Smears," I said, offering him the mug.

Mr. Smears looked up at me sideways, his eyes red and narrow. And after a moment he sniffled, took the mug, and gulped it down. He motioned for me to pour him another and then gulped that one down too. And after he'd gulped down yet a third, he dragged his shirtsleeve across his mouth and said:

"All right, then, Grubb. I suppose you're old enough now. But mind you carry your weight, or so help me it's off to the workhouse with you!"

And so I carried my weight for Mr. Smears—up and down the chimneys, that is. Mr. Smears called me his "chummy" and told everyone I was his apprentice, but all he was good for was sitting down below and barking orders up to me. Sometimes he'd sweep the soot into bags, but most often he left that part of the job for me to do too.

I have to admit that all that climbing in the dark was scary work at first. The flues were so narrow and everything was pitch-black—save for the little squares of light at the top and bottom. And sometimes the chimneys were so high and crooked that I lost sight of those lights altogether. It was difficult to breathe, and the climbing was very painful until my knees and elbows toughened up.

Eventually, however, I became quite the expert chummy. But sometimes when we arrived back at the cottage, Mr. Smears would knock me down and say:

"Job well done, Grubb."

"Well done, you say? Then why'd you knock me down, Mr. Smears?"

"So you'll remember what's what when a job *ain't* well done!"

There were lots of chimneys in our town for me to sweep back then, and I always did my best, but life with Mr. Smears was hard, and many times I went to bed hungry because, according to Mr. Smears, it wasn't sensible to feed me.

"After all," he'd say, "what good's a grub what's too fat to fit in his hole?"

Oftentimes I'd lie awake at night, praying for the Yellow

Fairy to take me away. "Please, Miss Gwendolyn," I'd whisper in the dark. "If only you'd leave me a little dust, just enough to sprinkle on my head so I can fly away, I'd be forever grateful."

Mr. Smears made me sleep in the back of the cart in the stable. I was too dirty to be let inside the cottage, he said, and what use was there washing me when I would only get dirty again tomorrow? There was a small stove in the stable for Old Joe, Mr. Smears's donkey, but on some of the chillier nights, when Mr. Smears neglected to give us enough coal, Old Joe and I would sleep huddled together in his stall.

Of course, many times over the years I thought about running off, but if I did run, where would I run to? I'd only ever been as far as the country manors on jobs with Mr. Smears, and since I knew no trade other than chimney sweeping, what was left for me besides the workhouse?

I suppose things weren't all bad. Every third Saturday Mr. Smears would allow me to wash at the public pump and sleep on the floor in the cottage. The following Sunday we'd dress in our proper clothes and attend service like proper folk. After that, we'd stop in the churchyard to pay our respects to Mrs. Smears. Sometimes Mr. Smears would sniffle a bit, but I would pretend not to notice so as not to catch a beating. Then we'd arrive back at the cottage, whereupon I'd pour him some beer and keep his mug full until he was pleasant enough to allow me outside to play.

For six years or so things went on that way, until one day I blundered into a stranger who changed my life forever. Indeed, we chimney sweeps have a saying that goes, "A blunder in the gloom leads a lad to daylight or to doom."

I just never expected to find either inside a lamb.

— T W O —

The Lamb

n a cool autumn Sunday when I was twelve or thereabouts, Mr. Smears and I returned from the churchyard to find a note pinned to the cottage door.

"What's this?" Mr. Smears grumbled. He tore off the note and opened it. "Well, well, well," he said, scratching his scar. "A bit of pretty luck this is, Grubb."

Mr. Smears couldn't read, so I was surprised he understood the note until he handed it to me. "You know what this means?" he asked.

"Yes, sir," I said, my heart sinking.

On the piece of paper was a drawing of a lamb inside a square. This, I knew, stood for the sign at the Lamb's Inn. Next to the lamb was a crude drawing of a sun and an arrow pointing upward. This meant that Mr. Smears and I were to report to the Lamb's Inn at sunrise the following morning.

"Ha!" said Mr. Smears, smacking me on the back. "Looks

like we've got our work cut out for us, Grubb. But also a handsome profit if we play it right."

What Mr. Smears really meant was that *I* had my work cut out for *me*. I'd worked the Lamb's Inn before, and not only did I know there were lots of chimneys to be swept, I also knew that Mr. Smears would spend most of the day

drinking up his wages in the tavern with the inn's proprietor, Mr. Crumbsby.

Mr. Crumbsby was a round man with a bald head and thick, red whiskers below his ears. He had a jolly, friendly air about him, but I knew him to be a liar and cheat, and at the end of the day he would waffle on about how much of Mr.

Smears's drink was to be deducted from his wages. Then he would trick Mr. Smears into thinking that he was actually getting the better of him.

That's not what bothered me, however, for no matter how many chimneys I swept, my wages were always the same—a half plate of food and a swig of beer, if I was lucky. No, what sent my heart sinking was the thought of Mr. Crumbsby's twins, Tom and Terrance.

The Crumbsby twins were the same age as me, but they were fat, redheaded devils like their father, and together their weight added up to one sizable brawler. I'd had my share of run-ins with them over the years, and the bruises to show for it, but most of the time Tom and Terrance were much too slow to ever catch me.

And so the next morning, Mr. Smears and I set out for the Lamb's Inn just before daybreak—me in the back of the cart with the empty soot bags and brushes, Mr. Smears up front in the driver's seat handling Old Joe. It was only a short distance through the center of town, over the bridge, and up the High Road. And when next I poked my head out from the cart, I spied the outline of the Lamb up ahead of us in the gloom.

Whitewashed, with a stone wall that ran around the entire property, the Lamb's Inn cut an imposing presence against the thick North Country forests that spread out behind it.

The inn stood three stories high and rambled out in every direction just as wide. A hanging sign out front bore a lamb, while coach-and-horse signs at each end advertised its stables.

The inn itself was said to be over two hundred years old, but it had burned down and been rebuilt a few times with more and more rooms. I only mention this because that meant the flues had been rebuilt too, resulting in a confusing maze of narrow passages that twisted and turned into one another so randomly that even an expert chummy like myself could get lost up there in the dark.

Indeed, I had just begun to imagine the grueling day ahead of me, when all of a sudden, farther up the road, a shadowy figure stepped out from the trees. It appeared to be a man in a long black cloak, but before I could get a good look at him, he dashed across the road and disappeared behind the Lamb's stone wall.

Nevertheless, with my heart pounding, I waited for Mr. Smears to say something. Surely, I thought, he must have seen the man too. But Mr. Smears mentioned nothing about it, and as he steered Old Joe for the Lamb's stables, I dismissed the black-cloaked figure as a trick of the early morning shadows.

"Well, what do we have here?" said Mr. Smears, and he pulled to a stop alongside an elegant black coach. Its driver's seat was flanked by a pair of large lanterns, and on its door was emblazoned an ornate letter *G*. The horses had already been unharnessed and bedded in the stable, which meant that the owner of the coach (a Mr. G, I assumed) had spent the night at the Lamb.

"Looks like old Crumbsby's got himself a fancy pants," said Mr. Smears, jerking his chin at the coach. "I'll have to remember that at the end of the day when the devil tries to chisel me for my drink. Ask him for how much he took the fancy pants, I will. That'll soften him up when he starts waffling on about being strapped for cash."

Mr. Smears chuckled to himself and scratched his scar.

"Shall I unhitch Old Joe, sir?" I asked. I wanted to have a look inside the stables, for certainly Mr. G's horses must be a breed apart to pull so fine a coach.

"Bah," replied Mr. Smears, climbing down after me. "Let Crumbsby's man do that. It's only right, us coming here on such short notice."

Mr. Smears and I crossed the yard to the Lamb's back entrance. But before Mr. Smears could knock, Mr. Crumbsby opened the door and gave my master's arm a hearty shake.

"I thought I heard you, Smears," said Mr. Crumbsby, smiling wide. His eyes were puffy with sleep, and his waistcoat was still unbuttoned. "Good of you to come. Business has been slow of late, so I thought it an opportune time to secure your services."

"Business been slow, eh?" Mr. Smears said suspiciously,

and he jerked his thumb toward the fancy black coach. "Looks like you've taken up collecting coaches, then, eh, Crumbsby?"

"A late arrival yesterday afternoon," Mr. Crumbsby said, then he lowered his voice. "An odd fellow that one is, too," he added secretively. "Him and his coachman. Like something out of the Black Forest, I tell you, what with their pale faces and gloomy dispositions."

"As long as their money ain't gloomy," said Mr. Smears, then he smiled knowingly and lowered his voice too. "And nothing gloomy about the price of lodging going up, I wager. A fine gentleman he is for inconveniencing you during your cleaning season—or some excuse like that you must've given him, eh, Crumbsby?"

Mr. Crumbsby smiled guiltily and ushered us inside. The fires were already roaring as we entered the kitchen, and Mr. Crumbsby's wife gave us each a slice of bread and cheese before she and her two daughters set about readying the rooms. Of course Mr. Smears protested my share, until Mrs. Crumbsby made her husband promise not to count it against our wages.

"Besides," said Mr. Crumbsby, "we'll settle our account in the tavern at the end of the day. But I warn you, Smears: you're too shrewd a businessman for the likes of me. I have your word you'll deal me plain?"

"That you do," said Mr. Smears, munching slyly. "That you do."

"As for you, Grubb, you'll remember that you needn't bother with the kitchen. And you'll leave the keeper's cottage until Mrs. Crumbsby tells you it's ready. I expect the twins should be up and about by midmorning. Understand?"

"Yes, sir," I said, my stomach turning. Mr. Crumbsby treated his lovely daughters, Anne and Emily, as little better than servants. Tom and Terrance, on the other hand, got a sizable allowance every week for doing nothing. But unlike their father, they made no pretense of being strapped, and carried themselves about town like a pair of haughty princes.

"As for our lone guest," Mr. Crumbsby continued, "he's lodged on the second floor. North side, corner room, east wing. He's paid up for two nights but plans on departing late this afternoon. Wishes not to be disturbed until then, is what he said. I warned him about the goings-on today, but he told me not to fret. 'Sleeps the sleep of the dead' is what he said—his words, not mine. You best mind your step up there today, Grubb, and leave the northeast flues for last. You hear me, lad?"

"Yes, sir."

"Grubb knows what's what," said Mr. Smears, "and knows even better the back of my hand if he steps out of line. Ain't that right, Grubb?"

"Yes, sir."

"Come along, then," said Mr. Crumbsby, and he led Mr. Smears and me into the tavern. The Crumbsby girls had moved all the tables and chairs away from the hearth and laid out sheets of brown paper on the floor. These extended across the tavern to the front door so that I could come and go without tracking soot about the inn.

"All right, get on with it," said Mr. Smears with his boot on my bottom. And into the fireplace I went and up the chimney I climbed. "Be mindful of the rooms," Mr. Smears barked after me. "You know what's waiting for you if I find so much as a speck of soot on Mrs. Crumbsby's furniture."

"Yes, sir," I shouted back. Then I heard Mr. Smears chuckle and Mr. Crumbsby offer him a drink.

All morning I climbed and crawled, scraping my way up through the chimneys on the western wing. A hard go of it I had, and I was thankful when it was time to sweep the hearths and haul the soot bags out to the cart. By noon I'd lost track of how many chimneys I'd swept, but Mrs. Crumbsby and her daughters took pity on me and gave me a slice of beef and a biscuit before I tackled the keeper's cottage.

When that was finished, it was back to the inn for the east wing. The flues on this side of the building were much more difficult to navigate, and once or twice I lost my way and popped down the wrong chimney.

However, as the afternoon wore on, I grew more and more tired, and soon I found myself lost in a pitch-black maze of narrow flues. I can't tell you how many times I seemed to crisscross back on myself, crawling and squeezing my way around like a worm in the dirt, when finally I saw a light coming from below.

Mindful of Mr. Crumbsby's guest in the northeast corner, I popped down the chimney ready to shoot back up. Lucky for me it was one of the chimneys I'd swept earlier. I recognized the rolled up carpet and the covered mass of furniture in the center of the room.

Not so lucky for me, however, was that the Crumbsby twins were now in the center of the room too.

"Well looky-look," Tom said sneeringly. "An invader come to storm our castle."

The twins' freckled faces were smeared with jam. And even though they were dressed alike, I could always tell which one was Tom by the chip in his left front tooth.

"I thought I smelled something foul coming from the chimneys," he added, rising with a stick in his hand. He'd obviously been playing at swords with his brother.

"I thought I smelled something too," said Terrance, smiling wide. "A rat gone up and died in there is what I thought."

"You don't look dead," said Tom, stepping forward. "But you look like a rat. A big black rat what's left his poop in our castle."

"A *little* black rat is more like it," said Terrance, stepping up also. "His bottom still smelly from pooping, I wager."

"But there's nowhere to poop now, is there, rat?"

"Nowhere to run now, either."

The boys were right. Even though the Crumbsby twins were slower than honey in winter, they were too close for me to dart back up the chimney. And before I could think of what to do next, fat Tom Crumbsby came for me with his stick.

He swiped for my head, but I ducked the blow easily and sent him flying past me into the hearth. His face hit the stone straight on.

"Ow!" he cried, his hands flying up to his mouth. "My *toof*!"

But Terrance was close behind, and the two of us collided in a cloud of soot. Terrance held me in a bear hug for a moment, but on his next breath he loosened his grip and started choking.

"Agh!" he coughed. "Soot!"

I twisted free and rushed from the room, leaving great patches of black everywhere I stepped and on everything I touched. My stomach squeezed with horror at the sight of it—Mr. Crumbsby'll have my head, I thought—and then Tom began blubbering behind me. "My *toof*!" he shrieked. "Grubb broke my uhffer *toof*!"

"Stop him!" his brother called, but I was already down the hallway and heading for the stairs. I took them two at a time and ran into Mrs. Crumbsby on the landing. I nearly knocked her over, and whether from the sight of me or the trail of soot in my wake, the kindhearted woman let out a shriek that I thought would collapse the stairs from under us.

"My apologies, ma'am," I said as I flew past, but I didn't dare look back to see if she was all right, for when I reached the bottom of the stairs, Mr. Crumbsby was already waiting for me.

"What's this, what's this?" he gasped.

"My *toof*!" Tom Crumbsby cried from above. "He broke my uhffer *toof*!"

"Why, you little rat," Mr. Crumbsby growled, grabbing for my collar, but I quickly dodged him and dashed down the hallway. Emily, the elder of the Crumbsby girls, stepped out from the parlor, her eyes wide with shock.

"Pardon me, miss," I said as I passed.

The only way out for me now was through the tavern. And as I ran for it, above the din I heard a voice in my head telling me the Crumbsbys were the least of my worries. No, nothing could compare to what Mr. Smears had in store for me when we got back to the cottage. And at the exact moment I saw him swinging for me in my mind, the hulking man with the scar appeared in the tavern doorway.

"What's the row?" he growled.

"Stop him!" Mr. Crumbsby shouted behind me. But the

drink had long ago done its work, and in his confusion Mr. Smears lost his balance and braced himself against the doorjamb.

"Grubb!" was all he could manage, and I dove straight between his legs.

I slid for a stretch on my stomach then sprang to my feet, nearly slipped on all the sooty brown paper, then found my footing again and headed for the front door. Mr. Smears must have fallen as he turned round, for behind me I heard a thud and a "Bah!" and then Mr. Crumbsby shouting, "Out of my way, you oaf!"

The afternoon light was quickly fading, but I could see the outside world through the open door ahead of me. Freedom was within my reach—but then I saw young Anne Crumbsby, eyes wide, mouth gaping, with her hand on the door latch.

"The door!" Mr. Crumbsby shouted. "Close the blasted door!"

But I kept running and—oh, Anne! Sweet Anne!

The young girl giggled and let me pass!

"Thank you, miss," I whispered as I burst outside, but I never knew whether or not she heard me.

"After him!" Mr. Crumbsby cried from within.

"After him!" Mr. Smears cried too.

A pair of men who were approaching from the road blocked my way at the gate, so I darted left and ran around the inn along the high stone wall. I remembered there was a break in the wall by the keeper's cottage, but when I got there, I spied Mr. Crumbsby's groom and stableboy heading straight for me. They'd been poaching rabbits at the edge of the forest, and each carried with him a long-barreled musket.

I hesitated, when suddenly I heard Mr. Crumbsby and Mr. Smears out front shouting, "Which way? Which way?" and "You go left; I go right!" And so I stepped back inside the yard and ran past the keeper's cottage toward the stables.

The fancy black coach with the *G* on its door had been readied for departure. Its curtains were drawn, and a pair of fine black steeds had been harnessed at the fore. Drawing closer, I noticed the door to the storage bed was down, and on the ground at the rear of the coach I spied a large, black trunk. The coachman, distracted by all the racket, had abandoned it to investigate, and as I glanced toward the inn, I caught a glimpse of his coattails as he disappeared around the corner.

"What's all the commotion, Nigel?" a man asked. His voice, deep and genteel, had come from inside the coach.

Mr. G, I thought—and then I realized I'd stopped running.

"Nigel?" Mr. G called again.

All at once, it seemed, I could hear footsteps and voices approaching from every direction. I thought about making a dash for the stables, but when the coach's silver door handle began to turn, I decided to try for the trunk.

It was unlocked, and along with some neatly folded clothes there appeared to be just enough space for me. I climbed inside, pulled my knees up to my chest, and closed the lid. My heart pounded at my ribs, and I hardly dared to breathe, but what little air I allowed my lungs in the cramped, dark trunk smelled musky and strange.

In the next moment I heard the coach door swing open and the sound of heavy footsteps approaching in the dirt.

"Pardon me, sir," came a voice, panting. It was Mr. Crumbsby. "But did you happen to see a young boy come this way?"

"A beggar, he looks like," growled another voice—Mr. Smears. "Black with soot and fit for the gallows, is what he is."

"I've seen no one of the sort," said Mr. G. "But whatever he's done to you, I'm sure you gentlemen deserved it."

"Bah!" said Mr. Smears.

"Come on, then," said Mr. Crumbsby. And as the men hurried off, I heard Mr. Crumbsby's groom yell, "I'll ready the hounds, sir! He can't have gone far!"

Then the sound of more footsteps approaching.

"What was that all about?" asked Mr. G.

"Don't know, sir," said another man's voice, this one higher and friendlier than Mr. G's. "Something about a chimney sweep. Didn't get all of it, I'm afraid."

"Very well, then, Nigel. Let's be on our way."

"Right-o, sir."

I heard the coach door close, some more shuffling in the dirt, and then I felt myself being lifted up off the ground. My head thumped against the inside of the trunk as Nigel loaded it onto the storage bed and closed the door.

A moment later we were off. And after I felt us swing onto the road and pick up speed, I dared to raise the lid just enough to prop open the door and peek out.

The light had grown fainter, and above the horses and the rattling of the coach wheels I could hear Mr. Crumbsby's hounds baying in the distance. The Lamb quickly got smaller and smaller as we sped away, but only when I saw it disappear behind a bend of trees did I allow myself a sigh of relief.

We were heading southeast along the turnpike, which would take us around town and into the country. A bit of pretty luck, as Mr. Smears would say.

Mr. Smears!

And just like that my relief turned to horror. What was I to do now? Where could I go? Surely never back to Mr. Smears, or to our town, for that matter. Mr. Smears would find me and send me to the workhouse for sure!

I sank back down into the trunk and closed the lid. The workhouse and all the rest of it were too scary for me to think about now. Besides, I was safe for the moment where I was. And where was that? Why, inside a trunk on the back of a speeding coach, thank you very much. Come to think of it, I'd much rather spend the night all warm and snug in a trunk than in a cold stable. However, when I thought about Old Joe having to spend the night alone in his stall, I began to feel sad.

Chin up, I said to myself in the dark. *Mr. Smears'll find another chummy for Old Joe to huddle up with. First thing is to get as far away from Mr. Smears as possible, which you're already doing. Next thing will be to jump from the trunk when the time is right. That's plenty for you to worry about now.*

But how far from Mr. Smears was far enough? And how would I know when the time was right to jump? These questions were enough to keep me occupied as we traveled on. And occasionally I'd peek as though I'd hoped to find the answers out there in the passing countryside.

The darkness came quickly, but the moon was full, and when next I peeked from the trunk I spied a great buttercup-filled meadow rolling past me. It looked like waves of sparkling silver in the moonlight, and for a moment I tried to remember if I had ever seen anything so beautiful.

"That's far enough, Nigel," called Mr. G.

I shut myself back inside and listened as we came to a stop. Nothing. No footsteps or jostling from the coach, either. So I dared to crack open the lid again.

"Ready, Nigel?"

"Right-o, sir," the coachman replied.

"It's all yours," Mr. G said gently. Then I heard a strange cooing sound—like that of a pigeon, only higher—but before I had time to wonder at it, I was startled by a loud crack and a flash of blinding yellow light.

I thumped my head on the top of the trunk and shrank back inside.

The horses whinnied, and I felt a great lurch forward. We were moving again, but unlike before, the coach was now shaking feverishly, up and down and side to side. I tried to open the trunk to see what was happening, but then the shaking abruptly stopped and a great force pulled me down.

Another lurch, this one more powerful than the first, and then everything became . . . well . . . *smooth* is the only way I could describe it. We were no longer moving, but it felt as if we were no longer stopped, either.

I cracked open the trunk and a great wind rushed past me, blowing the soot from my hair like the tail of some great black comet. I could see nothing but sky, and popping my head out a bit farther, I realized the sky was not just above me but all around me too.

I flung open the trunk, lifted the storage bed door, and peered out over the side of the coach.

It took a moment for everything to sink in.

There was the meadow of silver buttercups rolling beneath me; beyond that, great patches of jagged black trees; and farther still, clusters of tiny lights and the outline of our town against the sky. I recognized the steeple to our church, and for some reason felt sorry that I hadn't had a chance to properly say good-bye to Mrs. Smears before I went flying about the countryside.

That's when it hit me.

"I'm flying!" I gasped.

And then I was falling backward into the trunk again— the sound of the lid slamming down on me the last thing I remember before everything went black.

— THREE —

The Boy in the Trunk

I suspect Nigel must have awakened me when he unloaded the trunk from the coach. But as I came to, everything was so still and quiet there in the cramped darkness that I thought I'd fallen asleep inside one of Mr. Crumbsby's chimneys. The air was hot and stale, and my mouth was dry and tasted of soot.

"Oh no," I whispered. "Mr. Smears will box me good for sleeping on the job."

Then I realized something was different about this particular chimney. The bricks beneath me were soft and cushiony, the ones next to me as smooth as glass.

Suddenly the flue shifted, and the entire chimney seemed to be lifted off the ground. I sensed I was moving—*traveling again*, that was it—and in a flash everything came back to me. The Crumbsby twins, the chase from the Lamb, the fancy black coach—and the trunk in which I was hiding!

But what about that crack of thunder? What about the

flash of yellow light and all that flying about the countryside?

A dream? Well, of course it had to be a dream. After all, even a humble chummy like myself knew that people didn't just go flying about in fancy black coaches.

The coach! I was no longer on the coach speeding away from the Lamb. No sound of galloping horses, no sound of rattling wheels, only the thumping of my heart in my ears and footsteps beneath me. Yes, I was being carried on someone's shoulders!

Then I heard a heavy clang, like the sound of the iron gate at the churchyard, and the trunk came to a stop.

"Do you require anything else, sir?" asked a familiar voice. The coachman—Nigel, was his name.

"Take the trunk up to my chambers, will you?" said another voice—Mr. G, the owner of the fancy black coach. "And be sure you put a blanket on the horses when you return them to the stables. It's a bit chilly this evening."

"Right-o, sir," Nigel said, and then I was moving again.

The air was stifling, and I felt a tickle in my throat as if I would cough.

I swallowed hard, then swallowed again, and thankfully the tickle left me—but I hardly dared to breathe out of fear that at any moment the trunk's lid would swing open and Mr. Smears would haul me out by the hair.

But I'd left Mr. Smears behind at the Lamb, hadn't I?

Along with the Crumbsbys and Old Joe and the cart and the soot bags. The fancy black coach had taken me south along the High Road, which meant that I'd left behind the cottage and the stable and the churchyard—*the whole town*, for that matter—too.

The town! I remembered seeing it from the air, far beyond the meadow of silver buttercups just before I—but no, that couldn't be. I'd only dreamed all that. Yes, I must have fallen asleep inside the trunk on the way to . . . Well, that was the question now, wasn't it? On the way to *where?*

I was answered with the loud clang of another iron gate, more footsteps beneath me, and what sounded like an entire guild of blacksmiths hammering away in the distance. And as Nigel walked on, the racket grew louder and louder until finally the hammering came at me from every direction.

Then Nigel abruptly stopped and said, "Hallo, hallo, what's this?"

My heart leaped into my throat. I was sure he was speaking to me. But then a girl's voice answered jubilantly, "Why, hello there, Nigel. Back so soon?"

"Not soon enough, from the looks of it," Nigel said, annoyed. "You know right well you're not allowed down here without the boss!"

"Pshaw. You won't tattle on me, will you? I only wanted to have a quick look to see how things were coming along."

"Not my place to go tattling, Miss Cleona. And things look to be coming along quite nicely. Just about finished, from what I can tell."

"And from what *I* can tell, Uncle was successful on his trip to the North Country, was he not?"

"That he was, Miss Cleona, that he was."

"Splendid!" Cleona squealed. "Let's have a look at her."

"Now, hold up! No need to go flying off like that. The boss will introduce the two of you when he's good and ready. Come along, then, off to bed with—hallo, hallo, what do we have here?"

"What do we have where?"

"There in your hand tucked behind the folds of your gown?" No reply. "Now, now, don't go playing tricks on *me*, miss. I want no part of that business. Come on then, Cleona, cough it up." A brief moment of only hammering and then: "Just as I suspected. A book! You've been gadding about the library again!"

"I only wanted to read a little before bed."

"But the rules state clearly that no books are to leave the library without the boss's say-so. Them's the rules. *Period*."

"Pshaw. Uncle and his rules."

"Rules are rules for a reason, miss. And after your little trick of stacking all them books up to the ceiling, well, you're lucky you're allowed in the library at all."

"I know, but I'll return the book in the morning. I promise. I've been conducting research all week in case Uncle tries to trick me back." Another brief moment of only hammering. "Oh, please, Nigel," Cleona said. "I just wanted to make sure I knew everything before Uncle returned. Promise me you won't tell him, will you?"

"You're certain there's no trickery involved? I want no part of it."

"On my honor. No trickery involved whatsoever."

"Right-o, right-o," Nigel grumbled. "But I didn't see you, understand?"

"You're a gem, Nigel!" Cleona said, and her giggling trailed away.

Nigel giggled too, and then we were moving again.

Soon there came another loud clang, followed by a jumble of sounds that reminded me of the coal mines at the edge of town—chains and pulleys, winches and metal cranking against metal. Nigel set down the trunk, but it still felt as if we were moving—not sideways this time but upward into the air.

The hammering faded away, and when the cranking stopped, the sense of traveling upward stopped too. Another loud clang, and Nigel hoisted the trunk onto his shoulders with a grunt and started walking again.

"Hallo there, Mrs. Pinch," Nigel said, stopping. "Didn't expect to find you still up and about."

"Lots to do, lots to do," replied a weary voice. "And blind me if I haven't gone and misplaced my spectacles again."

"Shall I help you look for them, mum?"

"Certainly not. What kind of housekeeper keeps others from their beds because of her own carelessness?"

The trunk rose and fell quickly—Nigel shrugging, I assumed.

"Besides," said Mrs. Pinch, "they're in here somewhere. Got a speck of dust in my eye as I was laying out the linens, got distracted and—well, blind me if my head doesn't need oiling."

"You're sure it was you who misplaced them and not—"

"Oh, no, Cleona knows better than to play her tricks on me."

This Cleona seems awfully fond of tricking people, I thought, and Nigel shrugged again. "Right-o, then, mum," he said, setting down the trunk. "Off to the stables, I am."

"Head needs oiling, I tell you," Mrs. Pinch muttered distractedly.

"Good night, then, mum."

The coachman's heavy footsteps trailed away as Mrs. Pinch set about the room in search of her spectacles, all the while huffing and puffing and mumbling, "Blind me," when her search came up empty.

The tickle in my throat returned. I swallowed hard, but

the tickle only seemed to get worse. That's it, I was going to cough, no remedy for it now, so I pressed my face into Mr. G's clothes and let out a muffled, "Kipff!"

The tickle left me at once, but as I cocked my ear to listen, I noticed that all the huffing and puffing and blind me–ing outside had stopped. I waited, my heart pounding in terror, and then Mrs. Pinch began to hum pleasantly.

Dodged her for now, I thought. Yes, from the sound of things, it seemed as if Mrs. Pinch had set about the room again in search of her spectacles. Indeed, I'd just begun to entertain thoughts of an escape—when much to my surprise the trunk flew open and Mrs. Pinch screamed:

"Rat!"

Then she swung her broom and caught me square atop my head.

"Ow!" I cried.

Puzzled, Mrs. Pinch leaned cautiously over the trunk, her broom ready to strike.

"What on earth?" she said, squinting down at me. Then she slowly lowered her broom and exclaimed: "Why you're not a rat at all!"

"I'm afraid not, ma'am," I said, rubbing my head. "Though I must admit you're not the first person to call me that lately."

"Well, what on earth are you doing inside the master's trunk?"

I explained in short the circumstances surrounding my present situation, including how I came to live with Mr. Smears, as well as my apprenticeship as a chummy. Oftentimes I'd get ahead of myself, and Mrs. Pinch would become confused and ask me to go back. Her wrinkled face and squinty eyes seemed to soften when I told her about Mrs. Smears. However, when I got to the part about the trunk, her lips drew together so tightly that her nose nearly kissed her chin.

"Blind me!" she said. "You mean to tell me you're here by *accident*? A stowaway chimney sweep?"

I was about to reply, when I noticed the dimly lit room for the first time. The floors and walls were black, but at the same time glistened like polished coal. There were strange pipes of all shapes and sizes running everywhere, as well as curtains of purple and red velvet draped from floor to ceiling. The trunk had been set down at the edge of a fancy rug, and the furnishings, peppered about with knobs of silver and brass, were finer than anything I'd ever seen on jobs with Mr. Smears. There were statues and vases and all sorts of objects of which I didn't know the names. And at the center of it all, a grand four-poster bed. This, too, was draped in red and purple velvet, and emblazoned on the headboard, just like on the door to the coach, was a large silver letter *G*.

"Well?" Mrs. Pinch demanded. "What do you have to say for yourself?"

It was then that, glancing at the bed, I spied Mrs. Pinch's spectacles wedged between the coverlet and the bedpost.

"Spectacles," was all I could manage.

"Come again?" said Mrs. Pinch, squinting, upon which I reached out and gingerly retrieved them with my pinky finger.

"Humph," said Mrs. Pinch, snatching the spectacles from my hand. But once she slipped them on and saw how dirty I was, she opened her eyes wide and screamed.

"My apologies, ma'am." I closed my eyes and braced myself for the flurry of blows that I was sure would follow.

"Chin up, lad," Mrs. Pinch said after a moment. "A good thrashing is the least of what you need to fear here."

I opened my eyes to find the old woman standing before me with her broom tucked beneath her arm like a musket, the handle aimed straight at my heart.

"Now listen carefully," she began. "You're to step out of that trunk and march straight for the door. Once you're in the hallway, you're to turn left and keep marching until I tell you to stop. Understand?"

"Yes, ma'am."

"You're to keep your eyes straight ahead at all times. No peeking or ogling about, but straight ahead *at all times* no matter what. You hear me, lad?"

"Yes, ma'am."

"And you best mind my instructions, or blind me if you don't feel my broomstick on your bottom. Now march!"

And so I hopped from the trunk, turned left at the door, and set off down the hallway. Mrs. Pinch followed close behind, the tip of her broomstick lodged in the small of my back as if I were her prisoner. And I did try to obey her instructions, I truly did . . . but out of the corners of my eyes I couldn't help but notice a number of peculiarities.

The walls appeared to be of the same polished black as Mr. G's chambers, but they were lined with ornate sconces that burned with an eerie blue flame. Between some of the sconces were doors; between others hung large, gilded portraits that reminded me of ones I'd seen on jobs with Mr. Smears.

However, unlike the portraits in the manor houses, someone had marred the subjects with a bunch of swirly chalk mustaches. Even worse, on a portrait of a grim-faced little boy, someone had written: *A.G. has a spotty bottom!*

"That's far enough," said Mrs. Pinch. We'd come to a large, oaken door at the end of the hallway. The old woman scooted around me to give the brass handle a twist, and the door opened to reveal an iron gate behind it. Mrs. Pinch slid the gate sideways with a clang, and then scooted behind me with her broomstick at my back.

"Inside," she commanded.

The narrow chamber into which I'd stepped resembled a jail cell, the walls from top to bottom made of long iron bars. The cell itself appeared to be suspended inside a vast chimney, and as Mrs. Pinch closed the door and the gate behind me, I discovered the same eerie blue light shining down on me from higher up the shaft.

"Very well, then," said Mrs. Pinch. "You may turn around now."

As I did, the housekeeper shifted a large lever, which in turn set off the same cranking noise I'd heard earlier on my trip with Nigel. However, instead of moving upward, this time we were moving down!

Mrs. Pinch must have mistaken the expression of amazement on my sooty face for one of fear, for she stared down her nose at me and said, "Come, come now. It's only a mechanical lift. Surely you've seen something of the sort in your line of work."

"Only when they sank a down-shaft in the coal mines, ma'am," I replied. "And that lift had to be cranked by a pair of blokes, each one bigger than Mr. Smears!"

"Well, we won't be traveling far down as any coal mines. Although blind me if I shouldn't just move the master's bed down here, what with his nose always buried in his books."

The lift came to a stop, and Mrs. Pinch ushered me into a small parlor.

"Although you deposited most of your soot on the master's clothes," she said, pointing her broomstick again at my heart, "you'll stand here by the hearth without touching anything until the master says you may enter. That is, *if* he says you may enter. Understand?"

"Yes, ma'am."

"Once I introduce you, don't speak unless spoken to. Be sure to speak clearly and to the point, and do not say anything casual, obvious, or irrelevant."

"Irr-*elephant*, ma'am?"

"The master is a very proper man," the old woman said, ignoring me. "And while he's very fond of children, you'll do well to at least pretend you have some breeding in you. So let's start with that spine of yours and leave off slouching!"

"Yes, ma'am," I said, and stood up straight as a pencil.

"Very well, then." Mrs. Pinch made to leave, but then stopped short of the door. "It just occurred to me. To whom shall I say the master is being introduced?"

"Grubb, ma'am."

"Grubb?"

"Yes, ma'am. No first or last name, just Grubb. Spelled like the worm but with a double *b*. In case the master would like to write it down."

"I see," said Mrs. Pinch, her wrinkles softening. "And judging from the tale you told me upstairs, I assume it was Mr. Smears who bestowed this title upon you?"

"Yes, ma'am. Or so his wife told me, ma'am."

"And how old are you, lad?"

"I don't rightly know, ma'am."

"Humph," said Mrs. Pinch, looking me up and down. "To the untrained eye, your small stature and malnourished frame would suggest a boy of nine or ten. However, judging from your tale, I would guess your age to be twelve or thereabouts. So twelve or thereabouts is what I'll tell the master."

And with that Mrs. Pinch disappeared through a pair of pocket doors at the far end of the parlor. Gazing around, other than the coal-black walls and eerie blue light, to my eyes the parlor appeared no different than others I'd seen on jobs with Mr. Smears. However, stepping out from the hearth, above the mantel I spied a life-size portrait of a lady that, unlike the portraits upstairs, had not been defaced.

The lady's hair was black and done up beneath a wide-brimmed hat, and she was dressed in a flowing black gown. She sat at a dressing table with a silver-handled mirror in her hand, as if she were admiring the large, blue-stoned necklace that hung about her neck. But her black eyes seemed to stare past the mirror with an expression of deep sadness. I thought this odd at the time, but I also thought the woman to be the most beautiful I'd ever seen.

Presently I heard muffled voices coming from the next room, and I stepped back onto the hearth and stood up straight. I tried hard to hear what the voices were saying, but when I could make nothing out, I began to go over Mrs. Pinch's instructions again in my head. I so badly wanted to make a good impression.

But little did I know that nothing could have prepared me for what was waiting beyond the door.

— FOUR —

Good Evening, Mr. Grim

The master will see you now," said Mrs. Pinch, standing in the doorway. But as I made to pass her, she held me back by the shoulder and whispered, "Not so fast, lad. Remember what I told you."

We stood at the entrance to an enormous library. Books filled the walls from floor to ceiling—ceilings so high that rolling ladders had to be used to reach the upper shelves. More books lay tossed about on the furniture, while others were stacked on the floor as high as my head.

As in the upstairs chamber, there were statues and vases and curtains of purple and red velvet, but also clocks and swords and other weapons that I couldn't name. To my right I spied a large hearth with a pair of plush armchairs; above the mantel, a fierce-looking lion's head with glowing red eyes. The remainder of this wall was taken up by more bookshelves, some containing mechanical objects the likes of which I'd never seen.

"Master Grubb," Mrs. Pinch announced, pushing me forward with her broomstick. "Twelve years old or thereabouts and very dirty, sir."

As I stepped into the middle of the room, I noticed for the first time a large desk behind the stacks of books on the floor. On top of the desk were more books and mechanical objects, as well as a large lamp burning with the same eerie blue light.

"You may leave us now," said Mr. G, unseen behind the books on his desk.

"Very well, sir," said Mrs. Pinch.

And with that I heard the pocket doors close behind me.

"Now then," Mr. G began. "From the brief account given me by Mrs. Pinch, I take it you've had quite a journey. You'll find a pitcher and a goblet on the table there beside you. Please pour yourself some water and drink."

I hesitated. The pitcher and goblet were finer than any I'd ever touched.

"No need to stand on ceremony, Master Grubb. You're welcome to it."

As I drained my goblet, I searched unsuccessfully for Mr. G between the books on his desk. On the wall behind him, however, I spied a wide row of polished steel pipes running from the floor to the ceiling. These were bookended on either side by oaken doors, which in turn were bookended by a pair of knights. Each wore a red, bell-shaped helmet with a horned crest and a scowling black face mask. Their body armor was painted to match, but was plated in such a manner that they looked like a quartet of big red beetles standing on their hind legs.

"Ah, you've noticed my samurai," said Mr. G. "Just a little something I acquired in my travels. They stand guard in case any busybodies try to get inside from the balcony. The pair behind you is merely a second line of defense."

I glanced round at the pocket doors and discovered two more suits of armor behind me, each holding a long spear.

"The samurai are from Japan and are considered amongst the fiercest warriors in the world. Congratulations, Master Grubb. You are the first person to have ever gotten past them alive."

I swallowed hard, and the ticking of Mr. G's many clocks seemed to grow louder.

"So, you're the troublemaker from the Lamb's Inn, eh? The lad about whom the owner and that chap with the scar were making all that fuss?"

"Yes, sir," I said guiltily.

"And am I correct in concluding that you slipped into my trunk during their pursuit of you? Perhaps only moments before our departure?"

"Yes, sir."

"An intriguing turn of events," said Mr. G, more to

himself than to me. "Tell me, Master Grubb, at any point between your departure from the Lamb and your arrival here, did you happen to peek out from your hiding place?"

I made to speak, but then quickly stopped myself.

"I suggest you consider your answer carefully," said Mr. G. "Your sooty face speaks volumes, and I'll know at once if you're lying."

"Yes, sir," I said finally.

"And what exactly did you see?"

"Well, sir," I began slowly, "I peeked out when we were leaving the Lamb, heard Mr. Crumbsby's hounds setting off after me, and saw the inn disappear round the bend. I suppose I also peeked out a handful of times along the High Road, but then . . ."

I hesitated one last time, for upon remembering Mrs. Pinch's instructions, I decided that a proper gentleman like Mr. G would not be interested in my silly dream of flying about the countryside.

"Then what?" asked Mr. G. "What else did you see?"

"Nothing, sir," I said quickly. "What I mean is, I must've fallen asleep, sir. For the next thing I remember is being carried in the trunk on Mr. Nigel's shoulders."

I waited for what seemed like an hour of clock ticking. Finally a tall, slender gentleman dressed entirely in black rose from behind the mountain of books on his desk.

I took in the most obvious of his features at once: longish, slicked-back hair, black-ringed eyes, and a drawn, chiseled face that glowed whitish-blue like the moon. He looked me up and down as if inspecting a horse, but at the same time I sensed something dangerous beneath his cold appraisal— when without warning he lurched forward on his desk and snarled, *"Liar!"*

His eyes blazed, and his thin lips stretched wide around a toothy grin.

Terrified, I spun on my heels and made for the exit—but the pair of samurai beside the pocket doors crossed their long spears and blocked my escape.

I shrieked, turned round, and saw that the other samurai had left their posts and were now coming for me around the desk—armor clanging, their swords drawn, and their eyes glowing blue!

I shrieked again, and as I raised my arms to protect myself, discovered that the silver water goblet was still in my hand.

Clang, clang, clang! The four samurai marched closer and closer, and without thinking, I flung the goblet at the nearest one.

The goblet struck the samurai's helmet with a heavy clank, knocking it to the floor. But where the warrior's head should have been, there was only a shaft of blue light shooting up from his body.

I gasped in horror, and the samurai stopped. The three with their helmets still attached turned their glowing blue eyes to their headless companion, who promptly waved his armored hand back and forth above his shoulders. Finding nothing there, he shrugged, and the four samurai resumed their advance as if nothing had happened.

Clang, clang, clang!

I backed away, but the two samurai by the door grabbed me by the shoulders.

"Please, sir!" I cried, struggling against their viselike grip. "I wasn't lying, sir, I thought it was a dream!"

"You're at the Odditorium, lad," said Mr. G, grinning cruelly. "And dreams are all we have here!"

Clang, clang, clang!

I closed my eyes, steeling myself to receive the samurai's sword points, and then my ears cracked with thunder and I felt a flash of heat across my face.

So this is what it's like to die, I thought. But in the next moment, a high-pitched voice cried out: "YOU SHALL NOT HARM HIM!"

The grip on my shoulders released, and I opened my eyes to find the entire room bathed in a milky-yellow haze. Incredibly, all of the samurai were moving away from me, but there was something strange in their retreat.

They're not retreating, I realized. They're flying!

Light as goose down on a summer breeze, the samurai floated up into the air, over Mr. G's desk, and back to their posts.

I barely had time to wonder at it, and then a bright yellow ball of light quickly descended from the ceiling and wrapped me in a cloak of shimmering stars.

Much to my astonishment, it was now *my* turn to fly. And in a single bound I floated, eyes wide and mouth gaping, over the armchairs and landed on the hearth.

The light flashed and flickered and began to swirl about me like a cluster of yellow fireflies—round and round, faster and faster—until a great wind lifted me onto my tippy-toes. Then all at once the fireflies turned black, gathered in a great, rolling mass before my face, and whooshed off behind me, spinning me round on my heels as they shot up the chimney and out of sight.

"Cor blimey!" I gasped, gaping at my hands and coat sleeves.

All the soot, every last speck of it, was gone from my body. My gray chummy clothes were cleaner than I'd ever seen them, and my skin—well, I suspected my skin hadn't been this clean since the day I was born.

"Splendid, lad!" Mr. G exclaimed, and I turned to find him coming around the desk. The malice was gone from his smile, and in the crook of his elbow he held the samurai's helmet.

I just stood there, frozen in amazement.

"Terribly sorry about all that," said Mr. G, smiling. "But it was necessary, Master Grubb, I assure you."

"A trick?" the high-pitched voice cried out, and I spun around to discover an enormous dollhouse suspended from the ceiling in the corner behind me. The door to the doll-house was open, and there, hovering before it, glowed another fantastical ball of bright yellow light.

"Not a trick, but a test," said Mr. G. Then he turned back to me and whispered, "And quite an effective test, at that."

I tried to speak, but my tongue felt frozen—when all of a sudden the yellow ball of light streaked out from the doll-house and stopped, trembling in midair, only inches from Mr. G's nose.

"How about you pick on someone your own size!" the ball hissed. It began to grow bigger and bigger until, along the edge closest to Mr. G's face, there appeared the faint but unmistakable outline of teeth.

"Temper, temper," said Mr. G, unmoved. "I never doubted for a moment that you'd intercede to protect the child. But the test had to be authentic; the child's fear, genuine. How else could I be sure your magic was powerful enough?"

"Because I told you it was, you skinny little *twig*!"

The ball growled, its teeth becoming clearer and sharper as they parted into a monstrous, gaping crescent.

"Oh, very well, then," sighed Mr. G. "Go ahead and gobble me up. See where that gets us in the end."

The yellow ball just hovered there for a moment, shaking with fury until finally it zoomed back to the dollhouse. The light popped and fizzled, and then a little yellow girl with dragonfly wings and crystal-blue eyes materialized on the roof. "Silly twig," she muttered weakly, then slumped down and pouted with her back against one of the chimneys.

"Fairies," groaned Mr. G, rolling his eyes. The little yellow girl growled in reply and hurled a ball of light in his direction. Mr. G dodged it, and the ball burst apart against a large, colorful top upon his desk.

The top rose into the air and began to spin of its own accord. Mr. G quickly scooped it up with the samurai's helmet and turned the helmet over on his desk. A flash of bright green light exploded through the scowling face mask.

Mr. G removed the helmet, and the top was motionless again.

"It was *you* I saw coming out of the Black Forest," I said in astonishment. "You captured Gwendolyn the Yellow Fairy!"

"Captured?" said Mr. G. "Oh, I think not, Master Grubb. Brokered an alliance is more like it."

"An alliance," cried the Yellow Fairy. "Hah!"

"An alliance out of *mutual necessity*," Mr. G said for her benefit as well as mine. "But then again, we needn't get into all that now." He leaned back on the edge of his desk and folded his arms. "No, the most pressing matter at hand is what to do with *you*, Master Grubb. I must confess, I had no intention of acquiring a chimney sweep in my travels."

My gaze dropped to my shoes. Now my head had room for nothing but thoughts of what was to become of me.

"From what Mrs. Pinch tells me," said Mr. G, thinking, "I certainly can't send you back to that chap with the scar. And to turn an orphan like yourself out on the streets of London—"

"London?" I gasped, eyes wide.

"You mean to tell me that you had no idea you're in London, lad?"

"No, I didn't, Mr. . . . uh . . ."

"Grim," he said with a slight bow. "Alistair Grim. Pleased to make your acquaintance, Master Grubb."

"Likewise, Mr. G—I mean, uh, Mr. Grim, sir."

"As I was saying, to turn you out now in your present situation would no doubt ensure you a life of beggary and thieving. There are the workhouses, of course—"

I swallowed hard, my stomach in my throat.

"—but most would rather die than live in such places. Then again, I can't very well let you go around London babbling on about fairies and whatnot. Of course, anyone who listened to you would think you touched in the head. But there's always the chance someone might take you seriously and make trouble for us here at the Odditorium."

"The Odd—uh—I beg your pardon, sir?"

"Odd-ih-*tor*-ee-um," Mr. Grim repeated. "Go ahead. Give it a try, lad."

"Odditorium," I said slowly.

"Very good, Master Grubb. A word unlike any other for a place unlike any other."

I glanced over at the Yellow Fairy, who was now listening intently and batting her thick, black eyelashes at me.

"Begging your pardon, Mr. Grim, sir," I said, daring to

meet his gaze. "But, if you don't mind my asking, sir, what sort of place is this Odditorium?"

Mr. Grim smiled and replaced the helmet atop the samurai's shoulders. "Well, that remains to be seen, now, doesn't it, Master Grubb?"

"If you say so, sir," I said uneasily.

"Tell me. In addition to hiding in trunks, do you possess any other talent of which I should be aware?"

"Talent, sir?"

"Yes, Master Grubb, something at which you excel."

"Well, sir, I—if I may be so bold—I do fancy myself quite the expert chummy."

"Which would imply that you excel both at climbing and at squeezing through narrow spaces. What else?"

"Well, sir," I said, thinking, "I can run fast, especially when I'm being chased by blokes bigger than me. And, I can read a bit—the lady who took me in taught me that before she died, as well as how to count my fingers and toes. I've since taught myself to read better and count higher and . . . well, I'm afraid that's about it, Mr. Grim."

"A boy of twelve or thereabouts who excels at climbing and squeezing through narrow spaces, who can also read a bit and count higher than his fingers and toes? Well, then, perhaps we, too, can broker an alliance."

"An alliance, Mr. Grim?"

"An alliance, Master Grubb. We have many chimneys here at the Odditorium, all of which have not been swept in quite some time. Come to think of it, having a resident sweep on the premises might not be a bad idea. Having a boy around who can read a bit and count higher than his fingers and toes might not be a bad idea, either. Therefore, I have a proposition for you: how would you like to work here, Master Grubb?"

"*Here*, Mr. Grim?"

"Here at the Odditorium, Master Grubb. And in exchange for your services, you shall be given room and board and a small salary, which shall be deposited weekly in your name at the Central Bank—less your pocket money, of course."

"Pocket money?" I asked, amazed.

"But of course, lad. After all, a boy in London without pocket money—well, that simply won't do, now, will it, Master Grubb?"

I couldn't speak and just stood there, eyes wide and mouth gaping.

"There's only one catch," said Mr. Grim, and he squatted down so that our noses nearly touched. "You're never to speak to anyone on the outside about what goes on here. *Never.* Not a single word about the Odditorium ever. Do you understand me, lad?"

"Oh yes, sir, Mr. Grim," I said, nodding. "You can count on me, sir."

"Then again, you haven't much of a choice, now, do you? For if you refuse and decide to go blabbing"—he shot a quick glance at the dollhouse—"well, let's just say Miss Gwendolyn won't always be around to protect you."

I swallowed hard, for the look in Alistair Grim's eyes sent a chill down my spine unlike any other that day.

"What do you say, then?" he asked, his demeanor friendly again. "Do we have a deal, Master Grubb?"

"Yes, sir," I said, smiling. My fear was gone, and all I could do was marvel again at my good fortune.

"Good," said Mr. Grim, offering me his hand. "Gentlemen's shake on it."

And so for the first time I shook hands with Alistair Grim. It was the first time I'd ever shaken hands with anybody. But I wonder now, had I known then what I was getting myself into—samurai or no samurai—would I have tried again for the door?

FIVE

A New Friend

I spent the night in the shop. That's what Mrs. Pinch called it. The shop.

"You'll spend the night in the shop," she said. "There's a bed in there that Mr. Grim uses when he's working. That should suffice until we can figure out what to do with you." Then she opened the door and said under her breath, "But blind me if I can't think of a more proper place for you than here."

The room I entered resembled the others only in its blackness and blue sconce light. It was tiny compared to Mr. Grim's library, but appeared even tinier because of all the rubbish inside. There were shelves with oddly shaped bottles and workbenches stacked with books and tinkerer's tools. And tumbling out from every corner was all manner of scrap metals and strange mechanicals. At the center of the room was a large worktable piled high with cogs and springs and gears of every sort imaginable.

"Very well, then," said Mrs. Pinch, pushing me toward the bed. Then she placed a large bowl of gruel on the worktable and handed me a spoon. "Eat your fill and get some rest. And for goodness' sake, don't touch anything. Understand?"

"Yes, ma'am."

"You'll begin work in the morning," Mrs. Pinch said as she was leaving. "Until then this door will remain locked." She stepped into the hall, but then turned back and said: "After all, we wouldn't want you wandering about in the middle of the night, now, would we?"

I swallowed hard.

"There's nothing to be afraid of, lad," said Mrs. Pinch. "You're amongst friends here."

"Thank you, ma'am," I said. "For everything, that is."

Mrs. Pinch cracked a smile and closed the door. Then I heard her key clicking in the lock and her footsteps trailing off down the hall.

I looked around for a moment, and upon finding no fairies or glowing samurai staring back at me, quickly gobbled up my gruel and lay down on the bed. I didn't feel sleepy, but thought both the gruel and the bed pleasant enough. Indeed, I had just decided that I couldn't remember a more pleasant place to sleep—or a more pleasant meal, for that matter— when I felt myself being dragged under.

"I suppose I am sleepy after all," I yawned.

What must have been a second later, I was out.

My dreams came to me in fits of flickering pictures from the day before. But mixed somewhere in the middle of it all was the girl I'd heard outside the trunk—Cleona was her name. She sat beside me in a meadow of moonlit buttercups, but for some reason I could not see her.

"Do you have a family?" she asked.

"No, I don't, miss," I replied.

"Well, you're to live with us at the Odditorium, aren't you? So that makes you family."

"If you say so, miss," I said, searching for her amidst the flowers. "But how come I can't see you, miss?"

"Because you're not allowed to. But I can see you."

"I wasn't allowed to talk to the children in the manor houses, but sometimes we couldn't help seeing each other."

"Pshaw," Cleona said, giggling. "What a silly boy you are, Master Grubb. May I play a trick on you sometime?"

"A trick, miss?"

"I'm only allowed to play tricks on my family."

"Shall you bring me trouble, miss?"

"A trick well done brings joy to both the trickster and the tricked. Besides, who would want to bring trouble on one's family?"

"I wouldn't know, miss."

"So then, may I play a trick on you sometime?"

"If it brings you joy, miss."

"Thank you, Master Grubb."

"You're welcome, Miss Cleona."

"You know my name?"

"I heard you talking to Nigel outside the trunk."

"Well done," Cleona said, giggling. "A bit of a trickster yourself, are you?"

"Begging your pardon, miss?"

"Go back to sleep now."

"Miss?"

"Sleep."

I must have obeyed her. And if I dreamed about anything else that night, I couldn't remember, for I awoke the next morning with a feeling that I'd just leaped across some great black chasm.

"I slept after all," I said, sitting up. But for how long? Long enough, I thought, for I certainly felt rested. And as I gazed around the shop for some sign of morning, it occurred to me that I hadn't seen a single window in the Odditorium anywhere.

Just then there came a crackling noise, followed by a sputtering *tick-tick* and a flash of blue light from the center of the worktable. Rising from my bed and drawing closer, I spied a large red-and-gold-checkered pocket watch quivering amongst the scattered clock parts. I picked it up and opened it.

"What time is it?" the watch asked. Startled, I gasped and let it fall. "Ach!" the watch said, flopping about the table like a fish out of water. Then, with a crackle and a flash of blue light, the watch sprang upright on its case and shouted:

"Mind yer step, ya neep! If it's a fight ya want, McClintock's yer man!"

The watch's face bore a ring of Roman numerals—I'd learned these years ago by counting the bongs from the clock tower at the center of town—but between the X and the II there was a pair of smiling, mechanical eyes. The pupils glowed bright blue like the eyes of the samurai, as did the watch's wide, smiling mouth, and its curved hands hung down at the VIII and the IV so that the face appeared to be that of a jolly old chap with a large mustache.

"Well?" the watch asked. "You for fighting or gawking, neep?"

"Neither, sir," I said. "And I don't mean to stare, but I didn't expect to meet a talking pocket watch this morning. I apologize for dropping you, sir."

"Silly bam," the watch chuckled. "It'd take more than a wee bairn like yerself to rattle ol' McClintock."

"McClintock?"

"Aye. Dougal McClintock. Only surviving son of Dougal the Elder, and chief of the Chronometrical Clan McClintock. And who might you be?"

"Why, I'm Grubb, sir."

"Grubb?"

"Yes, sir. Just Grubb. Spelled like the worm but with a double *b*."

"Never heard of a Clan Grubb," the watch said. "Never heard of a grub with a double *b* either. A foreigner ya must be, then. But foreigners are always welcome amongst the McClintocks. A pleasure to make yer acquaintance, Mr. Grubb."

"Likewise, Mr. McClintock."

"Call me Mack, laddie. All me friends do."

"Very good, then, Mack."

"Would ya mind picking me up again? Me eyesight ain't what it used to be."

I did so, and the watch's bright blue eyes seemed to study me.

"Hmm," he said finally. "Yer outsides look all right. Got yerself some trouble on the inside, then, have ya?"

"Trouble, sir?"

"Aye, laddie. This is Mr. Grim's shop for Odditoria what's giving him trouble, so that would indicate ya being both Odditoria and trouble, would it not?"

"Well, I must admit I've been quite some trouble to Mr. Grim, but I thought the Odditoria was *where* I am, not *what* I am."

"Ya silly bam," Mack chuckled. "Odditorium is *where* you are. Odditoria is *what* you are. Ya follow?"

"I'm afraid I don't, sir."

"Loosely defined, the word *Odditoria*, at once both singular and plural, is used to classify any object living, inanimate, or otherwise what's believed to possess magical powers. Thus, Odditori*ummmm* is the place, and Odditori*aaaaa* are those objects *inside* the place. I dunno how much clearer I can make it, laddie."

"Oh, that's quite clear now, thank you. However, I'm sorry to disappoint you, Mack, but as far as my being Odditoria, I'm afraid there's nothing magical about me."

"Rubbish," Mack said, hopping into my hand. "Yer here in Mr. Grim's shop, ain't ya? And since this is the place for Odditoria what's giving him trouble, it's only logical to conclude that you, too, must be both Odditoria and—tick—tick—"

McClintock crackled and flashed, and then his eyes went black and he stopped ticking.

"You still in there, Mack?" I asked. "Mack?"

I shook him, opened and closed his case, then tapped him gently on the XII on his forehead. This last bit did the trick, and he started ticking again.

"What time is it?" he asked, the blue light returning to his eyes.

"Judging by your hands—er, by your face, I should say—well, I gather the time is twenty minutes past eight o'clock, give or take a bit since last we spoke."

"Ach, ya don't understand," Mack said sadly. "Me time is always twenty past eight. No matter how often Mr. Grim sets me, eventually I stop ticking and me hands go back to eight and four. And Mr. Grim can't for the life of him figure out why."

"So that's makes you Odditoria and trouble? A pocket watch what's not only magical, but what also can't keep Mr. Grim's time for him?"

"Aye, laddie," Mack said, hopping back onto the table.

"And I dunno if I'll ever get outta this shop in one piece. Mr. Grim's got bigger problems now, which leaves only the scrap heap for ol' McClintock."

"The scrap heap?"

"Aye. After all, what good's a talking pocket watch to Mr. Grim if it can't properly keep his time for him?"

"Well, you're very good at talking. That should count for something. And you can hop about and shine as bright as the lamps in Mr. Grim's library. That should count for something too, I'd think."

"Yer very kind," Mack said, turning away. Then he stopped. "Hang on. *You* have been inside Mr. Grim's library?"

"Yes, sir, I'm afraid I have."

"But that's where Mr. Grim keeps me cousins!"

"Your cousins?"

"Aye, me cousins the clocks!"

"Magical clocks?"

"Nah, ya silly bam, but clocks what's keeping their proper time *without* magic!"

"I don't know about that, but there certainly are a lot of clocks in there."

"Grubb!" Mack cried, hopping to the edge of the table. "Me new friend, you've got to get me inside!"

"Inside Mr. Grim's library, you mean?"

"Aye, laddie!"

"But what for?"

"What for?" asked Mack, jumping from the table and onto my shoulder. "What for? So I can keep me time correctly, that's what for!" I looked at him quizzically. "Don't you see, laddie? If I were to join me cousins in the library, I'd always know what time it was no matter how long I stopped ticking!"

"That's true," I said, thinking. "But Mr. Grim certainly wouldn't approve of my going in there without his permission. I suppose I could ask him, but come to think of it, why haven't you asked Mr. Grim yourself if you can join your cousins?"

"Well, uh," Mack stammered. "I, uh, well, it's just that—tick—tick—"

Mack crackled and flashed as before, then stopped ticking altogether, and his eyes dimmed to black. I caught him as he fell from my shoulder, and was about to tap him again on his XII, but then I heard Mrs. Pinch's key in the lock.

I quickly returned McClintock to the table and stepped back just as Mrs. Pinch entered the shop.

"Already awake, are you," she said. "No snooping about or touching anything, I should hope."

"Oh no, ma'am," I said. "And good morning to you, Mrs. Pinch."

"Humph," she replied. "Now off to the kitchen with you. Lots to do, and blind me if I'm going to waste my day playing hostess to a chimney sweep."

As Mrs. Pinch ushered me from the shop, I was tempted to ask her the time for Mack's sake. But when I glanced back at the worktable and saw none of his blue light amidst the clutter, I assumed he was still out and unable to hear me.

Good thing, I thought. Mrs. Pinch struck me as the sort who didn't like answering questions, never mind telling little boys the time.

SIX

Pocket Watches Can Be Trouble

I t was only a short distance down the hallway to the kitchen, but to me it seemed like miles. The smell of freshly baked bread had taken over me, and instantly my stomach began to grumble.

"You're on the first floor now, Master Grubb," said Mrs. Pinch, eyes forward and always two steps ahead of me. "In addition to Mr. Grim's shop, on this level you'll find the kitchen and the servants' quarters."

We stopped at the entrance to the kitchen and Mrs. Pinch turned around.

"You see that door down there?" she asked, pointing to a large red-painted door at the far end of the hallway behind me. "That door is off-limits to you, Master Grubb. You're never to go in there for any reason, you understand?"

"Yes, Mrs. Pinch."

"You better, or blind me if my broomstick shan't be the least of your worries."

I nodded and followed Mrs. Pinch into the kitchen. Unlike the rest of the Odditorium, the windowless chamber had hardly a speck of black paint anywhere. And instead of the eerie blue light, in the ovens there burned a brilliant bloodred fire unlike any I had ever seen.

Other than that, the Odditorium's kitchen was nearly identical to the Lamb's. However, I must say that Mrs. Pinch's bread tasted much better than Mrs. Crumbsby's. She served it warm with butter and jam, and allowed me to sit at the table rather than send me out to the stable, as Mr. Smears was wont to do.

"Easy, lad," Mrs. Pinch said as I stuffed my face. "You'll make yourself sick at the rate you're going."

"My apologies, ma'am," I said, but I kept on munching. I felt as if I hadn't eaten in weeks, and could not remember having ever tasted anything so delightful.

"I take it your Mr. Smears thought it ill-advised to feed you," said Mrs. Pinch, sitting down across from me. "Wanted to keep you small for your job, did he not?"

"I suppose he did, ma'am."

Mrs. Pinch's expression softened. "Well, you needn't worry about that here. Blind me if I'm going to let a lad like you go starving. Happy tummy, happy chummy, wouldn't you agree?"

"Oh yes, ma'am," I said, smiling. Then, unexpectedly, a

closet door cracked open and out slipped a broom sweeping away of its own accord.

"Just a moment, please," said Mrs. Pinch, and she hurried over to the closet and stuffed the broom back inside. "It's not polite to gawk, Master Grubb," she said, noticing my amazement, and I quickly went on with my munching.

After breakfast, Mrs. Pinch snatched her broom from the closet and ordered me into the lift with a scraper and chimney brush. And as we traveled upward, I waited for her broom to fly out of her hand and start sweeping again. But when it didn't, I began to wonder if my eyes hadn't been playing tricks on me earlier.

Mrs. Pinch brought the lift to a stop and we stepped out into the parlor. The furniture had been covered with sheets, and another had been laid out on the floor before the fireplace.

"You're to sweep this chimney and this chimney alone," Mrs. Pinch said. "No wandering off into the flues as is your habit. And when you're finished, you're to summon me on the talkback."

"The talkback, ma'am?"

Mrs. Pinch pointed her broomstick at a small panel on the wall beside the lift. "Just flick that red switch there and speak into the wire screen above it. I'll be able to hear you from the kitchen. You understand me, lad?"

"Er, yes, Mrs. Pinch," I said tentatively. "But—begging

your pardon, ma'am—might I have a soot bag and, er . . . a *broom* to sweep the hearth?"

Mrs. Pinch looked down at her broom as if my request puzzled her, and then stepped into the lift.

"You needn't worry about that, Master Grubb," she said. "And you'll be sure to keep out of the master's library. I needn't remind you why."

Mrs. Pinch smiled knowingly and disappeared with her broom up the lift.

My eyes immediately flitted to the library doors and then up to the portrait above the hearth. The Lady in Black, I christened her. What was she looking at past her silver mirror? And what could possibly make such a beautiful woman look so sad?

I looked more closely at the stones in her necklace, the blue of which seemed to glow a bit brighter than the rest of the painting. And as I stood there on the hearth, my eyes eventually wandered back to the library doors.

"The blue stones in the Lady's necklace look like the eyes of the samurai," I said to myself. Suddenly, I felt something rumbling in my chummy coat. I reached inside my pocket, and when I pulled out my hand again, there was McClintock the pocket watch.

"Mack!" I exclaimed as I opened him.

"What time is it?"

"You never mind that. What are you doing in my pocket?"

"Doing me duty, I figure. After all, what's a pocket watch without a pocket?"

"But how'd you get in there?"

"I dunno, laddie. I pretended to be out cold in the shop so's to distract ya, and then somehow I dropped off the table and into yer pocket while ya were gabbing with the old witch."

"That isn't very nice of you to call Mrs. Pinch a witch."

"Well, she *is* a witch."

"And," I said, raising my finger, "it isn't very nice of you to sneak into people's pockets and then go lying about it either."

"On my honor, laddie! I'm telling ya, something just picked me up off the table and dropped me in yer—" Mack stopped. "Hang on," he said, turning round in my hand. "Are we where I think we are?"

"You never mind about that. You're going to get me into trouble unless I get you back to the shop."

"I told ya yer trouble already, lad. So I hope you'll forgive me for what I'm about to do."

And before I could ask what he meant, with a crackle and a flash Mack leaped from my hand.

"McClintock!" he cried as he sailed across the room. Mack hit the floor with a grunt, tumbled a bit, and slid the rest of

the way on his case. He waited until the very last moment to close himself, and then slipped neatly under the doors and disappeared into Mr. Grim's library.

"Mack!" I called after him, dashing across the room.

"I've made it!" I heard him cry from within. "I've—Hey! What are you do—?"

Then all was silent.

I listened at the door. Nothing.

"You come out of there, Mack," I whispered, tapping gently. "You hear me?"

No reply. I pressed my ear to the door but could hear nothing but the ticking of Mr. Grim's clocks on the other side.

I was in for it now, I thought. If Mack fizzled out again, surely Mr. Grim would find him and know I had something to do with it. Perhaps, if I quickly stepped inside, snatched Mack, and then quickly stepped out again, what harm could come of it? Gwendolyn the Yellow Fairy had already protected me once, and surely, if the samurai tried to attack me, she'd do so again. Wouldn't she?

I listened for a moment longer, took a deep breath, and resolved at once to give it a go. I cracked open the library doors and immediately spied Mack lying on the floor only a few feet away. His case was open again, but his eyes were black as coal.

"Serves you right," I whispered, and I slipped inside and scooped him up. "No tapping you awake this time."

I closed Mack tight, returned him to my pocket, and instinctively glanced up at the ceiling behind me. The dollhouse that had hung in the corner was gone, and there was no sign of Miss Gwendolyn anywhere.

Surely the samurai will attack me now, I thought, making to leave. But when I saw their eyes were no longer blue, my curiosity got the better of me.

I stepped farther into the room, and amidst the library's fascinating contents, for the first time I noticed the books themselves. I began to wander about. Some of the books bore words I did not understand, while on others I was able to read the entire title. *The Science of* appeared on many of the books, as did *Secret, Wonder,* and *Legend.*

"'Legend of the Thunderbird and Other Tales from the Americas,'" I whispered, reading aloud the title of a large book that had been left on an armchair.

In addition to *Americas,* there were three other *A* words that kept popping up. I could read *Adventure,* but gave up on *Alchemy* and *Archaeology* until another time. And then, of course, there was one word that kept popping up more than any other.

Magic.

I wandered past the fireplace and gazed up at the roaring lion's head. Its eyes seemed to pulse and flicker as if a red fire was burning somewhere behind them. I thought this strange, but soon other objects caught my attention too.

In addition to the spinning top and the countless books piled high upon Mr. Grim's desk, I noticed a silver mirror resting facedown atop a narrow wooden box. I recognized it at once as the same mirror from the portrait of the Lady in Black.

Impulsively I picked it up. However, when I turned the mirror around, I discovered that the glass was entirely black.

"What an odd mirror," I whispered. "I should think the Lady in Black would have a hard time seeing herself."

I could have sworn I heard someone giggle behind me, but when I spun round, no one was there. Must be hearing things, I thought, my heart hammering.

I set the mirror down on its box and was about to leave, when out of the corner of my eye I spied one of Mr. Grim's notebooks lying open on his desk.

Suffice it to say, my curiosity again got the better of me.

"Cor blimey," I gasped, flipping through the pages. In addition to Mr. Grim's countless entries—some made up entirely of strange symbols that I did not understand—there were drawings of the most horrible creatures imaginable. Goblins. Trolls. A dragon or two. And yet, out of all the terrifying faces staring back at me, there was one drawing that sent a chill up my spine unlike any other.

"'The Black Fairy,'" I whispered, reading the caption. However, Mr. Grim's depiction of the creature bore little resemblance to any fairy I'd ever seen. Unlike Gwendolyn, the Black Fairy had the body of a man and a pair of massive bat wings. Its head resembled a large cannonball with a pair of empty white eyes and a wide crescent of long, pointed teeth. These, too, were black, and stood out like rows of daggers against the white inside of the creature's mouth. Beneath the drawing, Mr. Grim had written:

2 August. I regret to say that my search for the Black Fairy has ended in failure. According to my calculations, however, the location of his lair is correct. This leaves only two possibilities: either the Black Fairy is dead, or—as I feared—he has allied himself with the prince.

"The prince?" I wondered aloud. "Could Mr. Grim mean His Royal Highness, Prince Edward?" I flipped through the pages again, but could find no mention of him—or any other of Queen Victoria's children, for that matter. No drawings of this prince either. Only the name Prince Nightshade scribbled over and over again, and oftentimes followed by a series of question marks, as in, *WHO IS PRINCE NIGHTSHADE??????*

"Who is Prince Nightshade?" I muttered to myself—and then I heard the murmur of voices in the parlor.

My heart froze. Someone was outside.

Good heavens, how long had I been prying about? The murmuring grew louder—someone was coming, drawing closer to the door.

Panicking, I returned the notebook to its proper place and dashed over to the hearth—not enough time to make my escape up the flue—so I hid myself behind some stacks of books nearby just as the pocket doors slid open.

"After you," said Mr. Grim.

Peering through a narrow space between the stacks, I saw enter a squat, sharply dressed gentleman with a wide velvet collar and a starched cravat. His bulging face flushed pink behind his waxed white mustache. He carried his hat and a silver-pommeled walking stick in one hand; in the other, a blue silk handkerchief that he dragged repeatedly across his glistening bald head.

"But I demand an explanation!" the gentleman said frantically.

"May I offer you some sherry?" asked Mr. Grim. "Perhaps a spot of tea?"

"Miscellaneous liquids? Is that your only defense, Alistair Grim?"

"Come, come," said Mr. Grim, closing the doors. "All this huffing and puffing is unbecoming of you, Lord Dreary. Please sit down and let us discuss this in a more civilized manner."

The man with the white mustache heaved a heavy sigh, dragged his handkerchief across his head, and plopped into an armchair at the center of the room. Mr. Grim handed him a glass of water, and as the gentleman gulped it down, Mr. Grim placed the silver mirror back inside its box and cleared off a pile of books from his desk.

"Now, then, Lord Dreary," he said, sitting in his chair. "How has London been treating you while I was away?"

"You know very well this isn't a social call, Alistair Grim. But your leaving London so abruptly, with no explanation before the grand opening—well it smacks of unreliability, man!"

"I assure you, Lord Dreary, my trip to the North Country had everything to do with our business venture here."

"Well, I demand to know how."

"You know I can't tell you that."

"Just as I thought," Lord Dreary exclaimed. "Can't tell me that, he says!"

"That is a fundamental clause in our agreement. You're to leave all technical aspects of the Odditorium to me, no questions asked."

"Collecting more of that Odditoria rubbish, I wager!"

"Rubbish?" said Mr. Grim, offended. "How dare you, sir!"

Lord Dreary sputtered for a moment, and then sank back into his chair.

"Oh, Alistair," he sighed, fingering his collar. "You don't know what I've been through. Our backers are demanding an explanation for the delay. And when I saw your lack of progress downstairs—well, I'm afraid I let my frustration get the better of me. I hope you'll forgive me, old friend."

"Apology accepted," said Mr. Grim, smiling. "But rest assured I'm doing everything in my power to move things along in a timely manner."

"Then let me speak plain," said the old man, leaning forward on his stick. "Your father and I were good friends as well as business partners. And no one was happier than I to see

Grim's Antiquities fall to you upon his death. But that was almost fifteen years ago. And to be fair, for a couple of years you did well by him, dealing respectably and expanding your business. But after Elizabeth—"

Mr. Grim stiffened, and Lord Dreary's gaze dropped to the floor.

"Forgive me," he continued. "But after that I saw you change, man. You became a recluse. And your trips abroad, spending your father's fortune on Odditoria—the most remarkable, exotic objects I've ever seen—but never selling a stick of it? Well, I don't mind telling you that even our old friend Abel Wortley thought it madness, man."

"But Abel Wortley has been dead for some time now, hasn't he? And if you don't get to the point, I fear I shall join him soon out of sheer boredom."

Lord Dreary stammered and shook, but my mind was spinning. Who were these people they were talking about? This Elizabeth and this Abel Wortley?

"Now, Alistair," Lord Dreary said, wagging his finger. "Let us not forget that you came to *me* out of financial necessity. Five years ago you boasted of creating the most spectacular attraction on the planet. A house of mechanical wonders, you called it, at the heart of which would be your animus, this mysterious blue energy that surrounds us." Lord Dreary pointed at one of the sconces with his walking stick. "And because of what you showed me that day—a small model of the Odditorium, powered by the animus—I agreed to enter into a business venture with you."

"And you know how grateful I am for your assistance, Lord Dreary."

"However, since that time, you've refused anyone but me even the slightest glimpse of what you proposed. You've allowed none of our business associates inside, and you have sworn me to secrecy."

"The need for secrecy is of the utmost importance. Of all people, you should know that by now, Lord Dreary."

"I do, and therefore I needn't remind you that our business associates have continued to back our venture upon *my* reputation alone."

"I've already taken down the screens and the curtains outside. They can't buy that kind of publicity!"

"Oh yes, the outside of the Odditorium certainly lives up to its name, but it is the *inside* about which our associates are concerned. We're a year behind schedule. A *year.*"

"Tell them all I need is another month."

"Great poppycock!" Lord Dreary gasped. "But the grand opening has already been rescheduled six times."

"Wonderful, then you should be an old hand at it by now."

"But, Alistair, if you would only reveal to me the *source* of your animus and how it works, perhaps I could convince—"

"Out of the question. It is too dangerous for you to even speak of the animus outside the Odditorium."

"A demonstration, then. Something powered by the animus that I could show our backers—like that small model of the Odditorium you showed me five years ago."

"Again, out of the question. If my blue energy should fall into the wrong hands—no, it's too risky. Until everything is ready, until all the security measures are in place, the utmost secrecy is essential. You know that."

Lord Dreary sighed and sank back into his chair. "Then I'm afraid you leave me no choice," he said after a moment.

"No choice?"

"Notwithstanding the calamity that has become our business venture, the rumors about what goes on in here are not kind, old friend. Alistair Grim: inventor, fortune hunter . . . and some say, mad sorcerer."

"Nonsense," said Mr. Grim, chuckling. But as he raked his hand through his long black hair, I could tell Lord Dreary's comment had winged him.

"Perhaps it is nonsense," said the old man. "But you can hardly blame people for talking. You've become nothing short of a recluse. And on the rare occasions when you do appear in public, well, I needn't tell you that skulking about the streets in your gloomy black cloak doesn't help much either."

Mr. Grim was about to protest, but Lord Dreary raised a hand to stop him.

"Nevertheless," he continued, "any talk of madness, in sorcery or otherwise, is enough to spook even the heartiest of investors. And therefore I regret to inform you that even my impeccable reputation isn't enough to save you now."

"Save me?"

"Yes, Alistair Grim. I've been instructed by our business associates to tell you that, pending the outcome of this meeting, all your accounts at the Central Bank are to be frozen immediately."

"*What?*" cried Mr. Grim, rising. "They can't do that!"

"Oh, I'm afraid they can," said Lord Dreary, and he produced a document from his coat pocket. "Per the agreement you signed five years ago, and I quote: 'If party one'—that's you, Alistair—'fails to open the Odditorium by the agreed upon date'—that was a year ago yesterday, Alistair—'at the discretion of party two'—that's our backers—'all liquid assets and material holdings belonging to party one'—that's you again, Alistair—'shall be seized and sold at public auction.' There's more in here pertaining to me, but I assure you that my future isn't nearly as bleak as yours."

"But we're so close!"

"Then prove it!" Lord Dreary thundered, rising. "If you won't allow them inside, give me something I can show them—something to prove that their money has not been wasted on a madman's folly."

Mr. Grim wheeled away and, leaning on the wall behind his desk, hung his head low—his hair in his face, his arms rigid against the pipes. "So it's proof they want," he muttered, caressing the polished steel. "Proof that I'm not a madman?"

"Proof that Alistair Grim is still a man of his word," Lord Dreary said, his voice tight with emotion.

"Very well, then," said Mr. Grim, stiffening. He raked his hair back and turned to face Lord Dreary. "Tell our backers to gather outside at promptly three o'clock this afternoon."

"Outside the Odditorium, you mean?"

"Precisely," said Mr. Grim, sitting at his desk. He opened a drawer and removed a sheet of paper, dipped his pen in his inkwell, and began to write.

"What on earth do you have in mind?" Lord Dreary asked.

Mr. Grim held up a finger, seemed to think for a moment, and then finished writing.

"Here," he said, passing Lord Dreary the paper. "Have the printer rush off two hundred of these—large type, something dramatic—and return them to me by noon. I'll take care of the rest."

"Hm," said Lord Dreary, reading. "This had better not be another one of your confounded delays."

"On the contrary," said Mr. Grim. "I should think our backers will be quite satisfied with what I have in store for them." Lord Dreary looked unconvinced. "In fact, after today, I guarantee you they'll insist on giving us all the time we need."

"Hm," Lord Dreary said again, staring at the paper.

"Now, if you'll excuse me," said Mr. Grim, rising, "I've got a busy day ahead of me. Allow me to see you out, Lord Dreary."

The gentlemen left the library, but only when I heard the lift cranking away in the parlor did I dare come out of my hiding place. I quickly slipped from the room, dashed for the hearth in the parlor, and set about my work in the flue as if I'd been there all along.

I did not pay my respects to the Lady in Black as had become my custom.

I was so worried about Mr. Grim that I forgot she was there.

The Man in the Goggles

When McClintock began trembling again in my pocket, I did my best to ignore him. I truly did. "I'm not speaking to you, Mack," I said, and carried on with my scraping. The flue was cold and cramped, and a pair of soot-caked pipes ran along one of the walls and disappeared high above me into an adjoining shaft. I barely had any space to move, but the old pocket watch kept at it, jiggling up and down and side to side so violently that I finally gave in out of fear he might leap from my coat and tumble down the chimney.

"What time is it?" Mack asked as I opened him.

"Time to get you back to the shop," I said. "That's twice you tricked me."

"Ach!" Mack cried, spinning round in my hand. "This isn't Mr. Grim's library!"

"Lucky for you, it isn't."

"What's this yer gabbing about?"

"Don't pretend you don't know. You fizzled out when you slipped under the library doors. I had to fetch you and ended up hiding in there while Mr. Grim spoke with Lord Dreary."

"Dreary? Never heard of that clan before. Is he a foreigner like you?"

"You never mind about that. But rest assured you're never going anywhere near those library doors again."

Mack heaved a heavy sigh. "Ah, well. That was me last hope. Now it's the scrap heap for sure."

"Best thing for you, I should think. What with all the trouble you've caused me."

McClintock's hands sagged, his eyes dimmed, and his face turned downward into my palm.

"My apologies, Mack. I shouldn't have said that."

"Nah, yer right, laddie," he said. "Ol' McClintock's never been good for nothing but trouble. I only hope that someday you'll find it in yer heart to forgive me."

"Well, of course I forgive you. But friends don't go sneaking into one another's pockets."

"I told ya, laddie, I fell in there by accident!"

"And we're both lucky Mr. Grim's samurai didn't attack, although I must admit I'm a bit puzzled as to why."

"Perhaps they fizzle out like meself from time to time."

"Perhaps," I said, thinking. "But if I were Mr. Grim, I wouldn't want you in my library either. What with all your shaking and leaping about, you're liable to break something. I suspect that's why you're not allowed in there, isn't it?"

"Ya found me out," Mack said, his case slowly closing. "Well, it's been nice knowing ya, Grubb. I only ask that ya remember me as I was. Steadfast and true, the once-bright-'n'-fightin' Dougal, chief of the Chronometrical Clan McClintock."

Mack sighed again and sniffled.

"Oh, now stop that," I said, prying him open. "No need to get all gobby eyed and gloomy. We'll figure out something to keep you off Mr. Grim's scrap heap."

"Ya mean it, laddie?" Mack exclaimed, his eyes brightening, his hands twirling back to VIII and IV.

"Gentlemen's shake on it," I said, wobbling his case. Then, in the light from Mack's eyes, I noticed my fingers were still clean. "Hang on," I said, holding Mack up to the sleeves of my chummy coat. "I've been scraping for some time now, and there's not a speck of soot on me anywhere."

Indeed, as I shined Mack's light on the chimney wall, I discovered the soot there to be red and glistening. "That's odd. I've never seen soot like this before."

"Neither have I," said Mack. "Then again, I've never seen soot at all before, so I suppose I'll have to take yer word on that one, Grubb."

Suddenly a voice called out from below. "Hallo, hallo?"

"Ach!" Mack whispered, trembling. "It's Nigel. If he finds

out I've left the shop he'll tell Mr. Grim, and then it's the scrap heap for sure!"

"Stop your jabbering then," I whispered back.

"Hallo?" Nigel called again. "You up there, lad?"

"Yes, sir," I shouted. "Not quite finished yet, sir."

"Change of plans," Nigel said. "You need to come down at once. Master's orders."

From my position in the narrow flue, I couldn't see below me, but I knew from the sound of Nigel's voice that he'd stuck his head into the hearth.

"Quick, Grubb!" Mack whispered. "Help me climb up the chimney!"

"Nonsense," I said. "Just close yourself and get inside my pocket."

"Ya don't understand, laddie! Nigel is Odditoria too!"

"What's all the row, lad?" Nigel called.

"Coming, sir," I said, shifting my weight. This caused some soot to fall, and I heard Nigel grumble below me in the hearth. Then I whispered to Mack, "Did you say Nigel is Odditoria too?"

"Odditoria what's got animus like me! He knows I've left the shop—I've got to make a break for it!"

Mack squirmed in my hand and I almost dropped him, when without thinking I tapped him on his XII. He crackled and sputtered, and then his eyes went black.

That's good to know, I said to myself, and slipped him back into my pocket.

I quickly shimmied down the flue and landed in the pile of strange red soot that had accumulated in the hearth. The soot didn't burst into a dust cloud like normal soot; it had the feel of river sand. However, when I looked up and saw Nigel, all thoughts of soot and sand disappeared from my head at once.

"Well, well," he said. "You're the Grubb from the trunk, eh?"

The man staring down at me was even taller than Mr. Smears and twice as wide. His bald, elongated head jutted forward from a pair of massive shoulders, and his arms hung limply at his sides as if they were too long for his body. He was dressed entirely in black, with a pair of dark goggles wedged between his heavy brow and cheek. They covered his eyes and the top of his nose completely and were fastened snug around his head by a thick leather strap.

An odd-looking bloke, I thought. But he doesn't appear to be Odditoria, let alone powered by the animus like Mack.

"I asked you a question, lad," Nigel said. "Something wrong with your hearing? Or is the sight of me a bit too much for your tongue?"

"Yes, sir," I stammered. "I mean, no—I mean—yes, sir, I'm the Grubb from the trunk, and no, sir, my hearing is just fine, thank you very much."

"Right-o, then," Nigel said, extending his hand. "Nigel's the name, no need to call me sir. Gentlemen's shake if we're going to be working together."

"Working together?"

"That's right. Mr. Grim's orders."

Nigel's big beefy hand swallowed mine past my wrist. He shook it twice, his grip gentle but firm, then he picked up a stack of papers from one of the covered tables.

"You see these handbills here?" he asked, sliding one off the top for me. "We're to pass these out to people in the street. Public relations, Mr. Grim calls it."

I was able to recognize most of the words as Nigel read aloud:

MR. ALISTAIR GRIM,
DISTINGUISHED INVENTOR,
FORTUNE HUNTER,
& PURVEYOR OF ANTIQUITIES
PRESENTS
A SENSATIONAL & SPECTACULAR PREVIEW
OF HIS MECHANICAL WONDER,
THE ODDITORIUM!
ONE TIME ONLY!
THIS AFTERNOON! BEGINNING PROMPTLY AT
3 O'CLOCK!

YOU WON'T BELIEVE YOUR EYES!

"Right-o, then," Nigel said, heading toward the lift. "Let's be on our way—"

Presently a loud clanking noise rang out from the library— "Blast it!" cried Mr. Grim within—and Nigel and I rushed inside to find a pair of skinny black legs sticking out from the fireplace.

"Everything all right, sir?" Nigel asked.

"Oh, it's that blasted conductor coupling again," said Mr. Grim, shimmying out of the flue and onto the hearth. He had dressed down to his waistcoat and shirtsleeves, and in his right hand he held a small wrench. "And of course, today of all wondrous days, the loose connection is in a place I can't get to."

Frustrated, Mr. Grim tossed the wrench onto one of the armchairs, and as he stood up and brushed off his pants, some of that same, sandy red soot sprinkled down upon his shoes.

"Anything I can do, sir?" Nigel asked.

"Not in time for the preview," said Mr. Grim, raking back his hair. "In fact, unless the connection to the Eye of Mars is repaired, there's not going to be any preview."

"Oh dear," Nigel said. And as the men gazed up at the lion's head above the mantel, I noticed that the red light had gone out from the big cat's eyes.

So the lion's name is Mars, I concluded. Mr. Grim snapped his fingers and startled me from my thoughts.

"Master Grubb," he said. "Perhaps a lad of your experience is just what we need. Tell me, have you any knowledge of electromagnetic induction?"

"Er—uh—begging your pardon, sir?"

"Of course you don't," said Mr. Grim with a sigh. "Nevertheless, somewhere in that flue is a pair of pipes that need tightening. Under normal circumstances I would have to disconnect the entire network of pipes below in order to reach the faulty connection. However, given the immediacy of today's preview, there is simply no time for such an undertaking. Do you understand me, lad?"

"I believe I do, sir. You want me to climb up into that flue and get the eyes of Mars glowing again."

Mr. Grim looked confused, as if he hadn't expected my reply, and I pointed to the lion's head. "Mars," I said. "His eyes have gone black."

Mr. Grim and Nigel exchanged a look.

"But of course," said Mr. Grim, smiling thinly. "The lion's head, that's it."

I had the impression that he was hiding something, but him being Mr. Grim, I wasn't about to press the matter. "Well, what do you say, lad?" he asked, offering me his wrench. "You think you're up for the job?"

"You can count on me, sir!" I cried, snatching the wrench from his hand. And in a flash I was up inside the flue.

Almost immediately I was met with a tangle of pipes that took up nearly the entire shaft. None of them felt loose, however, so I squeezed myself past them and, feeling around in the dark, came upon a pair of pipes that rattled against each other.

"I think I've found them, sir," I called down, and set to work with the wrench. There was little space for me to move, but after a few minutes of twisting and turning, the pipes finally felt secure.

"I think that's done it, sir," I called again.

"Just a moment, please," said Mr. Grim. I heard a muffled hiss and what sounded like the squeak of a cabinet door opening in the library. Mr. Grim mumbled something in a language I did not understand, and then a low humming began and the pipes inside the flue grew warm.

"Ah, there we are," said Mr. Grim, relieved. Another squeak, another hiss, and Mr. Grim ordered me back down into the library.

Again I squeezed my way past the tangle of pipes, and as I emerged from the fireplace, I discovered that the light had returned to the lion's eyes.

"Job well done, Grubb!" Nigel said, patting me on the back.

Mr. Grim dashed across the room and flicked the switch on another one of those talkback contraptions beside the door. "Are you still in the kitchen, Mrs. Pinch?" he called. No reply. "Good heavens, Mrs. Pinch, where are you?"

"Blind me!" the old woman said finally. Her voice sounded muffled, but the irritation in her tone was clear. "Heaven forbid I should drop what I'm doing just to talk to you!"

"Are the ovens working again?" asked Mr. Grim, just as irritated.

"Why, yes they are," she said. "And I don't mind telling you that it's about time. Blind me if I'm going to spend my day—"

Mr. Grim flicked the talkback switch, and Mrs. Pinch's voice cut off.

"Splendid!" said Mr. Grim. "You have singlehandedly saved today's preview, Master Grubb. I am forever in your debt."

Mr. Grim gave a slight bow, and my heart swelled with

pride. I was feeling quite clever, too. From what I had seen in the kitchen, I gathered that, in addition to Mr. Grim's blue animus energy, there was some kind of *red* energy pumping through the Odditorium's pipes. Hadn't I felt its warmth in the flue, as well as seen it burning bright in Mrs. Pinch's ovens?

Come to think of it, I said to myself. *I'll wager all that soot I've been scraping comes from the red energy too.*

As to *how* all of it worked, well, I'm afraid I wasn't clever enough to figure that out yet. And it certainly wasn't my place to ask. I was just a chummy, and if there was one thing I learned from Mr. Smears, it was when to keep my trap shut.

"Now if you'll both excuse me," said Mr. Grim, sitting down at his desk, "there is much more work to be done."

"That there is, boss!" Nigel said, waving his stack of hand-bills. "Right-o, then. Come along, Grubb."

Following Nigel back into the parlor, I caught sight of something that stopped me cold. There on the hearth was Mrs. Pinch's broom, sweeping the soot into a bag all by itself!

"Good day to you, Broom," Nigel said, saluting. "Looks like old Mars left a mess for you in the library, too."

The broom parted its bristles and gave a slight curtsy, then carried on with its sweeping.

Nigel chuckled and said, "I wager you could've used a friend like Broom in your line of work, eh, Grubb?"

I just nodded, speechless, and followed Nigel into the

lift. Not a word was spoken as we traveled down to the floor below, but I was struck by how gentle the big man was in his movements, as if he was afraid he might break something.

We emerged into a small empty room about half the size of the parlor above, and as I followed Nigel to the door at the opposite end, I noticed for the first time not only how big his feet were, but also how unusually light and bouncy his step was.

Nigel produced a large key ring from his pocket and unlocked the door.

"This is the gallery," he said, waving me inside. "Stay close behind and watch your step. And don't touch anything, Grubb, or you might get yourself squished."

Nigel chuckled to himself and lead me through a dark and narrow maze of crowded wooden crates, some piled as high as the gallery's ceiling. Scattered between the crates was a most fantastical collection of objects: giant statues with animal heads, piles of shields and swords and helmets, a stack of oddly shaped brooms, and still another pile of colored glass balls as big as my head. In the center of the room was an enormous black cauldron, and finally, standing upright against the wall on the opposite side of the gallery, a pair of ornately decorated coffins.

"Bow your head, Grubb," Nigel said. "You're in the presence of Egyptian royalty."

"Begging your pardon, sir—I mean, Nigel?"

"Never mind," the big man snickered. "I'll explain it to you later."

We'd come to another iron door, and as Nigel unlocked the bolt, my eyes fell upon the pair of samurai standing guard there. Each held a sword like the samurai behind Mr. Grim's desk, and in the dim light of the gallery, I could see their eyes glowed blue behind their scowling black face masks.

"Good day, gents," Nigel said. The samurai did not respond, and we stepped out through the gallery door and onto a narrow landing.

As Nigel locked the door behind me, I peered over the balustrade. A pair of staircases curved down from either side of the landing to a grand reception hall below. Nigel chose the staircase on the right, and as I followed him down, he said:

"Now listen up, Grubb. You're to stick by me at all times. Most important, however, is to let me do the talking. If anyone speaks to you, you just say, 'Direct all questions to the man in the goggles.' That's me, you understand?"

"Yes, Nigel. Direct all questions to the man in the goggles."

Nigel nodded and we crossed the hall to the front door. Glancing behind me, I spied a life-size portrait of Mr. Grim on the wall between the two staircases. He sat proudly in an armchair—his face stoic, his black eyes piercing as in life— but in one hand he held a burning blue orb that glowed nearly as bright as the Odditorium's sconce light.

"Now, you remember what I told you?" Nigel asked.

"Yes, Nigel. Direct all questions to the man in the goggles."

"Right-o, then," Nigel said. Two more samurai stood guard at the front door. Nigel saluted them and unlocked the bolt. "Ready, Grubb?"

I took a deep breath and nodded, and then we stepped outside.

The sunlight blinded me for a moment, but still I was struck by the sense of bustling activity beyond my squinting—the clip-clopping of horses, the rattle of carriage wheels, the voices of people in the street. However, as Nigel and I descended the Odditorium's front steps, the street sounds began to die down. Indeed, by the time we reached the bottom, my eyes had adjusted well enough for me to see that everyone—including the horses and pigeons, it seemed—was staring at us.

Instinctively I turned around.

Gazing up at the Odditorium for the first time, I could hardly believe my eyes. There was an open-air balcony, on top of which stood an enormous pipe organ—its pipes twisting and stretching all the way up the front of the bulbous black building. A large silver letter *G* had been emblazoned on the door, and along the sides of the Odditorium four tall iron buttresses folded back on themselves like a quartet of mechanical legs.

"Any relation to Mr. Grim, young man?" a voice asked, and I whirled round to find a lady and a gentleman staring down at me. Londoners, I thought, looked just like people back home, only they were better dressed and spoke as if they were in a hurry.

"Have you been inside the Odditorium all this time?" the gentleman asked.

"Direct all questions to the man in the goggles," I said, looking up at Nigel. He smiled and gave me the stack of handbills.

"Start passing these out," he whispered. And in a flash, he sprang up the steps, spun round, and threw up his arms dramatically. "Ladies and gentlemen!" he shouted. "May I have your attention, please!"

A crowd had already gathered on the sidewalk, but I was able to gaze past it to the wonder of my surroundings. I had never seen such buildings, nor had I ever seen so many of them packed so tightly together. Most were as tall as the Odditorium itself, but some appeared even taller. Wrought-iron lampposts dotted the street in both directions, and the cobblestones themselves seemed to sprout people and coaches.

This whole place is magical, I thought, and decided at once that London was indeed the proper place for Alistair Grim's Odditorium.

"Ladies and gentlemen!" Nigel repeated. "Today, and only

today, comes the moment you've all been waiting for! At promptly three o'clock this afternoon, Mr. Alistair Grim shall present to you a sight unlike any other. A sensational and spectacular preview of his mechanical wonder, the Odditorium!"

A murmur of excitement spread among the crowd, and I took it upon myself to pace back and forth along the bottom step, waving my handbills.

"That's right," Nigel said. "Take a handbill! Take two, and give one to your neighbor! And be sure to tell your family and friends. Today, and only today, a sensational and spectacular preview of Alistair Grim's Odditorium!"

"What sort of preview?" a woman asked me.

"Is this another delay, lad?" asked another.

"Direct all questions to the man in the goggles," I said proudly. The crowd had grown thicker, everyone stepping closer and reaching for a handbill.

"That's right, ladies and gentlemen," Nigel shouted. "This afternoon's spectacular display will not only amaze you, but is also a preview of what to expect when the Odditorium opens exactly one month from Friday!"

"One month from Friday?" a man shouted. "You mean we can't come inside?"

"Not until the Odditorium's grand opening!" Nigel shouted. "Only one month from Friday!"

"But we've been waiting for over a year!" the man replied.

"We've been waiting over *five* years!" another man shouted.

"That's right," said someone else. "First it was the screens and curtains blocking the construction, and then that awful racket at all hours of the night—and still none of us has any idea what this blasted Odditorium is!"

The crowd grumbled in agreement. All the traffic in the street had stopped now, and I noticed for the first time a tall, well-dressed lad jostling for position only a few feet away from me.

"Let me see," he said, but a pair of gentlemen stepped in front of him and elbowed the lad back into the crowd.

"Now, now, ladies and gentlemen," Nigel said. "Your patience has been much appreciated. And believe me when I tell you that it shall be rewarded this afternoon! At promptly three o'—"

"Enough of this!" someone cried, and a small man with a top hat and a neatly trimmed beard stepped forward from the crowd.

"Why, if it isn't Judge Mortimer Hurst," Nigel said. "Retired city official and newly appointed director of the Queen's Museum Board of Trustees."

The judge sneered. "Oh, don't give me your pleasantries, Nigel Stout. Your boss knows better than anyone that such public displays require the proper permits. This is just another one of Alistair Grim's stall tactics—a trick to shift the blame for another delay onto city officials!"

As the crowd grumbled its displeasure, I felt a tug at my elbow. It was the tall, well-dressed lad I'd seen before.

"May I have one of them fancy papers, please?" he asked, and I slipped him a handbill from the top of my stack. "Thanks, chum," he said, and disappeared back into the crowd.

"I don't know nothing about no permits," Nigel said. "That's something you'll have to take up with the boss. You know I only work for Mr. Grim."

"Oh yes, I know your kind well, Nigel Stout," the judge said through clenched teeth. "I sentenced your brother William to hang for the murder of Abel Wortley, did I not?"

"That you did, Judge," Nigel said blandly. "That you did."

Abel Wortley, I said to myself. I had heard that name before in Mr. Grim's study. And to think that Nigel's own brother had murdered him!

"And furthermore," said Judge Hurst, "don't think for a second that I've forgotten how you appeared in London so soon after your brother went swinging. Doesn't take a market gardener to know that where one weed is pulled its twin will soon sprout."

"I might be William Stout's twin, sir," Nigel said, "but I'm not my brother. Been an upstanding citizen, I have.

Besides, William's done paid his debt. Done paid it and then some."

"All right, break it up!" a constable shouted, and he elbowed his way to the front of the crowd. "What's the trouble, Your Honor?"

"Hear, hear!" came another voice, and Lord Dreary emerged from the crowd too.

"Very good," said Judge Hurst. "Your timing is impeccable, Lord Dreary. I was just about to have that villain there hauled in for disturbing the peace."

"Disturbing the peace?" said Lord Dreary. "Have you gone mad, Hurst?"

"This Odditorium has been nothing but trouble from the start," said Judge Hurst. "An eyesore, a disgrace—and only two blocks from Her Majesty's museum!"

"There are no city ordinances against passing out handbills," Lord Dreary replied. "Mr. Stout cannot be blamed if these people stop and ask questions of their own accord."

"But this!" Judge Hurst exclaimed, holding up his handbill. "The laws are quite clear as to where such spectacles can occur!"

"Which is why I've personally filed all the proper permits on Mr. Grim's behalf."

"Call his bluff, Judge!" cried a voice from the crowd.

"Let Alistair Grim have his preview!" cried another.

More and more people began chiming in. Judge Hurst frowned and looked suspiciously at Nigel. The big man appeared sad—he just stood there, slouching at the top of the steps with his goggles turned down toward his enormous feet. Poor Nigel, I thought. All that talk about his brother William must have really winged him.

"What shall I do, Your Honor?" the constable asked. "That bloke's brother might've been a murderer, but I can't haul him in just for passing out papers."

"Very well," Judge Hurst said, crumpling his handbill into his pocket. "We shall see what Mr. Grim has in store for us after all."

The crowd cheered.

"Move these people along, constable," Judge Hurst said. "Life on our street needn't stop every time Alistair Grim spits."

The constable barked out his orders, and the men and women quickly dispersed, taking the remainder of my hand-bills along with them.

"Yes," said Judge Hurst, sneering up at the Odditorium. "We'll see what Alistair Grim has in store for us. And then Alistair Grim shall see what *I* have in store for *him*."

And with that, Judge Mortimer Hurst disappeared into the crowd.

"I was afraid of that," Lord Dreary said. Then he looked down at me and asked, "And who might you be, young man?"

"I, uh— Direct all questions to the man in the goggles."

"It's all right, Grubb," Nigel said, stepping down. He seemed his cheery old self again. "The lad here is just following orders, Lord Dreary. You see, sir, Grubb here works for Mr. Grim now too. Took him on last night, he did."

"Did you just call this boy a grub, Nigel?"

"Called him by his name is all. Ain't that right, Grubb?"

"That's right, sir. No first or last name, sir, just Grubb. Spelled like the worm but with a double *b*. In case you plan on writing it down, sir."

Lord Dreary narrowed his eyes at me. "Then you've been *inside* the Odditorium?"

"Yes, sir," I began, but then I remembered my discussion with Mr. Grim from the night before. "My apologies, sir. Mr. Grim told me not to talk about the Odditorium with anyone ever."

Lord Dreary chuckled. "That sounds like Alistair Grim, all right." He pulled out a pocket watch from his waistcoat and wound its knob. "Very well," he said. "If you wouldn't mind escorting me inside, Nigel?"

"Right-o, sir. Come along, then, Grubb. Our work's done here."

Lord Dreary returned his pocket watch to his waistcoat, and as I followed the men up the Odditorium's steps, I reached inside my chummy coat to check on Mack. In all the excitement, I'd completely forgotten about tapping him out in the chimney.

But when I felt inside my pockets, I discovered Mack was gone!

I spun on my heels, patting myself all over as my eyes darted down the steps to the sidewalk. There was no sign of Mack anywhere.

"What's the holdup, Grubb?" Nigel asked, and I turned back to see him and Lord Dreary staring down at me from the Odditorium's doorway.

My outsides froze, but my insides began spinning every which way—my heart racing as my brain frantically tried to retrace my steps. I knew at once Mack couldn't have leaped from my pocket somewhere inside the Odditorium. It was much too quiet in there and I would've felt him shaking.

But *outside* the Odditorium?

Yes, things had certainly been noisy enough—especially with all the yelling from Judge Hurst. But still, wouldn't I have felt Mack shaking inside my pocket?

Unless somebody snatched him, I realized in horror. Mack wouldn't need to shake himself free if someone else did the freeing for him.

Yes, that had to be it!

Thanks, chum, I heard the well-dressed lad say again in my head.

And all at once I knew what had happened.

A pickpocket! I said to myself.

"You all right, Grubb?" Nigel asked. "You look as if you've seen a ghost."

"Come on, lad," said Lord Dreary, annoyed. "I don't have all day."

Mr. Grim's words echoed in my head. *If my blue energy should fall into the wrong hands . . .*

And with that I bounded down the steps and took off down the street.

"Grubb!" Nigel cried.

"I'll come back!" I called over my shoulder. "I promise!"

"Grubb!" Nigel cried again, but I didn't stop to look at him.

At once I was swallowed up into the stream of pedestrians. I wasn't sure if I was headed in the right direction, nor did I know what Mr. Grim thought would happen if his blue energy should fall into the wrong hands.

Only one thing was certain: Mack had been right about me. I was trouble after all.

Shadows Fall

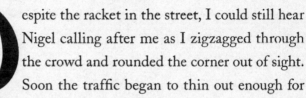

espite the racket in the street, I could still hear Nigel calling after me as I zigzagged through the crowd and rounded the corner out of sight. Soon the traffic began to thin out enough for me to see up ahead a stretch, and as I flew past row upon row of fashionable shops, I thought of the Crumbsby twins.

The pickpocket had worn a cap and a brown three-piece suit like fat Tom and Terrance wore on Sundays. He even had freckles and red hair like the Crumbsby twins, but his eyes were bright and mischievous, whereas Tom's and Terrance's eyes were little more than slits of coal-black malice.

A beating from Tom and Terrance is nothing compared to what's in store for me if I go back to Mr. Grim's without Mack.

Oh yes, Mr. Grim had been quite clear the night before about what would happen if I ever spoke to anyone about the Odditorium. And now I'd done something even worse. I'd gotten his animus lifted.

"It's all my fault," I muttered as I ran. "But no matter what, I've got to go back and tell Mr. Grim the truth."

The thought of returning to the Odditorium without Mack stopped me dead in my tracks. I had no idea where I was or how far I'd run. But as I gazed around trying to get my bearings, I saw a tuft of bright red hair sticking out from a lad's cap only a dozen or so paces ahead of me.

The pickpocket!

My heart leaped into my throat, but thankfully I thought twice about crying out. The pickpocket's legs were longer than mine, and he was still far enough away that he might be able to outrun me.

Suddenly the pickpocket stopped as if he'd felt my eyes on the back of his neck. I readied myself for a brawl, but the lad only patted his pockets and made for a shadowy lane to his right.

Following him at a distance, I rounded the corner just in time to see the heels of his boots disappear into a narrow alleyway between the shops. I ran after him, down a short flight of steps and through a winding maze of dirty passageways until I emerged into a cramped brick courtyard.

The pickpocket was waiting for me.

"I told ya lads I was tailed," he said, and I spun round to find that two other boys had closed in behind me. One was short and stocky with frog eyes and a gray woolen cap. The other was tall and thin with a square face and a flat nose. He wore a top hat cocked to the side and a fancy blue scarf around his neck.

"Look 'ere, me coveys," said the pickpocket. "If it ain't the little showman what was workin' outside of Mr. Grim's."

"I remember 'im," said the boy with the frog eyes.

"Me too," said the boy with the flat nose. "A proud bird he was, eh, Noah?"

"'At's right," said the pickpocket, stepping toward me. "I take it you ain't come 'ere to join our gang, birdie. Not with a posh job workin' for Mr. Grim."

I swallowed hard.

"'Owever," he went on, "I also take it we owe you a bit o' gratitude. What with all the commotion from you and your baldy friend, we took in quite a haul outside Mr. Grim's. Ain't that right, lads?"

"'At's right, Noah," said Frog Eyes and Flat Nose.

"Consider our debt paid, then," Noah said. "You turn 'round and fly on back to Mr. Grim's, and we let you take all your teeth with you."

Frog Eyes and Flat Nose laughed.

"You've something that belongs to me," I said, my voice tight.

"You mean *this*?" Noah said, producing Mack from his coat pocket.

"Yes. That's my pocket watch."

"Strange," Noah said, patting his pocket. "This 'ere is me pocket, ain't it, lads?"

"'At's right, Noah," said Frog Eyes and Flat Nose.

"And since this watch 'ere came out of me pocket," Noah said, dangling Mack in front of my face, "it's only logical that this watch belongs to *me*. Ain't that right, lads?"

"'At's right, Noah."

I made a grab for Mack, but Noah snatched him away. Frog Eyes and Flat Nose were on me at once, seizing me by the arms and pulling me back.

"The bird's a brawler," Noah said, smiling.

"Let 'im 'ave it," said Frog Eyes.

"'At's right, Noah," said Flat Nose. "Pluck his feathers."

Noah dangled Mack in my face again and said, "Time's up, birdie."

Frog Eyes and Flat Nose laughed, and Noah cocked back his fist. I clenched my teeth, bracing for his punch, but then the pickpocket began to bobble Mack like a hot potato. Noah quickly gained control of him and cautiously peered into his cupped hands. I couldn't see Mack, but I thought I glimpsed a flash of blue light on the pickpocket's dirty freckled cheeks.

"Don't open him!" I shouted—but it was too late.

"What time is it?" Mack cried, and all three boys let out a gasp.

"Cor blimey!" said Noah, his eyes wide. "A talking pocket watch!"

"Cor!" gaped Frog Eyes and Flat Nose.

"Made by Mr. Grim himself, I'll wager," Noah said.

"And who might you be, lad?" Mack asked.

"Give him to me!" I cried, trying to break free, but Frog Eyes and Flat Nose pulled me back.

"Is that you, Grubb?" Mack called, spinning round in Noah's hands. "Aye, laddie, there you are! What's all this about?"

"Mack!" I screamed, struggling.

"Pipe down, bird," said Frog Eyes, twisting my arm until I cried out in pain.

"What're you lads doing to me friend Grubb?" Mack asked.

"Come on, then," said Flat Nose. "Let us have a look, Noah."

"Naw," Noah said. "I pinched it from the birdie's pocket, so I gets to keep it."

"What's that?" Mack asked, spinning round. "Pinched me from me friend Grubb's pocket, did ya?"

"Quit yer jabberin', watch," Noah sneered. "You're mine, now."

Mack trembled and hopped—and without warning sprang from Noah's hand.

"*McClintock!*" he cried, and then clamped his case hard onto Noah's nose. The boy howled in pain, and his hands flew to his face.

"Get it off of me!" Noah cried, pawing at his nose in a flash of crackling blue.

Frog Eyes and Flat Nose just stood there gaping, but their grip on me released, and I quickly broke free and elbowed Flat Nose hard in the stomach.

"Oof!" he grunted, and then he dropped to the ground moaning.

Frog Eyes swung for my head, but I ducked and sent him stumbling past me.

Then, with a squeal of pain, Noah pried Mack loose and threw him down hard on the cobblestones.

"Mack!" I screamed, scrambling toward him—but the old pocket watch only laughed and said:

"Ha! It'll take more than that to scrap ol' Mack!" And then he flew up from the ground and cried, *"McClintock!"*

The pocket watch sailed past my head and smacked Frog Eyes square on his brow, whereupon Mack promptly fizzled out and tumbled to the ground.

Dazed, Frog Eyes collapsed on his bottom beside his mate, who was still moaning from my shot to his stomach. Then, unexpectedly, Noah knocked me down and went for Mack.

"Bite my nose, will ya?" Noah growled, and he raised his boot to stomp him.

"No!" I screamed—when out of nowhere a beefy hand clamped down hard on Noah's collar and lifted him clean off the ground.

"Nigel!" I cried, and the big man sent Noah flying backward.

The boy landed on top of his mates, and the three of them quickly scrambled to their feet and took off, running out of sight.

"Thank you, Nigel," I said. "But how did you find me?"

Nigel bent down and picked up Mack.

"Oh dear," he said, closing Mack's case. "Oh dear, oh dear, oh dear."

"I'm sorry, Nigel," I said. "I forgot he was in my pocket and—"

"Do you realize what you've done?"

I couldn't see Nigel's eyes behind his goggles, but the rest of his face was all fear.

"I know," I said glumly. "Mr. Grim told me what would happen if—"

"No, you don't know, Grubb," Nigel said, slipping Mack inside his coat pocket. "We need to tell the boss his animus has escaped. We've got to get back before—"

A strong breeze whipped through the courtyard, and what looked like a black cloud of smoke began billowing out from one of the darkened corners.

"Come on!" Nigel cried. "Let's get out of here!"

The big man scooped me up and slung me over his shoulder. And as he dashed with me from the courtyard, I caught sight of a pair of bright, burning red eyes blinking open amidst the smoke.

Nigel carried me back through the passageways, up the short flight of steps, and out into street. He paused briefly, and then dashed off in the opposite direction from which I'd followed the pickpocket.

"The Odditorium is the other way!" I cried. But then I saw another black cloud of smoke beginning to form in a shop doorway only a few yards away from us.

"There's no time to explain!" Nigel said, picking up speed. "Just tell me when we've lost them!"

"Lost who?"

"Just tell me!"

There was a handful of pedestrians milling about—and I was vaguely aware of their curious looks as we raced past them—but then a pair of burning red eyes slipped out from the shop doorway, followed by another pair from the passage we'd just left.

Both sets of eyes brightened as they caught sight of me, and I noticed for the first time that the smoke around them had taken on the shape of a pair of large black hounds. And yet at the same time I could see right through them, as if the beasts were made from the very shadows in which they moved.

My heart froze with terror as the pair of shadow hounds dashed off after us. But every time they came upon a shaft of sunlight that had managed to find its way onto the street, they slowed and skirted around it as if they were afraid.

"Do you see them?" Nigel asked.

Another red-eyed shadow hound joined the chase.

Then another!

And another!

"Yes!" I cried in horror. "There are five of them now!"

The other people in the street seemed not to notice them,

and soon the shadow hounds were right behind us, the five of them overtaking one another as if jostling for the lead on an invisible leash—when suddenly one of the hounds leaped straight for me.

Its paw swiped only inches from my face, the breeze ice-cold on my cheek. And then the hound landed in the street and tumbled toward a shaft of sunlight. Another hound immediately took its place at the head of the pack and made a leap for me too.

At the same time, Nigel rounded the corner and we emerged into a crowded open-air marketplace. The lead hound was close behind, but as soon as it hit the sunlight, the beast burst apart into a plume of smoke. Three more shadow hounds met the same fate and vanished one by one into thin air.

"Do you see them?" Nigel asked, panting.

"They're gone," I said, terrified.

"You're certain, Grubb?"

"Yes, the hounds broke apart as soon as they entered the square."

The marketplace was filled with the constant clamor of bell-ringing and shouting. From atop Nigel's shoulders I could see carts of hay and straw everywhere, while mounds of the same rose up amidst the endless stream of buyers and sellers like boulders in the middle of a babbling brook.

"That was a close one," Nigel said, setting me down. He stood bent over at the waist, gasping for breath with his hands on his thighs.

"What were they?" I asked, my throat tight with fear.

Nigel raised a finger to his lips, and when his breath had leveled off some, he stood upright, dragged his sleeve across his forehead, and stared up at the sky.

"We'll be safe here out in the open," he said. "At least until I can figure out the best way to get us back to the Odditorium."

Nigel felt inside his coat for Mack, then buttoned his pocket and led me to a large fountain at the center of the marketplace. Amidst the throng of peddlers who'd set up shop on the steps, Nigel found an opening for us to sit, and splashed some water on his head. Then he just sat there for a moment. Following his gaze through a break in the buildings at the far end of the marketplace, I spied a massive domed cathedral looming in the distance.

"A pity it's not a Monday," Nigel said. "Mondays and Fridays are the market days for livestock. You could rub yourself all over with their scent. That would make it harder for the doom dogs to track you."

"What are doom dogs?"

"Speak softly, Grubb," Nigel said, looking around. Then he leaned back on his elbows so that his mouth was close to my ear. "Doom dogs are what's after you now."

"After *me*?"

"That's right. And once a doom dog sets out after you, he's harder to shake than your own shadow."

I glanced around, terrified.

"Oh, it can be done, mind you. Especially during the day, when all you have to do is get them to follow you into the sunlight. You saw what happens to them then."

"Are those dogs spirits, Nigel?"

"A kind of spirit, yes, what can only roam about in the shadows."

I swallowed hard. Nigel stood up on the fountain's top step and gazed out over the crowded marketplace. After a moment, he nodded and sat back down beside me.

"Don't see any more of them, but they're hard to spot. And sunlight or no sunlight, once a doom dog latches on to you, you're as good as done for."

I shivered at the thought of how close the black hound's paw had come to my face—and then it dawned on me.

"It's because of Mack's animus," I said. "That's what Mr. Grim meant when he told Lord Dreary it was dangerous for his animus to leave the Odditorium. That's why those dogs came after me."

"You know about the animus?" Nigel asked in shock.

"I'm afraid I do."

I told Nigel the whole story—how Mack ended up in my

pocket, how I chased after him into the library and eavesdropped on Mr. Grim and Lord Dreary, and finally how I accidentally got him lifted. And when I'd finished, Nigel glared down angrily at his pocket.

"Oh, please don't be cross with Mack," I said. "He was only afraid you'd come looking for him because you'd found him missing from Mr. Grim's shop."

"What would I be doing in Mr. Grim's shop?"

"Well, since that's the place for Odditoria—"

I stopped.

"The place for *what*?" Nigel said, turning to me, and I saw my terrified face reflected in his goggles. Now I'd really gotten Mack into a pickle, I thought.

"Well?" Nigel pressed.

"Well," I sputtered, "I know it's not proper to repeat things, but Mack told me the shop is for Odditoria what's giving Mr. Grim trouble. And, well . . . silly as it may sound, Mack said that you were Odditoria too."

"Oh he did, did he?" Nigel said, glaring down again at his pocket.

"Please try to forgive him, Nigel. He was only afraid Mr. Grim would scrap him for wanting to be with his clock family in the library. And I suppose you can't blame him for that. I know if I had a family, even a family of clocks, I'd want to be with them too."

Nigel's whole body sagged, and as he stared off at the cathedral, his face grew even sadder than it had looked outside the Odditorium. I suspected he was thinking about his brother William again, but I did not think it proper to pry.

"Did I say something wrong, Nigel?" I asked after a moment, but the big man appeared lost in thought. "Nigel?"

Startled, Nigel smiled. And just as before, he instantly became his cheery old self again. "Right-o, then. All's forgiven on my part. As for Mr. Grim, I suppose you'll have to cross that bridge later. Come to think of it, what I wouldn't give for a bridge to throw you off."

Nigel's comment winged me, and I looked down sadly at my feet.

"No, no, Grubb," he said, chuckling. "I don't mean it like that. Just wish I had a bridge over a river in which I could wash your scent off."

"There's the fountain," I said, relieved.

"It's against the law to wash in there. And the last thing we need is the law on our backs, what with Judge Hurst looking for any excuse to make trouble for Mr. Grim."

The two of us sat there thinking hard amidst the clamor.

"May I ask you a question, Nigel?"

"Go ahead, Grubb."

"If the doom dogs can sniff out Mack's animus, how come they can't sniff out the animus inside the Odditorium?"

"Because the Odditorium is protected by the boss's magic paint."

"Magic paint?"

"The Odditorium is just a big machine powered by the animus—like Mack, only more complicated and without all the jabbering. However, it's safe to use the animus inside the Odditorium because the whole place is protected by Mr. Grim's magic paint. Mack, unfortunately, is not. Understand?"

"So that's why everything is black! The magic paint blocks the doom dogs from sniffing out the blue animus!"

"That's right. A concoction of dragon scales, troll's blood, that sort of thing. With great power most often comes danger, and one always has to be mindful of danger."

Made sense to me. I was used to being mindful of things that were dangerous. Fire, soaring heights, and crumbling old flues—not to mention Mr. Smears and the Crumbsby twins.

"I'm sure the boss will explain it to you someday—"

A rumble of thunder, barely audible above the din of the marketplace, stopped Nigel cold. He bounded up to the top of the fountain steps. "Oh dear," he said, staring off at the sky. "Oh dear, oh dear, oh dear."

"What is it, Nigel?" I asked, rushing up to him, and I spied a thick swath of black clouds rolling in behind the cathedral.

"He was closer to London than we thought."

"Who?"

"The prince," Nigel said weakly.

Another rumble of thunder—this one a bit closer—and then Nigel grabbed my arm and dashed off with me into the crowd.

— N I N E —

Unexpected Guests

M aybe that was the last of them," Nigel said, gazing about. "Or maybe they've lost track of our scent and are roaming about someplace else for us."

There had to have been over a dozen streets and alleyways that branched off from the marketplace, some so narrow that not even a single ray of sunshine managed to find its way to the ground. However, even down the darkest, narrowest passages, we could spy no sign of the doom dogs anywhere.

"What are we going to do?" I asked, beginning to panic. "What if there are more of those horrible hounds out there waiting for us?"

We'd stopped in front of a shop at the edge of the maketplace, trying to determine the safest way back to the Odditorium. The black clouds were quickly closing in on the great dome, the thunder rumbling more frequently now. And as the marketgoers whirled about their business in anticipation of the coming storm, Nigel squatted on his haunches so that his mouth was level with my ear.

"Now calm yourself, lad," he whispered. "And try not to let your fear get the better of you. After all, there's a natural balance of both good and evil in our world, and the doom dogs are only doing their job."

"What do you mean?"

"You see, sometimes spirits what belong in the Land of the Dead escape into our world, and it's the doom dogs' job to bring them back."

"But what does that have to do with the blue animus?"

"When the animus is used in a machine what's unprotected by Mr. Grim's paint, the doom dogs think it's an escaped spirit and come into our world to fetch it."

"Why would they think the animus is an escaped spirit?"

"Er, well, uh," Nigel stammered nervously, "all that's a bit complicated to explain right now. Suffice it to say that, once the doom dogs realize the animus is *not* a spirit, they still want a spirit to take back with them."

"You mean—?"

"That's right, Grubb. They snatch the spirit of the person what used the animus."

I gulped.

"Doom dogs are very good at what they do," Nigel continued, "so usually only a handful of them come over into our world at a time. There's a good chance we've seen the last of them."

"Do the doom dogs belong to the prince?"

Nigel snickered and shook his head. "Of course not," he said. "Doom dogs work on their own to keep the natural order of things—ruthless and independent with allegiance to no one. Even the prince can't control the likes of them. Which is why I'm more worried about those crows."

Nigel pointed up at the clouds, and I spied a large flock of the big black birds circling near the cathedral dome.

"Crows can sense when doom dogs have come into our world," Nigel said. "And so the prince has trained himself a flock to follow them. Most of the time they only lead him to doom dogs what's tracking a spirit. But *today*—"

"The crows will lead him to *me!*"

"So you see? All the prince has to do is send out his flock to follow the doom dogs, and then they'll lead him straight to you and the Odditorium."

"And by 'the prince,' you mean Prince Nightshade?"

Nigel gasped and clamped his big hand over my mouth.

"Mind your tongue, lad!" he hissed, and for the first time that day I was terrified of him. "Mr. Grim has forbidden anyone to speak of him outside the Odditorium." Nigel removed his hand. "Now tell me," he said, holding me by the shoulders. "How does a lad like you come to know the prince's surname?"

I swallowed hard and promptly confessed to what I had seen in Mr. Grim's notebook, including the drawing of the Black Fairy and all the question marks after the prince's name. Nigel pondered this for a moment, and then a smile hovered about his lips.

"Well, I suppose I can't blame you for being curious," he said. "However, I think it best we don't tell the boss you've been admiring his artwork. Wouldn't you agree?"

"Thank you, Nigel," I said, relieved, and the big man mussed my hair.

"Right-o, then. Let's get moving."

"But what about Mr. Grim's preview?" I asked, pointing to the clock tower at the center of the marketplace. "It's nearly three o'clock already."

"Yes, we've got to get back to warn him about the escaped animus before everything starts. Come on, then. Stay in the sunlight, watch out for coaches, and tell me if you see any red eyes lurking about the shadows."

Nigel started off, but I didn't move.

"What's the matter?" he asked.

"I just remembered that I saw only four doom dogs vanish in the marketplace."

"That's good. If only one is tracking you, he shouldn't be too hard to shake."

"But what if he's not tracking *me*?"

"What do you mean?"

"Well, if the doom dogs go after a person what's used the animus, wouldn't the doom dogs go after Noah and his gang, too?"

Nigel's brow furrowed and his body sagged. "Oh dear. I'm afraid in all the excitement I forgot about those lads. Should one of those dogs catch hold of them—"

Nigel swallowed hard and quickly shook off the thought.

"Right-o. That's another bridge we'll have to cross when we come to it. On our way, then, Grubb."

The two of us set off quickly—street after street, block after block—drawing angry words from pedestrians whose paths we abruptly crossed in order to remain in the sunlight. The closer we drew to the Odditorium, however, the closer the thunder drew too. And by the time I spied the Odditorium's big black chimneys above the rooftops, the skies had gone almost completely dark.

The crows, however, were nowhere to be seen.

"If there were any doom dogs on your tail," Nigel said,

looking up at the sky, "I'd wager those crows would be following you too."

"That's a relief. But do you think those clouds might scare people away from Mr. Grim's preview?"

"Not likely. Folks here in London have been waiting for years to see the Odditorium at work. A soak and a sniffle is a small price to pay, I should think."

As we approached the street on which the Odditorium was located, Nigel and I were met with a wall of people—everyone pushing and shoving each other amidst a great racket of shouts and police whistles.

"Stand back!" a constable commanded.

"Don't push!" cried another.

"Up you go, then, Grubb," Nigel said, and with one hand the big man scooped me up onto his shoulders. The Odditorium was clearly visible farther down the block, and the crowd in the street stretched out in every direction as far as I could see.

"Make way, make way!" Nigel shouted. "We're with Mr. Grim! Make way!"

Intimidated by Nigel's size, the crowd quickly parted before us without a word of protest. However, upon reaching the Odditorium we discovered Lord Dreary and Judge Hurst in the midst of a commotion. A handful of smartly dressed gents stood nearby (Mr. Grim's backers, I assumed) while a line of constables barked at the crowd to stay back.

"Look!" someone shouted. "It's Alistair Grim!"

All eyes turned upward, and there stood Mr. Grim, glaring down at us from the Odditorium's balcony—his expression steely, his bony fingers splayed out like tree roots upon the polished steel pipes of the balustrade.

The entire crowd immediately fell silent. Lightning flashed, and a loud clap of thunder exploded above our heads, but Mr. Grim gave it only a passing glance before he turned his back on us and sat down at his pipe organ.

"We're too late," Nigel said.

And amidst another rumble of thunder, Mr. Grim began to play.

A shiver of excitement rippled through the crowd. Mr. Grim's playing was magnificent, and after a quick series of expertly fingered flourishes, something strange began to happen. At first I thought my eyes were playing tricks on me. But once I heard the sound of creaking hinges and cranking gears, I knew it to be real.

The Odditorium was *moving*!

The crowd gaped and gasped, and as Mr. Grim's fingers picked up speed, the Odditorium picked up speed too—all of it twisting and turning and bobbing and weaving as if the entire building were alive and dancing to the music.

"It works," Nigel said to himself. "It actually *works*!"

We all stood there in awe as Mr. Grim played on, and

finally, when the music reached a fever pitch, the Odditorium appeared to lengthen upward an entire story. It held there for a moment on a single high note, and then slowly settled down again as Mr. Grim's fingers traveled to the opposite end of the keyboard.

All of a sudden, a woman's scream rang out above the crowd and the music stopped.

"Help! Help!" she cried.

Mr. Grim stood up and looked out over the balcony. There was a fuss brewing farther down the street. I couldn't see exactly what was happening, only that people were frantically moving aside.

Then, from amidst the commotion, a constable went flying up into the air. He sailed backward over the crowd, his arms and legs pinwheeling. A moment later, another constable went flying up after him!

More heads turned and people screamed, and everyone began backing away from something in the street—something that was clearly making its way toward Nigel and me—and then the crowd parted to reveal a trio of lads staring up at us.

It was Noah, Frog Eyes, and Flat Nose. Their skin was deathly white, their mouths set in snarls, and their eyes, ringed with black circles, glowed a devilish purple.

"Oh dear," Nigel said. "They belong to the prince now."

And with that the three lads pointed up at Mr. Grim and uttered the most terrifying noise I'd ever heard—a low, inhuman moan that sounded as if it had come from Mr. Grim's pipe organ.

Mr. Grim met their glowing purple eyes with a strange expression of both defiance and confusion. And then, in a flash of thunder and lightning, a screech echoed above our heads.

Gazing upward, I spied a line of crows perched atop a nearby building. At first I thought the screech had come from them, but then, high above us, a large, black-winged creature emerged from the clouds, circled there like a hawk, and began to dive.

I recognized the monster immediately from the drawing in Mr. Grim's notebook.

"The Black Fairy," I gasped.

Whether or not Nigel heard me, I cannot say, for the big man immediately lifted me off his shoulders, tucked me under his arm, and made a dash for the Odditorium. I caught one last glimpse of Mr. Grim as he fled from the balcony, and then all around us the street erupted into bedlam.

The crows took flight and the crowd screamed and scattered. The line of constables in front of the Odditorium tried to hold us back, but Nigel easily pushed them aside and made for the steps—when without warning the Black Fairy swooped down and snatched Judge Hurst from the sidewalk.

"Help!" he cried as he was carried off—but I lost sight of him as Nigel scooped up Lord Dreary, tucked him under the same arm as me, and bounded with us both up the steps.

"Great poppycock!" Lord Dreary shouted, squirming. "Put me down!"

Nigel ignored him. And as the big man reached the Odditorium's front door, he hunched over a small black dome covered with buttons. Wedged as I was between his arm and Lord Dreary, I couldn't exactly see which combination of

buttons Nigel pressed, but when he'd finished, the front door to the Odditorium swung open and Nigel carried us inside.

"Defense! Defense!" he shouted, and as he set down Lord Dreary and me, the samurai drew their swords and dashed for the door.

Noah and his gang were heading up the steps outside.

"No!" I cried, and Nigel covered my eyes with his hand.

"It's for the best, Grubb," he whispered.

And then the samurai's swords went whistling through the air.

"Great poppycock!" Lord Dreary exclaimed. "Those lads just *disintegrated*!"

"They weren't lads, sir," Nigel said. "Not anymore."

Nigel removed his hand from my eyes. Noah and his gang were gone, all right. But as the samurai made their way back up the steps, the Black Fairy landed with a heavy thud in the street behind them.

Squatting on its haunches, the creature was at least as tall as Nigel—its massive bat wings spreading out far beyond the outline of the door frame. And just like the drawing in Mr. Grim's notebook, the insides of the Black Fairy's eyes and dagger-filled mouth were completely white.

"Good heavens!" Lord Dreary gasped.

The Black Fairy screeched and flapped its wings, then turned its white eyes upward and opened its mouth wide.

"Hurry up, gents!" Nigel screamed. The samurai rushed back inside. However, just before the big man shut the door behind them, I caught sight of what looked like a long stream of black fire shooting out from the Black Fairy's mouth.

"Mr. Grim!" Nigel cried. "The monster's aiming for the balcony!"

The Odditorium shook violently and I fell to the floor. Nigel pressed a button beside the front door and a second inner door slid sideways into the frame. At the same time, a panel slid open in the ceiling, and down dropped Mr. Grim inside a giant birdcage.

"No need to worry, Nigel," he said. "I lowered the shield on the balcony just in time. The control room is safe for now."

Another blast hit the Odditorium, and I staggered to my feet.

"What on earth is going on?" cried Lord Dreary. "I demand an explanation!"

"No time for that," replied Mr. Grim, then he turned to Nigel and said, "Looks like we'll have to leave sooner than planned."

"Right-o, sir," Nigel said, and he began pushing Lord Dreary into the birdcage.

"What's that?" the old man sputtered. "Leave? Great poppycock, man! You're not planning on taking me out there with that—that—*thing*, are you?"

"That thing, as you so eloquently call it, is the Black Fairy."

"The Black—?"

"Fairy, yes. Quite an unpleasant chap as you might have gathered, but a shrewd one, nonetheless."

Another blast shook the building, and the Black Fairy shrieked outside.

"It won't take him long to figure out that the Odditorium is impervious to his fire," Mr. Grim went on. "Therefore, I suggest we get moving before Prince Nightshade arrives to help him."

"Prince Nightshade?" asked Lord Dreary, stunned. "What are you—?"

Nigel shut the old man inside the birdcage. Mr. Grim threw a lever, and then he and Lord Dreary quickly began their ascent.

"Take the boy with you to the engine room, Nigel," Mr. Grim called down. "Gwendolyn is fond of him, and we don't have time to risk her temper."

"Right-o, sir," Nigel said, and Mr. Grim and Lord Dreary disappeared into the ceiling. "Come on, then, Grubb," Nigel said, and I followed him over to the large portrait of Mr. Grim that hung between the staircases.

"Stand back," Nigel said. He placed his palm on the glowing blue orb in Mr. Grim's hand and pushed it gently, upon which, along with the muffled sound of gears grinding under the stairs, the portrait slid sideways to reveal a secret chamber beyond.

"Cor blimey!" I gasped.

The cavernous space into which we entered was spherical in construction, with a small landing and a steep staircase leading down to the floor below. A line of red-burning furnaces ringed the outside walls, and hanging from the domed ceiling was the Yellow Fairy's dollhouse. Directly beneath it, at the center of the room, was an enormous crystal sphere with a massive tangle of pipes branching out from it in every direction. At the top of the sphere, a porthole with a hinged steel cover stood open.

"It's time, miss," Nigel said as we descended the stairs, and the Yellow Fairy appeared in one of the dollhouse's upstairs windows.

"Oh really?" she said mockingly, batting her eyelashes. "The Black Fairy has got your twiggy boss worried now, has he?"

"Now, now, Gwendolyn," Nigel said. "No need to call Mr. Grim names."

"And what are you going to do about it, *baldy*?"

The Yellow Fairy hurled a shimmering ball of her fairy dust and hit Nigel square in the chest, encasing him in a glowing yellow bubble. The bubble began floating up into the air with Nigel inside, but the big man appeared unconcerned, and calmly lifted his goggles to reveal a pair of eye sockets filled entirely with blue animus.

My mouth fell open in amazement.

Mack had told the truth. Nigel *was* Odditoria after all.

The big man blinked once, and beams of bright blue light shot from his eyes. They burst apart in sparkles against the inside of the Yellow Fairy's bubble, and then the bubble turned green and began to fizzle and pop until it dissolved completely and Nigel dropped to the ground.

"We don't have time for this, miss," he said, replacing his goggles. And as if on cue, another blast from the Black Fairy shook the Odditorium.

"What's going on down there?" shouted Mr. Grim, his voice crackling behind me. "Why don't we have power?"

Nigel rushed over to the wall, where he flicked the switch on yet another of the Odditorium's mechanical talkbacks.

"It's Gwendolyn, sir!" Nigel shouted. "She won't get into the sphere!"

"Good heavens! Tell her she can't break our alliance now!"

"I can hear you loud and clear, *twig*!" the Yellow Fairy shouted. "And our alliance said nothing about me spinning around in some big glass ball!"

"The Black Fairy is retreating!" Lord Dreary said on the talkback. He sounded farther away than Mr. Grim.

"Gwendolyn, please," said Mr. Grim. "If you don't get into that sphere and start spinning, the Black Fairy will return with the prince and destroy us all!"

"Ha! A big bully is all he is. Besides, I'd rather stand and fight than run away like a bunch of lily-livered humans!"

"Be reasonable, will you?" said Mr. Grim. "Even a fairy of your power is no match for Prince Nightshade and his army!"

"So says you, twig! But I'm beginning to think this Prince Nightshade doesn't even exist. Just another one of your tricks to use me—like that jig yesterday with the samurai!"

"Alistair, look!" Lord Dreary shouted in the background. "There's something happening in the clouds!"

"Gwendolyn, I beg of you!" cried Mr. Grim. "We don't have time for this nonsense!"

"You talk to her, Grubb," Nigel said, pushing me forward. "You're a child. She'll listen to you."

"But what shall I say?"

"Well, you might start by asking her to get in that sphere!"

"Er, uh, begging your pardon, miss," I said nervously. "But would you be so kind as to get into that sphere?"

"Ha!" said the Yellow Fairy. "Playing the child card, are you? Nice try, baldy!"

"No one's trying to trick you, miss," I said. "You see, all of this is my fault."

"Your fault?" asked Gwendolyn and Mr. Grim together.

"Yes, sir—uh, miss," I stuttered, spinning in place. "You see, it was I who tipped off the doom dogs."

"Doom dogs?" asked Mr. Grim from the talkback. "Did you say doom dogs, Master Grubb?"

"Yes, sir. It's a long story, but the nub of it is I accidentally brought Mack outside and got my pocket picked. The lads what done it opened him, and, well—"

"He's telling the truth, Miss Gwendolyn," Nigel said, holding up Mack. "This pocket watch here runs on the blue animus."

Mack must have been shaking in Nigel's pocket, because when he opened him, the watch cried, "What time is it?"

Nigel immediately tapped Mack's XII and closed his case.

"Let me guess," Gwendolyn said, her disposition softening. "Without the magic paint to protect them, the lads who used the animus fell victim to the doom dogs."

"That's right," Nigel said, slipping Mack into his pocket. "And after those devil hounds took their souls to the Land of the Dead, Prince Nightshade turned their corpses into Shadesmen."

"Shadesmen?" asked the Yellow Fairy.

"The walking dead. Soulless creatures what serve only their master. The lads knew Mack here had come from the

Odditorium, and so they led the Black Fairy straight to our doorstep."

"And where are these lads?" Gwendolyn asked sadly.

"Mr. Grim's samurai put them to rest. They're at peace now."

The Yellow Fairy pondered this a moment. She looked close to giving in, I thought.

"I know you to be a protector of children, miss," I said. "It's too late to save them other lads, but should you find it in your heart to save this one"—I pointed to myself—"well, I'd be forever grateful, miss."

The Yellow Fairy batted her eyelashes and studied me. Then, without warning, she flew from her dollhouse, circled it once, and hovered above the sphere.

"If this is another one of Grim's tricks," she said, her eyes locking with mine, "child or no child, I'll gobble you up too!"

And with that the Yellow Fairy swooped down into the sphere and, closing the porthole behind her, began to twirl herself into a whirlwind of sparkling yellow light. For a moment she changed into the monstrous, toothy ball that I had seen the night before in the library. But just as quickly the teeth disappeared, and the ball expanded and brightened until it filled the entire sphere.

"Thank you, Gwendolyn!" Mr. Grim cried from the

talkback, and all at once the Odditorium began to tremble. "Nigel, you and the boy get back up here immediately!"

"Right-o, sir," Nigel said, and we dashed across the engine room and up another flight of stairs, at the top of which was a large red door.

Suddenly I heard a muffled burst of organ music, and the entire Odditorium tilted and shifted—first to one side, and then the other.

"Is the Black Fairy attacking again?" I asked, steadying myself.

"Not yet," Nigel replied. "But he will soon. Come on, Grubb. Through here."

Nigel opened the door, and once we were on the other side, I realized it was the same red door that Mrs. Pinch had warned me about earlier that morning. Nigel and I hurried down the hallway past Mr. Grim's shop and into the lift. Nigel shut us inside and pulled the lever, and as the lift began its ascent, I couldn't help but ask: "What shall become of me now, Nigel?"

"What do you mean?"

"Mr. Grim said that if I told anyone about what goes on inside the Odditorium, Gwendolyn wouldn't always be around to protect me."

"But certainly the boss didn't mean protection from *him*.

More likely he meant protection from something like what's going on outside."

"You think so?"

"Of course. Everyone makes mistakes, Grubb. Even Mr. Grim. But you owned up to it without being asked. And that takes courage and character. And if there are two things Alistair Grim prizes above all else in a person, it's courage and character."

"Courage and character."

"Besides, if it wasn't for you, Gwendolyn might never have gotten into that sphere." Nigel pulled the lever again and the lift came to a stop. "Then again, if it wasn't for you, we might never have needed her to do so in the first place."

Nigel chuckled and slid open the doors. But as we stepped out into the parlor, we nearly tripped over Mrs. Pinch. She was on her hands and knees, searching for something on the floor, and upon her head she wore a samurai helmet.

"Pardon us, mum," Nigel said. "On your way down, are you?"

"I *was*," the old woman said, irritated. "But blind me if all this thrashing about hasn't knocked off my spectacles."

Another burst of organ music caused the Odditorium to shift. Nigel and I lost our balance, and I heard a distinct crunching sound beneath my feet. The three of us froze, and then I bent down and peeled something from the sole of my shoe.

"Oh dear," Nigel said. "I think Grubb found your spectacles, mum."

The hearth was now ablaze with the same strange red fire I had seen in the kitchen, and in its light I could see that Mrs. Pinch's spectacles had been completely crushed.

"My apologies, ma'am," I said, terrified.

Mrs. Pinch rose to her feet, snatched back her spectacles, and stared down at me crossly.

"Nigel, where are you?" called Mr. Grim from the talkback by the lift.

Nigel flipped the switch and said, "In the parlor, sir. We've run into a little problem with Mrs. Pinch's spectacles."

"You mean she's not at her station?"

"No, she's not, sir. And from the looks of her spectacles, she won't be much use to us there."

"Oh, what next!" cried Mr. Grim. "All right, then, you take the lower gunnery. Mrs. Pinch can go up to your station with Lord Dreary."

"Don't change the subject, man!" shouted Lord Dreary in the background. "What's all this about magic paint?"

"What shall I do with the boy?" Nigel asked.

"Oh yes, the boy. Send him into the control room with Mrs. Pinch. I could use an extra pair of eyes. And be sure

170

you take the stairs. I don't want you getting stuck in the lift should the Black Fairy return."

"Right-o, sir," Nigel said. He flicked off the talkback and twisted one of the blue burning sconces above it. A secret panel slid open in the wall next to the lift, and inside I could see a narrow shaft containing a spiral staircase.

"You heard him, Grubb," Nigel said, descending. And as the secret panel began to close, he called back, "And don't let Mrs. Pinch go bumping into anything!"

"Of all the nerve," she said with her hands on her hips. "Why, I could find my way around the Odditorium blind-folded!"

And as if to prove it, she took me by the elbow and led me into Mr. Grim's library.

The room itself had come alive with movement. The desk was in the process of sliding back into its original position over a hidden trapdoor in the floor, and disappearing into the ceiling above it was the large birdcage in which Mr. Grim had dropped down into the reception hall below. The wall behind Mr. Grim's desk had been raised so that the library now opened directly onto the balcony. All the samurai were gone, and a wide, glowing blue energy shield had been lowered over the balcony's balustrade. Finally, Mr. Grim's pipe organ had turned around so that it faced the street.

Mrs. Pinch and I stepped out onto the balcony to find Mr.

Grim and Lord Dreary in the midst of a heated discussion.

"Magic paint made from dragon's scales and troll's blood?" Lord Dreary exclaimed. "You can't be serious, man!"

"Don't you see? Without the protection of my magic paint, the Odditorium could not exist. Even the smallest use of the animus would have given me away years ago!"

"But—but—"

"I don't have time to argue with you," said Mr. Grim, and he tossed the old man a samurai helmet. "How's your aim, old friend?"

"How's my *aim*?" Lord Dreary gasped, confused.

"Mrs. Pinch is the only person who knows how to operate the upper gunnery. You'll have to talk her through her targeting."

"Talk her through her *targeting*?"

"Mrs. Pinch," said Mr. Grim, ignoring Lord Dreary, "you'll be able to find your way to the upper gunnery and operate the controls effectively?"

"I outfitted the gunneries myself, didn't I?" replied the old woman. "Blind me if I couldn't operate the entire Odditorium with my eyes closed!"

"Very good. On your way, then."

"Yes, sir. Come along, Lord Dreary."

"But—but—" the old man sputtered, but Mrs. Pinch took him by the elbow and quickly led him out.

Mr. Grim sat down at his organ and flicked the switch for the talkback on the keyboard. "Are you in place, Nigel? Do you have a visual?"

"Ready, boss," Nigel replied.

I stepped closer to the edge of the balcony. Gazing down through the transparent blue energy shield, I discovered that not only had the buttresses unfolded themselves into a set of mechanical spider legs, but also the entire Odditorium had risen a full two stories off the ground.

"Very well, then," said Mr. Grim. "We'll discuss your part in all this later, Master Grubb. But for now you must act as my lookout. Do you understand?"

"Yes, sir. But, begging your pardon, sir—what am I looking out for?"

Out of nowhere, an armored skeleton swooped down atop a skeleton steed and swiped a huge battle-ax at me as he passed. The blue energy shield flashed like lightning, and I let out a shriek and fell backward onto my bottom. Mr. Grim calmly turned to me and said:

"Something like that, I should imagine."

TEN

The Battle in the Clouds

lthough many of the Odditorium's secrets had only been revealed to me in the moments immediately following the Black Fairy's attack, I would not actually get to see Mr. Grim's gunneries until much later. Nonetheless, I think it best to skip ahead a bit and describe them so you won't be as confused as I was when the battle began.

The Odditorium had two gunneries, one upper and one lower. The upper gunnery was the larger of the two and consisted of a turret with four cannons. When not in use, the cannons stood upright in the guise of the Odditorium's chimneys, while the turret appeared as just another inconspicuous black dome at the center of the roof. Once everything was activated, however, the chimneys tilted sideways and locked into place around the turret, a portion of the turret gave way to a blue energy shield, and the entire contraption began to track across the Odditorium's roof.

The lower gunnery, on the other hand, was outfitted with just two cannons, and could only be accessed through a porthole directly beneath the great sphere in the engine room. And just as the upper gunnery could track atop the roof, so too could the lower gunnery glide along the Odditorium's belly.

Of course, I didn't know this at the time, and as more armored skeletons began to attack, I had only a vague sense of Mrs. Pinch and Lord Dreary being somewhere above me, and Nigel being somewhere down below.

"Can you hear me, Cleona?" said Mr. Grim into the talk-back on his organ. "Why aren't you at your post?"

"I'm here," replied a gentle voice that I immediately recognized as belonging to the young girl I'd heard outside the trunk. Cleona the trickster. "I was looking for my comb," Cleona said. "You wouldn't happen to know where it is, now, *would you?*"

"Oh, thank goodness you're safe," said Mr. Grim with a sigh. "I thought for a moment that—"

"Pshaw. You worry too much, Uncle."

"Then you're aware of what's happening outside? You know this is not a trick?"

"Much too elaborate a trick for the likes of you. But as for hiding my *comb*, that's going a bit far, don't you think? After all, it was just a little chalk on your paintings. It comes right off."

Of course! I thought. The portraits I saw last night in

the upstairs gallery—it was Cleona the trickster who drew all those chalk mustaches. And *A.G. has a spotty bottom*—A.G. stood for Alistair Grim, which meant the portrait must be of Mr. Grim as a little boy!

"We'll talk about your comb and my spotty bottom later," said Mr. Grim, flicking another switch. "How about you, Mrs. Pinch? Are you and Lord Dreary settled in the upper gunnery?"

"Good heavens!" Lord Dreary exclaimed over the talk-back. "There are hundreds of those skeleton soldiers coming our way!"

"I'll take that as a yes."

Mr. Grim pressed some buttons on his organ and the Odditorium began to tremble.

"All right, everyone," he began. "Wish we could've had time for another drill, but things being what they are, I'm hoping you're not rusty."

"Pshaw," Cleona said. "We've drilled this so many times I'm full of holes."

Nigel and Cleona snickered over the talkback, but Mr. Grim ignored them.

"Now remember, gunners," he said, "until we're clear, I ask that you take great care when firing at Nightshade's soldiers. No need to turn our beloved London into rubble over an army of Shadesmen."

Shadesmen, I said to myself, terrified. Those armored skeletons out there were the walking dead, just like Noah and his gang, only these Shadesmen had glowing *red* eyes instead of purple, and looked to have been dead much, *much* longer.

"They're everywhere!" Lord Dreary cried, and another one of the armored skeletons swiped the shield with his battle-ax. I yelped with fright, but Mr. Grim appeared cool as a cucumber.

"Stiff upper lip, old man," he said. "We're counting on you to help Mrs. Pinch. As for the rest of you, if for some reason we don't make it, well I just want to say what a privilege it's been knowing you."

"Likewise, boss," said Nigel, his voice coming from the organ.

"Humph," said Mrs. Pinch.

"But—but—!" sputtered Lord Dreary, and Mr. Grim flicked off his talkback.

"I'm opening the dampers now, Cleona," he said. "Not sure if you'll feel any pushback from Gwendolyn, but let me know if you sense a power drain, will you?"

"No worries, Uncle. I can hold my own against her kind."

"Very well, then," Mr. Grim said, and he flicked some more switches. "Hold on to your helmets, people. Here goes nothing."

As soon as Mr. Grim began playing his pipe organ, the

Odditorium began to tremble and shake. At the same time, I could hear a low rumbling noise coming from somewhere below my feet. It grew louder and louder until, much to my astonishment, the buildings outside began sinking into the ground.

Gazing down through the shield, I could see a massive cloud of sparkling green smoke billowing out below us. And as the mechanical spider legs folded back into their original positions, I realized that the buildings were not sinking, but that the Odditorium was rising—no, *flying*—up into the air above them!

"I was right," said Mr. Grim, his eyes wide. "The proper ratio of fairy dust and animus makes the perfect propellant."

Of course, I thought. Yellow and blue make green, which meant that the smoke down there was a mixture of Gwendolyn's fairy dust and—

"Oh no!" I cried. "The animus will summon the doom dogs!"

"Nonsense, lad," said Mr. Grim. "The blue animus is quite harmless when mixed with Yellow Fairy dust. Even the most amateur of sorcerers knows that!"

I remembered the headless samurai's helmet from the night before—how it had snuffed out Gwendolyn's fairy dust and stopped Mr. Grim's top from spinning. It was the same with Nigel shooting his animus at Gwendolyn's big yellow bubble a few minutes ago in the engine room.

"The two energies cancel each other out, then?" I asked, staring down at the swelling cloud of sparkling green smoke. "Like fire and water, Mr. Grim?"

"Something like that, Master Grubb," he said. "But unfortunately we don't have time for a chemistry lesson at present."

More and more armored Shadesmen began swooping down on us—some striking the blue energy shield with their battle-axes, while others just wailed and steered their steeds around the Odditorium out of sight. And yet, despite the racket, the different functions of Alistair Grim's multicolored energies suddenly became clear to me. The blue animus energy powered the Odditorium's mechanical features. The Yellow Fairy dust energy gave the Odditorium its power to fly. And the red energy—

Without warning, a hissing bolt of bright red lightning rained down from above and struck one of the Shadesmen, turning him and his skeleton horse at once into a dissipating cloud of thick black smoke.

"Cor blimey!" I gasped.

Yes, come to find out, not only did the red energy fire up the Odditorium's ovens, but it could also be fired out of the gunnery cannons to blow up Shadesmen.

"Great shooting, Mrs. Pinch!" Mr. Grim shouted into the talkback. "You too, Lord Dreary!"

"Humph," said Mrs. Pinch, and Lord Dreary chuckled modestly.

"Well, now," he said, "you know I wasn't awarded first prize in the Duke's annual pheasant hunt for noth—"

Mr. Grim cut off his talkback again as the army of Shadesmen whizzed past us like a swarm of angry hornets. All of them, as well as their horses, were outfitted in bronze breastplates and helmets, the latter of which were topped with red-bristled crests that reminded me of my old chimney brushes. And the skeleton steeds' eyes, just like those of their riders, glowed red in their skulls.

Presently, the clang of battle-axes on the outside walls echoed throughout the Odditorium from every direction.

"We've got climbers!" Nigel called out from the talkback, and I spied a Shadesman's feet scrambling for purchase near the top of the shield. Some of the skeleton horses were now circling the Odditorium without their riders, too.

"Are the samurai on the battlements?" asked Mr. Grim.

"They are, sir," replied Mrs. Pinch, "but I can't see how they're faring against—"

"Help us, Alistair!" cried Lord Dreary in the background. "We've lost two of our warriors over the side!"

"Even a samurai is no match for a cavalry charge," mumbled Mr. Grim. "Order them back inside, Mrs. Pinch! I'll take care of the climbers with the levitation shield."

"The *what*?" cried Lord Dreary—but Mr. Grim cut him off again.

"Any sign of the Black Fairy, Master Grubb?" he asked.

"Yes, sir," I said, pointing. "He's up there, hanging back in the clouds."

"He knows better than to tangle with our energy bolts. You see anything else?"

"No, sir, just more Shadesmen jumping from their horses."

"Good," said Mr. Grim, changing his organ tune to something more festive. And as the Odditorium rose higher and higher, it began to move forward, too—the rooftops quickly rolling beneath our glittering green tail.

"Eyes upward, Master Grubb," said Mr. Grim, and he flicked on the talkback again. "Lord Dreary, are the samurai safe inside?"

"Yes!" the old man replied. "But I don't see what you can do against these climbing skeletons from down there!"

As if to answer him, Mr. Grim pressed a button on his pipe organ. In a blinding flash of yellow, a powerful buzz shot through the floor and tickled my toes. A moment later I spied a dozen or so of the armored skeletons floating up past the shield, their bony arms and legs flailing about in scores of Gwendolyn's glowing yellow bubbles!

"The levitation shield," said Mr. Grim. "A quick burst of Yellow Fairy dust that surrounds the Odditorium and thus repels anything not nailed down. Don't mind telling you how relieved I am to find out it actually works."

Mr. Grim winked, and then more bolts of hissing red lightning shot out from the Odditorium in every direction, turning the Shadesmen and their horses into smoke, in some places ten at a time.

"Huzzah!" cried Lord Dreary. "Take that, you blasted bone bags!"

"That's the spirit, man!" said Mr. Grim. "All right, then, people, let's make a concerted effort to keep those climbers off the walls, shall we?"

Mr. Grim changed his tune again, his fingers moving even faster across his pipe organ. And as the Odditorium picked up even more speed, the armored skeletons and their steeds gave chase.

Bolts of red lightning crackled all around us as countless Shadesmen were vaporized into smoke. We were high above the city now and moving out toward the countryside. Far off in the distance, at the edge of the clouds in which the Black Fairy and his army had arrived, I could see the blue of the afternoon sky.

But as Mr. Grim steered the Odditorium toward it, I noticed a shower of glowing red lights whizzing through the air straight for us.

"He's sending out his archers!" Nigel cried from the talk-back.

Mr. Grim looked up from his organ just in time to see the first volley of red-tipped arrows strike the shield. The Odditorium trembled violently, and the shield appeared to fizzle and pop purple as if it would blink out. But in the end it held.

"Those arrows are tipped with red energy!" cried Mr. Grim. "Prince Nightshade must have found the other Eye of Mars!"

"Begging your pardon, sir?" I asked.

"The power source for the gunneries. Legend has it that the god had two Eyes. And since I found only one in my travels, I always worried Prince Nightshade had found the other!"

I glanced back at the lion's head above the fireplace. As far as I could tell, old Mars still had both his eyes. In fact, the big cat's peepers were glowing brighter than ever. So what was all this talk about gods and whatnot?

"Focus all your efforts on the Shadesmen's arrows," Mr. Grim said into the talkback. "It appears Prince Nightshade has found the other Eye of Mars!"

"Oh dear," said Nigel.

"Another volley!" Lord Dreary shouted. "No, no, no! To the right—farther to the right, woman!"

Crackling bolts of bright red lighting rained past us in every direction. Mr. Grim played some of the pipe organ's lower keys, and the Odditorium banked hard to the left.

"That's it," said Mr. Grim. "Lay down some strafing fire while I—"

The Odditorium rocked violently, and I was nearly thrown to the floor again as a mass of crumbling brick bounced off the energy shield.

"Good heavens!" cried Lord Dreary. "Those arrows knocked out one of our cannons. We're down to only three!"

Mr. Grim pulled a lever on his organ and the Odditorium picked up even more speed. More red lighting shot out from Nigel's station below, and a line of approaching Shadesman was instantly turned to smoke.

"Gunners," shouted Mr. Grim, "I need you to hold them off while Cleona gets into position!"

"Right-o, sir."

"Is it time, then?" Cleona asked from the talkback.

"Yes, love," said Mr. Grim. "The energy panels in your chamber should have more than enough charge to sustain the Odditorium's steering systems while we make the jump. Get into position and open the porthole, but remember to deactivate the shields only when you're ready. If one of those arrows should get inside—"

"Pshaw," Cleona said. "You worry too much, Uncle."

"Be careful, Cleona. You're our only hope now."

Cleona giggled, but then Lord Dreary shouted, "Another volley!"

Sprays of red lightning shot out from above and below, wiping out an entire front line of Shadesmen and their arrows at once.

"Huzzah!" Lord Dreary exclaimed. "Great shooting, woman! You too, Stout!"

"Thank you, sir," Nigel replied.

"Keep those arrows away from Cleona's porthole!" cried Mr. Grim.

The red energy bolts picked off Shadesmen left and right, and as Mr. Grim made some adjustments on his keyboard, the Odditorium spun halfway around so that we were flying backward. The Black Fairy was far away from us now, and yet a great shadow appeared to be looming up in the clouds behind him.

"Mr. Grim!" I shouted. "Look!"

And with that a huge chariot burst forth from the clouds with a team of four black horses leading the way.

Mr. Grim swallowed hard. "Prince Nightshade, I presume."

As if in reply, the monstrous black steeds neighed with a deafening screech. Fire flashed from their mouths, smoke billowed from their nostrils, and all at once it seemed as though the world grew darker, and the air was thick with fear.

Most terrifying of all, however, was the figure in the chariot. I could make out only the outline of his form—his chunky black armor, the spiked crown upon his head, and a flowing black cape that swelled like a sail behind him. In one hand he held the horses' reins; in the other, a fiery red whip that, when cracked, exploded with lightning and thunder.

"He's here!" Mr. Grim cried into the talkback. "Hurry, Cleona! Open the porthole! I daren't turn my back on the prince for long!"

The prince cracked his whip. Lightning flashed and thunder boomed, and Mr. Grim spun the Odditorium around again until it faced the clear blue sky.

"What are you waiting for?" cried Lord Dreary. "Why aren't you firing at him, woman?"

"No!" said Mr. Grim. "Any shot from the Eye of Mars will only make Prince Nightshade stronger. Continue firing on the Shadesmen if you can, but keep your energy bolts away from the prince, do you hear?"

A screech from the Black Fairy, a neigh from the steeds, and another crack of the whip behind us—the lighting and thunder closer now.

"He's gaining on us!" Nigel shouted. I could see only blue sky ahead of us, and were it not for the deafening racket, I wouldn't have known anything was amiss.

"The Odditorium might not survive a crack from his

whip," said Mr. Grim. "Please hurry, Cleona! What are you waiting for?"

Without warning, a thick bolt of bright blue light shot out from somewhere above the shield. It traveled only a short distance and then burst apart into an enormous swirl of sparkling silver stars, at the center of which appeared what I could only describe as a hole in the sky.

"Thank you, darling!" said Mr. Grim. "Back inside with you and close the porthole!" Mr. Grim flicked some switches and played some keys. "Maintaining forward thrusters and coming about to port," he said, and once again the Odditorium spun around in place, traveling backward, it seemed, as we turned to face our attackers.

The prince was leading the charge now, and his steeds sped toward us at full gallop as the Black Fairy and the remaining cavalry brought up the rear.

They were closing quickly.

"I've lost my cannon!" cried Mrs. Pinch from the talkback. "It won't fire, sir!"

"It's that blasted conductor coupling again!" cried Mr. Grim, and I glanced over my shoulder to discover the lion's eyes were blinking on and off above the mantel.

"Activating the levitation shield one more time," said Mr. Grim, changing his organ tune, and once again the floor buzzed and the world flashed yellow. "That will take care of any Shadesmen who try to come through the hole with us."

I couldn't believe what I was hearing. Did Mr. Grim intend for us to pass through that hole in the sky?

Prince Nightshade's steeds were almost upon us, and for the first time I could clearly see the prince's face looming up behind them—a bottomless black pit with only a pair of glowing red eyes beneath an open, black-crowned helmet.

A blue light began flashing on Mr. Grim's pipe organ.

"Hang on, everybody," he said. "Here we *gooooo*!"

The Black Fairy shrieked.

The steeds spit fire.

And as Prince Nightshade raised his whip, the glowing red gash that was his mouth stretched apart into a deafening, black-fanged roar of "MINE!"

I froze in terror, certain that my soul had just been snatched from my body—but then the prince brought down his whip, and in a burst of thunder and lightning the Odditorium shook violently, knocking me once again to the floor.

Dazed, I thought for certain I was dead. Everything had become peaceful and glowing, as if the world had been enveloped in a brilliant white mist.

Mr. Grim rushed over to his pipe organ.

"I'm here!" he cried, gazing out over the balcony. "I'm here!"

I tried to scramble to my feet, but the Odditorium suddenly lurched forward and knocked me back down.

A great *whoosh* sucked the air from my lungs.

And before I could breathe again, everything went black.

A Lesson in Power

hen I came to, I found myself sitting on the floor with my ears ringing and my head thick with cobwebs. I tried to shake them off, and discovered Mr. Grim on the floor beside me shaking off his cobwebs too.

"Are we dead, sir?" I asked.

Mr. Grim shot me a look of surprise, then scrambled to his feet and gazed out over his organ. The shield was gone now and the wind whipped freely across the balcony.

"I was there, Elizabeth," Mr. Grim whispered to himself. "I was there."

Elizabeth? This was not the first time I'd heard that name—Lord Dreary had mentioned an Elizabeth this morning in the library, hadn't he? But then I noticed Mr. Grim's eyes, sad and distant, as if he was longing for something out there in the sky.

"Is everything all right, sir?" I asked tentatively.

Mr. Grim looked startled at first, then smiled and motioned for me to approach the balustrade.

I could hardly believe my eyes. The sky was clear and blue. And far below the Odditorium I spied an endless sea of rolling whitecaps. I had never seen the sea before, but nonetheless knew what I was looking at. And I must confess that seeing it for the first time awed me as much as anything I'd seen at Mr. Grim's.

"Congratulations, Master Grubb," he said. "You have just successfully navigated an interdimensional space jump."

I looked up at him dumbstruck and he gave me a wink.

"Cleona?" he called, flicking on his talkback. "Cleona, are you there?"

"I'm here, Uncle," she replied. "Is everyone all right?"

"Not sure yet, but how are you faring?"

"Pshaw, nothing I can't handle. Although, I am a bit sapped, I must admit."

"I can imagine. The space jump has all but drained the Odditorium's animus. Something to do with the balance of spiritual energies, do you think?"

"Forgive me, Uncle, but my brain's too gooey now for thinking scientifically."

"Forgive *me* for being insensitive. Yes, you must rest before you recharge the animus. We'll get by on the reserves until you're ready, and then you and I will have to figure out a way to stay longer next time."

"Very well, then," Cleona said with a yawn.

"And thank you, love."

"You're welcome, Uncle."

"Gwendolyn?" Mr. Grim said, flicking another switch on the talkback. "Are you there?"

"I'm here, twig!" the Yellow Fairy snapped crossly. "But don't you dare ask me to start spinning again—my head's gone all loopy, thanks to you!"

"By all means, rest. We've more than enough of your fairy dust to remain airborne. You've gotten us out of quite a scrape, and I'll be sure to have Mrs. Pinch bring you down some chocolates."

"Oooh!" Gwendolyn said, and Mr. Grim flicked off his talkback.

"Oooh, indeed," he said to me. "Never met a fairy who didn't like chocolate."

I was just about to ask if Cleona was a fairy too, but then Lord Dreary called out, "Alistair! Where the devil are you, Alistair Grim?"

"Oh dear," said Mr. Grim, and I followed him into the library to find Lord Dreary, still in his samurai helmet, entering with Mrs. Pinch.

"Great poppycock!" the old man shouted. "Would you mind telling me what in blazes all that was about?"

"What in blazes was what all about?"

Lord Dreary pointed frantically at the balcony. "*That!* Out there!"

"Just an interdimensional space jump. Nothing to be alarmed about."

"A *what?*"

Mr. Grim crossed to the table that held the pitcher and silver goblets.

"Mrs. Pinch," he said, righting one of the goblets, "after you take Gwendolyn her chocolates, would you mind bringing up that bottle of Asterian nectar I've been saving? I'd like to make a toast in honor of the Odditorium's maiden voyage."

"If I can find it amongst all your other bottles," said Mrs. Pinch.

"A toast?" asked Lord Dreary. "Maiden voyage, did you say?"

"And when you see Nigel," Mr. Grim continued, ignoring him, "please be sure he inspects the gunneries for leaks before the two of you join us down here for a drink."

"Yes, sir," said Mrs. Pinch, and she was gone.

"Made only a bit of a mess," said Mr. Grim, picking up his spinning top from the floor. "Nothing broken, as far as I can tell."

"Nothing broken?" Lord Dreary said, storming over to the desk. "Flying all over London with skeletons and black fairies! An armored devil trying to whip us to shreds, and you say nothing's broken? How about *your word*, man?"

"My word?"

"Maiden voyage, indeed!" Lord Dreary thundered with his fists on the desk. "I heard what you said. All your talk of drills! You've been planning to leave London all along. You swindled me you—you—*charlatan*!"

"How dare you, sir!" cried Mr. Grim, aghast.

Lord Dreary's cheeks huffed and puffed like a blacksmith's bellows, and then he collapsed into a chair. He made to drag his handkerchief across his brow, but upon finding the black samurai helmet still on his head, he jumped and sputtered and flung the helmet across the room.

"Please try to understand," said Mr. Grim, sitting on the edge of his desk. "After discovering what I'm about to tell you, I had no choice but to make a temporary change of plans."

"Oh, Alistair," sighed Lord Dreary, fingering his collar. "Alistair, Alistair, what have you done?"

"To be sure, I never meant to swindle you. And you have my word as a gentleman that I shall pay back every cent I owe you. You must believe me, old friend."

Lord Dreary dragged his handkerchief across his head. "After what I've seen today, I don't know what to believe."

"Very well," Mr. Grim began, crossing to the fireplace. "As you know, for some time now I have been traveling the world collecting Odditoria. What you *do not* know, however, is that the word *Odditoria*, at once both singular and plural, is used to classify any object living, inanimate, or otherwise that is believed to possess magical powers."

"Did you say *magical* powers?"

"That I did."

"Then the rumors are true," said Lord Dreary in astonishment. "You *are* a mad sorcerer!"

"Madness notwithstanding, I suppose I am deserving of such a title. But my interest in Odditoria has been mostly scientific. After all, when one understands the science behind a magical object, one can harness its power for practical use."

Mr. Grim pressed a button on the mantel, and the lion head with the glowing red eyes immediately swung open to reveal a hidden compartment behind it. At the center of the compartment was a miniature version of the glass sphere contraption down in the engine room. However, instead of a fairy, inside the sphere floated a glowing red orb about the size of a billiard ball.

"Behold the Eye of Mars," said Mr. Grim. Standing on his tippy-toes, he opened a small porthole and removed the orb from the glass sphere.

My eyes grew wide and my jaw gaped. The lightning from

the gunnery cannons, the fires in the ovens and engine room furnaces, even the soot in the chimneys had nothing to do with the lion's head. All of it had come from this little, glowing red ball!

"Good heavens," said Lord Dreary. "You mean to tell me that is—"

"The source of the Odditorium's firepower," said Mr. Grim. "You see, according to a little known legend, Mars, the Roman god of war, was said to have given a magical weapon to each of his twin sons, Romulus and Remus, so that they would always be equal in power. These weapons were known as the Eyes of Mars."

"And by Romulus and Remus, you mean the legendary founders of Rome?"

"Very good, Lord Dreary. However, according to the legend, Romulus still managed to kill his brother Remus, steal his Eye of Mars, and name the city of Rome after himself. Incensed by this treachery, Mars took back both his Eyes and buried them separately somewhere deep within the Earth. Just another Roman legend, scholars thought. *I,* on the other hand . . ."

Mr. Grim smiled modestly and offered the orb to Lord Dreary, but the old man hesitated to take it.

"Go ahead," said Mr. Grim. "I assure you that, even in its activated state, the Eye of Mars is quite harmless unless one knows how to use it."

Lord Dreary tentatively took the Eye of Mars in his hands, his face instantly glowing red as he stared down at the orb in amazement. "It's warm."

"Quite an effective source of heat on a cold London evening," said Mr. Grim, nodding. "And so you see, Lord Dreary, the Eye of Mars is only one of three magical entities for which I have built conductors to harness their power."

"You mean there are other conductors here inside the Odditorium? Contraptions with which you harness the yellow and blue energy, too?"

"Precisely."

"Hang on," Lord Dreary said. "Your trip to the North Country—Gwendolyn, the girl you told to get into the sphere —you can't possibly mean—"

"You are correct, old friend. The legendary Yellow Fairy. Her magic dust, harnessed in one of my conductor spheres, gives the Odditorium its power to fly. I'll introduce the two of you shortly."

Stunned, Lord Dreary again dragged his handkerchief across his brow. I could tell the old man's head was spinning, but it all made perfect sense to me. Different kinds of Odditoria gave you different kinds of energy. Yellow flying energy came from Gwendolyn. Red blasting energy came from the Eye of Mars. And blue mechanical energy came from . . . Well, that was the question now, wasn't it? Where *did* the blue energy come from?

Mr. Grim waved his hand over the orb, and upon uttering a strange incantation, the glow from the Eye of Mars went out.

"What have you done?" Lord Dreary cried.

"Just an ancient Roman spell," said Mr. Grim, taking the sphere back to the fireplace. "You see, in its deactivated state, the Eye of Mars appears to be nothing more than a worthless glass ball. Then again, I've found that the most powerful Odditoria are usually things that, on the surface at least, appear to be ordinary."

Mr. Grim placed the Eye of Mars back inside its conductor,

pressed the secret button, and the lion's head swung back into place. Its eyes had gone black again.

"But how—where did you find it?"

"To make a long story short," said Mr. Grim, "I tracked down the Eye of Mars to a dormant volcano on the Italian peninsula where, shall we say, I *persuaded* the dragon who lived there to give it to me."

"*Dragon*, did you say?"

"Well, naturally when one travels around the world collecting magical objects, one stands a good chance of running into the magical creatures who guard them. However, early on in my quest for Odditoria, I realized that *someone else* was traveling around the world collecting Odditoria too."

"Prince Nightshade!"

"Indeed," said Mr. Grim, fetching his notebook from his desk. "On more than one occasion, in fact, it appeared as if the old prince had snatched my Odditoria right out from under my nose—and in some cases, the magical creatures who guarded them, too."

Mr. Grim opened his notebook and handed it to Lord Dreary. I could not see the page from where I was standing, but the fear in the old man's eyes made it clear which one of Mr. Grim's drawings had caught his attention.

"The Black Fairy," Lord Dreary said weakly.

"The prince's second in command," said Mr. Grim. "You'll find many other nasty creatures in there too—all of whom have allied themselves with the prince."

Lord Dreary scanned a few more pages and then quickly closed the notebook and handed it back to Mr. Grim, out of fright.

"But who *is* this Prince Nightshade?" asked Lord Dreary.

"I'm afraid I don't know *who* he is," said Mr. Grim, returning his notebook to his desk. "But it is clear to me *what* he is: a master of the Dark Arts, someone who has learned to harness the power of Odditoria much as I have. And to make matters worse, it appears this Nightshade character also has the power to absorb magical energy into his body. The more energy he absorbs, the more powerful he becomes."

"Great—"

"Poppycock, yes," Mr. Grim said quickly. "And judging from the armor worn by the prince's Shadesmen, I am convinced that he used his Eye of Mars to resurrect the ancient armies of Romulus and Remus."

Lord Dreary gasped. "You mean those blasted bone bags are actually dead Latin soldiers?"

"Precisely," said Mr. Grim. He snatched a book from one of the shelves and began flipping through its pages. "It makes sense that the Eye of Mars could *only* resurrect the armies of

Romulus and Remus. One brother could not possibly conquer the other if he could not destroy his army, and thus they would always be equal in power. Or at least that's what Mars thought."

"So those Shadesmen cannot be killed?"

"Oh no, they can be killed with the right weapons," Mr. Grim said absently, reading. "A blast of red energy. A swipe from an animus-infused samurai sword . . ."

Mr. Grim flipped a few more pages and then, unable to find what he was looking for, tossed the book onto his desk and raked back his hair in frustration.

"So that is why Prince Nightshade has come after you?" asked Lord Dreary. "Because you possess the other Eye of Mars?"

"Unfortunately, no," said Mr. Grim. "Although Prince Nightshade has been even more successful than I in his quest for Odditoria, it appears there is one magical entity that has continued to elude him: a source of the animus."

"A *source* of the animus?"

"Yes, old friend," said Mr. Grim, thinking. "Judging from the eyes of the lads that led Prince Nightshade to the Odditorium, it appears that Nightshade has discovered a magical means by which to combine the red energy from the Eye of Mars with the animus residue from our escaped pocket watch. Red and blue make purple, you see—"

"And the lads who led him here," Lord Dreary exclaimed, "their eyes glowed purple!"

"Correct. If the Eye of Mars can only resurrect the ancient armies of Romulus and Remus, then the number of red-eyed Shadesmen the prince can gather for his army is limited. However, if he were to get his hands on a source of the *animus*—"

"Then the number of *purple*-eyed Shadesmen he can gather is *unlimited*!"

"Correct again, Lord Dreary," said Mr. Grim. "Prince Nightshade wants the animus so he can create a purple-eyed army of the dead."

A heavy silence fell over the room. I couldn't help but feel sorry for Noah and his gang, but just the thought of an entire army of those moaning purple-eyed devils gadding about the world sent a shiver up my spine—not to mention that I had almost become one of them myself.

"So, this pocket watch," Lord Dreary said finally. "Is *that* the magical object from which you harness the animus?"

"Good heavens, no!" cried Mr. Grim, laughing, but then he abruptly stopped and gazed about the room. "Come to think of it, where *is* old McClintock?"

"Nigel has him, sir," I said, and Mr. Grim started as if he'd forgotten I was there.

"Thank you, Master Grubb," he said, smiling wryly.

"However, I must admit that your knowledge of Mack's whereabouts would have been much more useful to us about an hour ago."

Mr. Grim shot me a wink, but it did little to ease my guilt. In all the commotion, I'd nearly forgotten that this whole mess was entirely my fault.

"I beg your pardon, sir," I said, looking down at my shoes, at which point Mrs. Pinch's broom unexpectedly swept past me into the room. Lord Dreary cried out in surprise, but the broom ignored him and began tidying up the hearth. Evidently, more of the sandy red soot had fallen out of the flue during the battle.

"Not now, Broom," said Mr. Grim, and the broom gave a quick curtsy and disappeared into the parlor. "Odditoria," said Mr. Grim with a shrug, and Lord Dreary sighed and fingered his collar.

"Speaking of which," said the old man, "if the red energy comes from the Eye of Mars, and the yellow energy comes from Gwendolyn the Yellow Fairy, from what Odditoria do you harness the blue animus?"

"Now, now," said Mr. Grim, smiling, "what kind of mad sorcerer would I be if I went about revealing everything in my bag of tricks at once?"

"Great poppycock, man, don't play games!"

"I assure you, Lord Dreary, it is not my intention to be evasive. However, I should think any attempt to explain the source of my blue energy without an accompanying demonstration would be futile. And given the state of the Odditorium's systems, such a demonstration is impossible at the moment."

"Yes, but Alistair, I—"

"Besides," said Mr. Grim, rising, "it looks as if Mrs. Pinch and Nigel have arrived with our Asterian nectar."

Lord Dreary and I turned to find them standing in the entrance to the library. The old woman held a tray, on top of which rested a slender black bottle and five small glasses.

However, I could not help but stare at Nigel. He was Odditoria too, was he not? Odditoria powered by the animus just like Mack. But Nigel most certainly wasn't a machine. Which meant that *people* could be powered by the animus too. Maybe Nigel was the *source* of the animus. After all, odder things had happened at Alistair Grim's, even though I had yet to come across a sphere big enough to hold a man like Nigel Stout.

"Allow me, Mrs. Pinch," said Mr. Grim, and he took the tray and set it on his desk. "Don't want you pouring this without your spectacles."

Mrs. Pinch furrowed her brow and drew her lips together tightly.

"Asterian nectar," said Mr. Grim, holding up the bottle. "A rare delicacy I picked up in Greece." Mr. Grim popped the cork and filled each glass with the thick, black liquid. "Gather 'round," he said. "You too, Master Grubb."

All of us took our glasses.

"Alistair, I—" Lord Dreary began, but Mr. Grim quickly cut him off.

"There'll be plenty of time for show-and-tell later," he said. "Let us now enjoy the peace and quiet of this moment with a toast to the Odditorium."

Mr. Grim raised his glass. Nigel and Mrs. Pinch followed suit, but both Lord Dreary and I hesitated.

"Are you not going to join us, Lord Dreary?" asked Mr. Grim.

The old man looked back and forth between Mr. Grim and the others—then heaved a heavy sigh and said, "When in Rome."

I wasn't quite sure what he meant by that, since we were nowhere near Rome as far as I could tell. But nonetheless, when Lord Dreary raised his glass I did the same.

"To the Odditorium," said Mr. Grim.

"To the Odditorium!" replied the others.

"You, too, Master Grubb," said Mr. Grim.

"To the Odditorium," I said, and we all sipped from our glasses.

I had never partaken in a toast before, nor had I ever tasted anything as delicious as Mr. Grim's nectar. And as a salt-scented breeze blew in from the balcony, I gazed out past the pipe organ to the clear blue sky and understood at once that what I had tasted was adventure.

— TWELVE —

Nigel's Secret

fter our toast, Lord Dreary continued to press Mr. Grim to reveal the source of his animus, upon which Mr. Grim once again insisted that, until the Odditorium's systems were recharged, such a revelation would be impossible. Besides, he explained, there were more pressing matters at hand now that Prince Nightshade was on our tail. The first order of business: to find out where the space jump had taken us.

"Right-o, then," Nigel said. "Come along, Grubb."

"Just a moment, Nigel," said Mr. Grim. "If you and Lord Dreary would care to step into the parlor, I'd like to speak to Master Grubb for a moment. *Alone.*"

I swallowed hard and my heart began to hammer. For a while there I thought Mr. Grim was going to let me off the hook about McClintock.

"Begging your pardon, sir," Nigel said. "As far as I can tell, this whole Mack business was an honest mistake."

"Yes, Alistair," said Lord Dreary. "Try not to be too hard on the lad, will you?"

"I'll take your advice into consideration," said Mr. Grim, ushering them out. But as Nigel and Lord Dreary retreated to the parlor, Mrs. Pinch lagged behind.

"May I help you, Mrs. Pinch?" asked Mr. Grim.

"Well, sir, I . . ."

The old woman's eyes darted back and forth between Mr. Grim and me.

"Yes, Mrs. Pinch?"

"Well, sir," she began again. "I may not have my spectacles, but I know a good lad when I see one. And blind me if I'm going to stand by without putting in a word for Master Grubb here."

"Your word is duly noted," said Mr. Grim, and he motioned for her to leave.

"Humph!" said Mrs. Pinch. And with that the old woman picked up the tray of dirty glasses and stormed out of the library.

"Well now, Master Grubb," said Mr. Grim, closing the pocket doors. "Looks like your little jaunt with McClintock has brought us a bit of trouble, has it not?"

"I'm afraid it has, sir," I said guiltily.

"Nothing to be afraid of just yet," said Mr. Grim, and he crossed to his desk. "Turn your back, please," he said.

"Sir?"

"Turn your *back*."

I gulped. Here comes a beating for certain, I thought, and I slowly turned round to face the door. However, as I braced my bottom for his blows, I caught sight of Mr. Grim's reflection in the silver water pitcher on the table. He reached into the wooden box on his desk, took out the Lady in Black's mirror, and stared at it for a long time.

"What's to become of him?" he whispered into the mirror —and I could have sworn I saw it flash—but then Mr. Grim frowned. "Temperamental trinket," he muttered, and quickly returned the mirror to its case.

"You may turn around now," he said, and I obeyed. "Very well, then, no more suspense. All is forgiven, Master Grubb."

"Cor blimey!" I said, relieved. "You mean you're not going to beat me, sir?"

"Beat you?" said Mr. Grim, aghast. "Certainly not, Master Grubb. Everyone makes mistakes, but you have shown courage and honesty in the face of adversity—not to mention quite a bit of resourcefulness—which is why I'd like to offer you a job as my apprentice."

"Your *apprentice,* sir?" I asked, amazed.

"I'm not getting any younger, and I'd be lying if I said all this Nightshade business hasn't made me mindful of my own mortality. I could use a boy like you to help carry on here, should something happen to me. And so, I am promoting you from resident chummy to sorcerer's apprentice—that is, if you want the job."

"But of course, sir!" I cried, my heart swelling. "Oh, thank you, sir!"

"Very well, then, we'll work out the particulars later." Mr. Grim pulled down on a nearby sconce, and his desk slid back to reveal the trapdoor in the floor. "But for now, you run along with Nigel. And send in Lord Dreary, will you? I did promise him an introduction to Gwendolyn, did I not?"

Mr. Grim winked, and the giant birdcage began its descent from the ceiling.

"Yes, sir, oh, thank you, sir!" I cried, and I dashed out into the parlor. "Mr. Grim would like to see you now, Lord Dreary, sir!"

Lord Dreary, oblivious to my happiness, muttered something about a stiff upper lip and then hurried into the library.

"Looks like you swallowed a bucket of sunshine," Nigel said. "Everything turn out all right, then?"

"Oh yes, Nigel! Mr. Grim asked me to be his apprentice!"

"Well done, lad!" Nigel said, patting me on the back. "A wise choice, I might add, but no time to celebrate now. We've got work to do."

Nigel motioned for me to follow him.

"Where are we going?" I asked.

"Why, to the garret. If the boss wants to find out where the Odditorium has jumped to, the garret is where we must begin."

Nigel opened the secret panel beside the lift, and I followed him inside. The shaft was pitch-black. Nearly all of the Odditorium's blue sconce lights had gone out—a result, Mr. Grim had explained earlier, of having to run on the power reserves. And as we climbed the stairs, Nigel removed his goggles to light our way.

"Watch your step, Grubb," he said.

The animus from his eyes certainly was bright enough, and as we passed the first landing, I spied a door that I determined to be a secret entrance beside the lift on the fourth floor—the same floor on which the long hallway with the marred portraits was located. I so badly wanted to ask Nigel about Cleona the trickster; but as we pressed on, I decided it was not the proper time to talk about swirly chalk mustaches and A.G.'s spotty bottom.

"Here we are, then," Nigel said as we came to a trapdoor in the ceiling. Nigel pushed it open, and the two of us hoisted ourselves up into the garret.

As with most garrets, the ceiling was low, and Nigel had to hunch over to keep from bumping his head. In the center of the room was a pair of ladders, each leading up to a hatch that opened onto the roof. Beside each ladder stood a pair of samurai with their swords drawn. The late afternoon sunlight shone down on them from the hatches, casting their face masks in shadow so that only the blue of their eyes could be seen.

"Hallo, hallo," Nigel said. "You gents still hanging about?" The samurai, as usual, did not respond. "Carry on, then. Back to your posts."

The samurai promptly sheathed their weapons and shuffled past us, one by one disappearing down through the trapdoor.

Nigel stepped over a large pipe and skirted around one of the ladders. The garret was nearly filled to capacity with a massive tangle of clockwork gears and flues—all of it packed together so tightly that it seemed impossible that any of it could actually work.

"Over here, Grubb," Nigel said. And as I joined him beside the ladder, I noticed that he was staring up at a colony of bats hanging upside down from the ceiling.

I gasped and backed away. Being a chummy, I'd had my share of run-ins with bats, thank you very much, and I knew better than to go bothering with them—unless, of course, I wanted to get my ears bitten.

"Don't be afraid, Grubb," Nigel said, unhooking a bat from the ceiling. "These ain't your typical belfry bats."

As Nigel held the bat close to his glowing blue eyes, I

could tell right away that the creature wasn't a real bat at all, but a mechanical bat made entirely of black metal.

"Wake up, sleepyhead," Nigel whispered, and a thin bolt of animus shot out from each of his eyes, enveloping the bat in a shimmering ball of sparkles. The bat instantly sprang to life, its eyes aglow with animus as it flapped its inky black wings and let out a screech.

"Cor blimey!" I gasped. Perhaps Nigel was the source of the animus after all.

"Good morning, child," Nigel said, and then he set the bat atop his shoulder. Nigel did the same for all of them, one by one bringing them to life and wishing them good morning until he had a dozen or so of the black mechanicals perched atop his massive shoulders.

"Come along then, children," he said. He replaced his goggles and headed for one of the ladders. "That means you, too, Grubb."

The big man climbed up and squeezed himself through the open hatch. I followed him, and as I stepped out onto the roof, I spied the upper gunnery for the first time. One of its cannons had indeed been blown off, and the turret's blue energy was deactivated.

"Over here, Grubb," Nigel said, and I joined him at the edge of the roof just as he set down the last of the bats on the Odditorium's castlelike battlements. Nigel didn't seem worried about their animus attracting the doom dogs, and so I knew that the tiny mechanicals had to be covered in Mr. Grim's magic paint. Just like the Odditorium.

"Be mindful of danger, children," Nigel said. "I expect all of you to come back safe and sound, do you hear?"

The bats nodded their mechanical heads and chomped their mechanical jaws.

"Right-o, then, off you go!" And with a loud clap of his hands the big man sent the bats scattering away in every direction. "Safe and sound, children!" he called after them. "Safe and sound!"

The bats screeched their good-byes, and the two of us watched them fly away—their cries quickly fading as they grew smaller and smaller in the distance. Finally, when the last of the bats had disappeared into the setting sun, I asked, "Where are they going, Nigel?"

"In search of land," he replied. "It'll be dark soon. Mr. Grim can steer the Odditorium by the stars, but first we need to know how close we are to land. Wouldn't be sensible for us to travel west if land was closer east."

Nigel heaved a heavy sigh and leaned with his elbows upon the battlements. I wasn't tall enough to do the same, so I just stood there gazing up at him.

"Will they be able to find their way back?" I asked.

"Oh yes," Nigel said. "That is, if they don't run out of animus first."

"You mean they fizzle out like Mack?"

"No, the bats have to be recharged from time to time, as does everything else what runs on the animus. Mack, on the other hand, fizzles out but then comes back. He *never* has to be recharged. And for the life of him, Mr. Grim can't figure out why."

"Is that why he's always in the shop?"

"That's right, Grubb. So, until the Odditorium is up and running again with blue animus, we won't be able to go anywhere."

"But if that space jump drained the Odditorium of its blue animus, how come it didn't drain you of yours too?"

Nigel shot me a look of surprise—not the best way to ask him about his blue energy, I had to admit—but then the big man heaved a heavy sigh, as if he knew this question had been coming.

"The animus works differently in a person than it does in a machine," he said simply. "Same reason why the doom dogs don't come for me. The animus is safe inside my body. However, unlike Mack, I have to be recharged from time to time."

Guess I was mistaken, I thought. If Nigel has to be

226

recharged, then he cannot possibly be the source of the animus.

"I suppose you're afraid of me now, eh, Grubb?" Nigel said quietly.

"But of course not! Why would I be afraid of you? Animus or no animus, you're still my friend, aren't you, Nigel?"

"That I am, Grubb," Nigel said, smiling. But as he gazed out over the sea, once again his face took on the same sad expression that I had seen in the marketplace.

"Begging your pardon, Nigel," I said after a moment. "But since we're friends, may I ask what you're thinking about when you look so sad?"

The big man turned to me. "You can tell I'm sad without seeing my eyes?"

"I suppose I can, yes. Is it because you miss your brother William?"

Nigel hung his head a bit, then turned back toward the sea. "No, not William," he said. "I don't give him much thought anymore. The one I'm missing is Maggie."

"Who's Maggie, Nigel?"

"Maggie is William's daughter."

"Oh," I said, swallowing. "Is she—?"

"Dead?" Nigel asked, and I nodded. "No, Grubb. Maggie is as alive as you are. A little older than you, in fact, and healthy as one of Mr. Grim's horses."

"Where is she?"

"It's all a bit complicated, Grubb. But since you're going to be Mr. Grim's apprentice, I suppose I'll have to explain it to you sooner or later."

Nigel and I sat down with our backs against the battlements.

"Maggie's mum," Nigel began, "died in childbirth, so right from the start it was up to William to raise Maggie on his own. He had a hard go of it at first, but eventually he managed to make a comfortable life for the two of them working as a coachman for Judge Mortimer Hurst."

I gasped. "The same Judge Hurst what caused all that fuss today?"

"That's right, Grubb. William used to work at the stables where Judge Hurst boarded his horses. The judge took a liking to William and offered him a job—took a liking to little Maggie, too, and would often let her ride with him in his coach.

"But you see," Nigel went on, "Judge Hurst, when he wasn't sentencing people to hang, was also a collector of antiquities. And along with Mr. Grim and Lord Dreary, he sometimes did business with an elderly gentleman by the name of Abel Wortley."

"Abel Wortley—the man Judge Hurst said your brother William done in!"

"Right-o, Grubb. Abel Wortley was a purveyor of antiquities just like Mr. Grim used to be. And oftentimes Judge Hurst would send William to fetch the old man for society meetings where they could show off their latest acquisitions.

"Well, one night when William went to pick up Mr. Wortley at his house, the old man didn't come down. Neither did his housekeeper, for that matter. William thought this strange, of course, but Judge Hurst told him not to bother about it and gave him the rest of the night off. And so William spent the evening playing with Maggie at his lodgings. She was just shy of four years old at the time but smart as a whip, she was, and the apple of her father's eye."

Nigel smiled, but I could hear in his voice that he had grown sad again.

"Anyhow," he said with a sigh, "an inspector from Scotland Yard met William at the stables the next morning. You see, Abel Wortley and his housekeeper had been done in the night before. Stabbed to death and robbed, they was, around the same time William was there. And so he became the prime suspect. William protested his innocence, of course, but when the inspector found some of the stolen items in the judge's coach—"

"Oh no!"

"Oh yes, Grubb. Judge Hurst could easily account for his whereabouts, so who else had been at Wortley's around the time the old man got himself done in?"

I swallowed hard, speechless.

"Needless to say, the evidence against William was damning. However, when Judge Hurst visited him in the clink, he told William that if he went quietly to the gallows, Maggie would be provided for. Gave William his word that he would send her off to live in the country with his sister. A proper lady, she is, what can't have children of her own. So you see, that's where Maggie lives today. With Judge Hurst's sister."

"So then William confessed his guilt?"

"Either way, he was going to hang, so why not give his daughter a better life? The judge's sister could provide for Maggie in ways that William never could. And best of all, she could set Maggie on the path to becoming a proper lady."

"But Nigel, if William didn't murder Abel Wortley, then who did?"

"Well, that's where things get a bit tricky. And that's where Mr. Grim comes in."

"Mr. Grim?"

"You see, Mr. Grim had been a friend of Wortley's too. And being his friend, he spent a lot of time in the old man's study. Even after Elizabeth—" Nigel abruptly stopped and cleared his throat. "That is, even after Mr. Grim removed himself from society and began collecting Odditoria, Mr. Wortley was one of the few friends with whom he still associated. And being that he spent so much time in the old man's study, when he visited the crime scene, he had a fair idea of what the robbers had taken."

"The items found in the coach?"

"All that, yes, but also a couple of other items that were *not* found in the coach. Items that appeared ordinary—unless one had knowledge of Odditoria."

"Ordinary," I whispered.

"What's that you say?"

"Ordinary. Mr. Grim said that the most powerful Odditoria are usually those things that, on the surface, appear ordinary."

"He's right. And so Mr. Grim knew that Abel Wortley's killer had to have knowledge of Odditoria too. Why else would a thief steal such ordinary objects and leave the more valuable ones behind? And since William didn't seem the sort to be familiar with Odditoria, Mr. Grim suspected he had been framed by someone who was."

"Good heavens!"

"But you have to remember that, back then, no one knew Mr. Grim was gadding about the world collecting Odditoria. Consequently, if he spilled the beans about the missing objects, he would endanger his entire quest."

"Because he would have to reveal that the objects were magical?"

"That's right, Grubb. Not to mention that he would risk

revealing his knowledge of Odditoria to the real culprit too."

"So what happened, Nigel?"

"Well, when Mr. Grim visited William in the clink, he told him that he not only thought William was innocent, but also that he thought he'd been set up by someone."

"Judge Hurst!" I exclaimed.

"Right-o, Grubb. But Mr. Grim had no proof, you see. And there was also Maggie to think about. Mr. Grim did offer to take her in, but even he had to admit that the kind of life he could provide for her was nothing compared to the life she'd lead in the country—what with all his quests in search of Odditoria and whatnot."

"That would be a problem," I said, but I was thinking about Cleona the trickster. She lived at the Odditorium, didn't she?

"But besides Judge Hurst," Nigel continued, "Mr. Grim had plenty of reasons to suspect that one of his other society friends might recognize Odditoria too. And without the proof of the stolen items . . . well, you see poor William's predicament?"

I stared down sadly at my shoes. Poor William, indeed. Not only had he been hanged for something he didn't do, but also the sister of the very man who hanged him was raising his daughter. On the bright side, however, at least William was at peace and no longer missed her. But what about Maggie?

How dreadful all that must have been on the child—and she being just shy of four years old. At least I was six or there-abouts when Mrs. Smears died. But even if Maggie missed her father half as much as I missed Mrs. Smears, well . . .

The tears began to rise in my throat, but I quickly swallowed them down. *Chin up*, I told myself. *This is no time to get all gobby eyed and gloomy. Nigel needs a friend, and if I'm going to be Mr. Grim's apprentice, I need to be strong about such things.*

And so I forced myself not to cry. "So that's when you came to London, Nigel?" I asked finally. "After your brother was hanged?"

"Yes and no, Grubb. You see, just before William was led to the gallows, Mr. Grim offered him a bargain."

"A bargain?"

"That's right. A bargain in which Mr. Grim offered to bring William back from the dead."

I gasped.

"Of course," Nigel went on, "William thought Mr. Grim had gone touched in the head. But then again, what did he have to lose? So he listened carefully as Mr. Grim laid down the terms of his bargain. One, that upon his resurrection, William would come work for him. Two, that he would always keep his work secret. And three, that he would never reveal his true identity to anyone until Abel Wortley's killer was found."

"And did William agree to Mr. Grim's terms?"

Nigel grew silent. And looking back, I suppose I should've put it all together much sooner. But only when he lifted his goggles and stared at me with his animus-filled eyes did the nub of Nigel's story finally hit home.

"You!" I cried. "You're William Stout!"

"That's right, Grubb. And as I'm sure you've guessed, there never was a brother Nigel. Nigel was the name I took after Mr. Grim brought me back from the dead. Played the role of William's twin, I did, so as to keep the terms of my bargain."

Nigel replaced his goggles, and a long silence passed in which his secret gradually sank in. A million questions raced through my mind at once, and as I searched among them for the proper one to ask, for some reason I settled on perhaps the silliest question of them all.

"So if you were brought back from the dead," I said, "does that mean you're a Shadesman, too, Nigel?"

The big man laughed heartily. "Don't worry, Grubb," he said. "Unlike those bone bags, people what's been brought back with the animus wind up much as they were in life—except for their bright blue peepers, of course. In fact, Mr. Grim says the animus is the closest one can get to the scientific recreation of the human soul."

"Cor blimey," I said. "But, Nigel, if you're really William Stout, that means that Maggie—"

"Is really *my* daughter."

Nigel's words stopped me cold, for despite everything I'd learned about him that day, I never imagined my new friend might have a child.

"So you see, Grubb?" he said after moment. "When I'm looking sad, it's because I'm missing Maggie."

"Have you seen her since . . . well . . . since you came back from the dead?"

"Only from a distance. Mr. Grim sometimes sends Mrs. Pinch to the country with gifts for her, and I hang back in the coach hoping to catch a glimpse of her. Sometimes I do, sometimes I don't, but I send out the bats nearly every night to check up on her. The judge was true to his word, Grubb, and Maggie's been growing up quite happy. There's comfort for me in that."

"But, Nigel, if everyone thinks you're William's brother, wouldn't Maggie think so too? I mean, couldn't you visit her in the country as her Uncle Nigel?"

"Being that everyone fancies me the brother of a murderer, her new family thinks it best she not associate with my sort. Besides," Nigel added, pointing to his goggles, "what sort am I, anyway? Not alive, not dead, but a freak in between what can't even look at his daughter with his own eyes."

I swallowed hard, unsure of what to say.

"No," he said firmly. "It's best for everyone if things stay as they are now. At least until Abel Wortley's murderer is brought to justice. Who knows? Now that Prince Nightshade has finally reared his ugly head, we might end up killing two birds with one stone."

"What do you mean?"

"Well, it's entirely possible that the first time the prince got to his Odditoria before Mr. Grim was ten years ago at Abel Wortley's. Meaning, Abel Wortley's killer and Prince Nightshade might be the same person."

Cor! I was about to exclaim, when something occurred to me. "I saw Judge Hurst with the Black Fairy!"

"What?"

"When the Black Fairy attacked, he snatched up the judge and carried him off. Not long afterward Prince Nightshade appeared from the clouds."

"Hm," Nigel said, thinking. "An intriguing turn of events. Especially since Mr. Grim could never prove that Judge Hurst framed me. Then again, after seeing this Prince Nightshade for the first time today, I don't know what to believe anymore."

Presently, McClintock began rustling in his pocket, and as Nigel made to take him out I cried, "Don't, Nigel! The doom dogs will come after us again!"

"No need to worry about them," Nigel said. "The Odditorium's magic paint is powerful enough to protect us even up here."

"What time is it?" Mack asked as Nigel opened him. But

as soon as he caught sight of those big goggles staring down at him, Mack let out a terrified, *"Ach!"*

He crackled and flashed, gave a quick *tick-tick,* and then his eyes went dim.

"Don't try that on me," Nigel said. "I know your fizzling-out routine all too well, you coward!"

"Coward?" Mack cried, lighting up immediately. "You calling the chief of the Chronometrical Clan McClintock a coward?"

"Just as I thought. Playing possum again! Why, I've got a good mind to toss you off the roof and be done with you!"

"Well, if yer gonna scrap me, then yer gonna have to fight for it!"

Mack leaped for Nigel's nose—*"McClintock!"* he cried—but Nigel caught him just in time. "Let me go!" Mack shouted, and Nigel made to tap him on his XII.

"Don't!" I cried.

Nigel and Mack stopped their scuffling and turned to me.

"There's no sense in fighting about it now," I said. "After all, it was I who accidentally brought Mack outside. So I suppose if you're going to toss him off the roof, you'll have to do the same with me, Nigel."

"Hang on," Mack said, spinning round. "What are we doin' on the roof?"

"A lot has happened since you got pinched, Mack," I said.

"Nevertheless, I should think it more sensible for Odditoria to stick together rather than fighting all the time. Especially now that Prince Nightshade is after us."

"Prince Nightshade?" Mack asked. "What's a Prince Nightshade?"

"I'll explain it to you later. But what do you say, Nigel? Do you think you and Mack can be friends?"

"Grubb's right," Nigel said, sighing. "We Odditoria have to stick together. Sorry I said I was going to scrap you, Mack. You know I'd never go through with it."

"And I'm sorry I tried to bite yer nose," Mack said. "Especially since you know I *would* go through with it."

Nigel laughed. "Gentlemen's shake on it, then," he said, wobbling Mack's case.

"Odditoria and friends to the end," Mack said.

"Right-o," Nigel said, and then he extended his hand to me. "You too, Grubb."

"Me?"

"Of course," Mack interjected. "Yer Odditoria and a friend, ain't ya?"

"A friend, yes, but—"

"Then stop yer jabberin' and put it there, laddie!"

Mack wobbled his case, and rather than arguing with him about being Odditoria, I shook Nigel's hand and Mack's case at the same time.

"Friends to the end, lads!" Mack cheered.

"Friends to the end!" Nigel and I repeated.

Then, out of the corner of my eye, I saw something flash on the far side of the roof. "Look!" I said, pointing.

"One of my bats come back already?" Nigel asked.

"I don't think so," I said, searching. All I could see now was the toothy outline of the Odditorium's battlements against the twilight skies. And for a moment I thought my eyes had been playing tricks on me, but then—

"There!" I said as the light flashed again. "Did you see it?"

"Yes, I did!" Nigel said, scrambling to his feet. "Looks like it's coming from the other side of the battlements. Come on!"

The three of us dashed across the roof, and the light flashed again.

"I see it now too!" Mack exclaimed. And upon reaching the opposite battlement, Nigel leaned out over the side of the Odditorium.

"Oh dear," he said.

"What is it?" Mack and I asked.

Nigel didn't answer right away, but the look of terror on his face told me we were in big trouble just the same.

"We've got to find Mr. Grim," he said finally.

And then we ran for the gunnery.

—THIRTEEN—

Sirens' Eggs and Banshees, Please

What is it?" asked Lord Dreary, out of breath. "An explosive of some sort?"

Fortunately there was enough animus left in the Odditorium's reserves to power the talkbacks, so all Nigel had to do to summon Mr. Grim was hop down into the gunnery. Nigel reached him in the engine room with Lord Dreary, and when the gentlemen arrived on the roof moments later, I could tell by the old man's disposition that his introduction to Gwendolyn had done little to ease his bewilderment.

"Not an explosive, old friend," said Mr. Grim, peering over the battlements. "No, judging from its shape and size, I would suspect that the object down there is some sort of tracking mechanism."

"A tracking mechanism?" asked Lord Dreary.

"Yes," said Mr. Grim, turning around. He leaned with

his back against the battlements and folded his arms. "Have a look for yourself."

Lord Dreary did so, his face flickering red as the mysterious object flashed again beneath him. "Great poppycock!"

"One of the prince's Shadesmen, no doubt," said Mr. Grim. "Must have attached it before I activated the Odditorium's levitation shields."

"It looks like a giant serpent's egg."

"A *Siren's* egg, to be precise."

"A Siren, did you say?"

"Yes. Those beautiful but dangerous sea witches whose songs lured ancient sailors to their deaths. The prince must have convinced one or more of them to join his evil menagerie of living Odditoria."

"Good heavens! You really think one of those singing sea witches could have allied herself with the prince?"

"I shall have to enter a sketch of the creature in my notebook," said Mr. Grim, thinking. "Nevertheless, if a Siren has the power to lure, Prince Nightshade has no doubt discovered a magical means by which to fashion a tracking mechanism out of her eggs—a tracking mechanism that will lure him straight to us!"

"But, Alistair!" cried Lord Dreary. "If the Siren's egg is luring Prince Nightshade to the Odditorium, then surely it is only a matter of time before—"

"Time!" Mr. Grim exclaimed. "What time do you have, Lord Dreary?"

"Why—I—" he sputtered, removing his pocket watch from his waistcoat. "Hang on. Having a hard go seeing in this light . . ."

Without thinking, I held up Mack to assist him, and as soon as his blue light illuminated Lord Dreary's pocket watch, Mack twirled his hands to ten and twelve.

"It's ten o'clock!" he cried, spinning round in my hand and jumping for joy. "Look at me, laddies! I know what time it is! Just ask me! Why, it's ten o'clock! It's ten o'—tick—tick—"

Mack crackled and flashed blue, and then his eyes went dark and his hands spun back to VIII and IV.

"Good heavens!" gasped Lord Dreary. "Is that the pocket watch that caused all the trouble?"

"Never mind that," said Mr. Grim, gazing out over the battlements. "Does it look like ten o'clock in the evening out there to you, Lord Dreary?"

"Well, I—judging from the position of the sun, the time of year, I would say it's closer to six o'clock."

"Precisely. Therefore, if your watch reads ten o'clock London time, we cannot be in the London time zone."

"Remarkable!" said Lord Dreary. "The space jump instantly transported us to a place four hours behind London time!"

"And yet *seven* hours have gone by on your watch."

"What do you mean?"

"If you'll recall, we left London shortly after the preview began at three o'clock. That means *seven* hours have gone by on your watch—three o'clock plus seven hours makes ten o'clock. However, by my calculations, only *two* hours have passed since we popped out of the sky wherever we are now."

"You're right," said Lord Dreary, thinking. "And if only two hours have passed, regardless of wherever we are now, my watch should read five o'clock. Three o'clock plus two hours makes five o'clock."

"That is correct," said Mr. Grim. "But since your watch reads *ten* o'clock—"

"We've lost five hours!" I cried, and both Mr. Grim and Lord Dreary started as if they had forgotten I was there.

"Very good, Master Grubb," said Mr. Grim. "That would explain the power drain. Not only did the force of the space jump knock out nearly all of the Odditorium's animus, it also knocked out all of us for five hours!"

"Good heavens!" cried Lord Dreary.

"I should have realized this immediately," said Mr. Grim, thinking. "Everybody's heads had gone all loopy. But blast it! I didn't think to check the time!"

"But, Alistair, regardless of whether or not we were

unconscious for five hours, how could a hole in the sky instantly transport us so far from London?"

"How should I know?" cried Mr. Grim. "I'm a sorcerer, not a physicist!"

"Yes, well—"

"Nevertheless," said Mr. Grim. "I now realize that the strain of a space jump is much greater than I anticipated. This is something I will have to account for if we are to ever try it again."

"But, Alistair," gasped Lord Dreary, panicking. "If you add on two hours to the five we were asleep, that means that—"

"Prince Nightshade has been tracking us for seven hours!"

"Oh dear," Nigel said.

Mr. Grim rushed across the roof and jumped down into the gunnery. He flicked on the talkback and shouted, "Cleona, are you awake?"

"I am now," Cleona yawned. "What is it, Uncle?"

"Sorry to disturb you, but you need to come up to the roof immediately!"

"Is this a trick? Payback for scribbling on your paintings?"

"I've already hidden your comb in retaliation for that," said Mr. Grim. "Thus, as far as I'm concerned, we are even until the paintings are clean again."

"Pshaw."

"Now, please, Cleona. I need you up here on the roof immediately. It truly is a matter of life and death."

"No tricks?"

"On my honor, Cleona."

"All right, Uncle."

Mr. Grim scrambled up from the gunnery and back to the battlements.

"Uncle?" said Lord Dreary. "Did I just hear that girl call you Uncle?"

"I'm afraid you did."

"But who on earth could possibly call you Uncle? You're an only child!"

Mr. Grim was about to answer, but was stopped short by the glowing blue figure of a girl rising up through the roof.

"Here I am," she said.

Lord Dreary spun around and gasped.

The girl appeared to be a bit older than me, with delicate features wrapped in skin the color of ivory. Her hair was white and fell from her head in a pair of long braids that reached her knees. She wore a simple white gown cinched at the waist, and on the hem and neckline was a square maze pattern that glowed bright blue like the halo of light surrounding her.

"Over here," said Mr. Grim, indicating the battlements. And as the girl glided past me, I noticed that I could see straight through her to Lord Dreary on the other side.

Lord Dreary must have seen me through her too. And as the girl floated up and peered out over the battlements, the old man staggered back and cried: "A ghost!"

"I beg your pardon," said the girl, turning round in mid-air. "I should think a gentleman of your breeding would know better than to go around calling people names, Lord Dreary."

"You—you know me, miss?" the old man sputtered.

"Only by sight, of course. But I must admit, I've found your constant bickering with Uncle over the years quite amusing."

"My apologies," said Mr. Grim. "I forgot the two of you have yet to be introduced. Cleona, meet Lord Dreary. Lord Dreary, this is Cleona."

"A pleasure to officially make your acquaintance," Cleona said. "I hope I didn't startle you, Lord Dreary. After all, now that you know the true nature of the Odditorium, I no longer thought it necessary to hide myself."

"Hide yourself?" asked Lord Dreary, stunned.

"What Cleona is referring to," said Mr. Grim, "is her annoying habit of making herself invisible in order to eavesdrop on our conversations in the library."

"You mean like this?" Cleona said, and she vanished into thin air.

"Good heavens!" cried Lord Dreary, and Mr. Grim rolled his eyes.

"Darling, please, we don't have time for this," he said, but Cleona only giggled, seemingly from nowhere. "You see?" said Mr. Grim, exasperated. "This is what I get for indulging her eccentricities over the years. Case in point: her fixation on calling me Uncle when she knows very well that I am no such relation. This has been going on for—well, what's it been, now, Nigel, ten years?"

"Twelve," he said. "I've been here ten myself, sir."

"Anyhow, if there's one thing I've learned since Cleona's arrival, the only way to neutralize a spirit's mischievous nature is to beat them at their own game."

"Did you say *spirit*, Alistair Grim?"

"That I did. And like most spirits, Cleona is very fond of

playing tricks on people. For instance, drawing mustaches and writing nasty comments on my family portraits."

Again, Cleona giggled from nowhere.

"So you see," said Mr. Grim, "in order to beat Cleona at her own game, I've hidden her comb and will only reveal its whereabouts when the portraits are clean. And speaking of games, Cleona, as we now have an evil necromancer on our tail, I humbly request that you end this game of hide-and-seek at once."

"Pshaw," she said, and appeared again where I last saw her, hovering just above the battlements between Mr. Grim and Lord Dreary.

"Then she *is* a ghost!" cried Lord Dreary.

"Not a ghost, but a banshee."

"A banshee?"

"Yes, Lord Dreary," Mr. Grim said impatiently. "You're familiar with the old Irish legends regarding such entities?"

"Yes, well, if I remember correctly, a banshee is said to be a harbinger of death, is she not? Known for her excessive wailing just before someone is about to die?"

"Just before or just afterward. In addition, banshees often attach themselves to a specific family, and are thus seen as messengers from the beyond—a bridge, if you will, between our world and the Land of the Dead. However, when not in mourning, banshees are actually quite playful. Now, if there are no more questions, I'd like to move on to the matter at hand."

"I have a question," Cleona said, and Mr. Grim heaved a frustrated sigh. "It's for Lord Dreary, actually."

"Er, uh—yes, miss?"

"Has Alistair Grim always had this annoying habit of talking about people in the third person when they are present?"

"Well, I . . ." Lord Dreary chuckled. "Why, yes, I believe he has, miss."

"Peachy. I have a feeling you and I are going to get along quite smashingly, Lord Dreary." Then Cleona turned to me and said, "And I have a feeling you and I are going to get along quite smashingly as well, Master Grubb."

You know me, too? I wanted to say, but my voice got stuck in my throat. And as Cleona's crystal-blue eyes met with mine, I felt a flutter in my stomach that said, *Banshee or no banshee, Cleona the trickster is the most beautiful girl I've ever seen.*

"And look," Cleona said, pointing to my hand. "You still have the pocket watch I gave you!"

"Oh dear," Nigel said.

"Of course," said Mr. Grim. "I should have known!"

It was then my voice came back to me. "You mean you—?"

"That's right, Grubb," Cleona said, giggling. "This morning, I made myself invisible and slipped Mack inside your pocket while you were talking to Mrs. Pinch in the shop."

"Then Mack was telling the truth," I said—when suddenly I remembered my dream from the night before. "You!" I cried. "You asked to play a trick on me when I was asleep!"

"That sounds like her," said Mr. Grim, and he leaned back wearily against the battlements. "Cleona only plays tricks on her family."

"And quite an amusing trick this one was," she said, giggling. "Especially when you went chasing after Mack in the library, Grubb."

"So I did hear someone giggling in there!"

"Yes. I was in the library when Mack slipped under the door. I thought he might give me away, so I tapped him on his twelve to knock him out. Then I returned the book I borrowed and made myself invisible just before you came in."

Mr. Grim stiffened. "*Book*, did you say?"

"I'm sorry, Uncle. I know the rule about borrowing books, but I just wanted to read up on fairies in the event you and Gwendolyn teamed up to play tricks on me."

Mr. Grim was silent, and Cleona gazed round at us.

"Why is everyone looking at me like that?" she asked. "It was just a trick."

"On the contrary," said Mr. Grim. "Your little trick is what set this whole mess today in motion!"

"Whatever do you mean, Uncle?"

"Master Grubb?" said Mr. Grim, gesturing for me to

explain, and I quickly related the events leading up to Prince Nightshade's arrival in London.

"My apologies, everyone," Cleona said, when I'd finished. "And especially to you, Master Grubb. I meant no harm by it." Then she sank guiltily back down to the roof and said, "I'll go clean off the mustaches and your spotty bottom now, Uncle."

"Not so fast," said Mr. Grim, crossly. "It seems that the prince's Shadesmen have attached a tracking mechanism to the Odditorium. I don't suppose you could find it in your heart to pass through the downstairs wall and dislodge it?"

Cleona steeled herself, as if she was summoning up the courage to honor Mr. Grim's request. "I'll do my best, Uncle," she said.

"Oh, no you don't," Nigel said firmly. "Begging your pardon, Mr. Grim, but being that the Odditorium is over the ocean at present, if Cleona were to materialize beyond its walls, it would take nearly all her strength just to stay airborne, never mind trying to dislodge a tracking mechanism at the same time."

Mr. Grim heaved a heavy sigh. "You're right, Nigel. What was I thinking. . . ."

"Perhaps if I hugged the Odditorium's outer shell," Cleona said, "I might be able to pry off the tracking mechanism without losing too much of my strength. At least I can give it a try."

"Certainly not," said Mr. Grim, softening. "It's too much of a risk in your present condition. Forgive me for even asking, love, and I thank you for your selflessness. As always."

"What on earth are you talking about?" asked Lord Dreary.

"Being a land-dwelling spirit," Mr. Grim began, "a banshee does not have the power to cross large bodies of water unless she is enclosed in something that protects her. The Odditorium's magic paint does just that, same as it protects us from the doom dogs. Without it, Cleona's life force would drain away and she would cease to exist."

"Good heavens," said Lord Dreary.

"The same goes for Gwendolyn. Just one of many laws of the supernatural universe that I'm afraid is unalterable."

"The magic paint is very powerful, Uncle," Cleona said. "And really, I'm feeling quite myself again. Perhaps if I—"

"Out of the question," said Mr. Grim. "Even if you were successful in dislodging the tracking mechanism, you'd be so drained afterward that it'd take you forever to regain your strength and transfer the animus."

"Wait a moment," said Lord Dreary. "Are you saying that Cleona controls the source of the animus?"

"No, old friend," said Mr. Grim. "Cleona *is* the source of the animus."

Lord Dreary and I gasped.

"Hence," Mr. Grim went on, "now that you have seen the conductor spheres for my other Odditoria, you understand in theory how I've been able to harness Cleona's supernatural essence to create the very spirit of the Odditorium itself."

"Odditoria," said Lord Dreary, thinking. "Used to classify any magical object that is living, inanimate, or *otherwise*. That is what you said, Alistair. *Otherwise*—as in something that is neither alive nor dead."

"In Cleona's case, yes," said Mr. Grim. "So you see, Lord Dreary, without our banshee here, the Odditorium's mechanical functions simply could not exist—including the machine that facilitated the space jump."

"But the space jump," said Lord Dreary. "How does Cleona—?"

"A banshee, by her nature, is a bridge between our world and the Land of the Dead. And so I've invented a machine that harnesses that nature to create an interdimensional bridge of my own. Unfortunately, the machine takes quite a toll on poor Cleona, and thus we find ourselves in our present situation."

"I don't mean to interrupt, sir," Nigel said. "But getting back to the tracking mechanism?"

"Thank you, Nigel," said Mr. Grim. "Unfortunately, even if Cleona or Gwendolyn were successful in dislodging the tracking mechanism, it wouldn't do us much good if there are others flashing away out there."

"You mean—?"

"If Prince Nightshade allied himself with more than one Siren, then it's only logical to assume that he fashioned more than one tracking mechanism from their eggs."

"I'll do it," Nigel said. "Tie a rope around my waist, and I'll climb down and start looking for them."

"A valiant proposition, Nigel. But it would take you much too long to make an adequate sweep of the Odditorium's perimeter. Speaking of sweeping, even Broom wouldn't have the strength to pry off something like that tracking mechanism. And given the fact that Mrs. Pinch's spectacles are smashed . . ."

Broom? I said to myself. *Was Mr. Grim implying that Broom could fly as well as sweep? And what did Mrs. Pinch have to do with anything?*

"No," said Mr. Grim. "The most efficient way to embark on our search-and-destroy mission would be to use—"

"The wasps!" Nigel said.

"Very good, Nigel. My thoughts exactly."

"The wasps?" said Lord Dreary, confused.

"Cleona," said Mr. Grim, ignoring him, "do you think you're strong enough to charge the energy panels in your chambers?"

"I think so, Uncle," she said. "But since the space jump drained the Odditorium's systems almost entirely, I won't be able to give you much power for the reserves until I get all my strength back."

"Can you get the wasps going for us?"

"Yes, but if you'd like me to charge the rest of the Odditorium too, I should think I'd have only enough energy left over for one."

"One wasp will be sufficient," said Mr. Grim.

Just then we heard a loud screech above our heads. Lord Dreary let out a shriek and dove for the battlements, but the rest of us gazed upward and spied a cluster of tiny blue lights headed our way.

"The bats!" I cried, and the entire colony screeched as if in reply.

"Good heavens!" exclaimed Lord Dreary. "We're under attack!"

"Don't be afraid, old friend," said Mr. Grim. "They work for us."

The bats circled the roof once, formed a single line, and then swooped down through the porthole and into the garret —all except one, which broke off at the last moment and lighted on Nigel's shoulder.

"What do you have here?" Nigel said, reaching into the bat's mouth. "Look, sir," he said, handing it to Mr. Grim. "It's a leaf."

"Yes," said Mr. Grim, examining it. "A red-oak leaf, to be precise. We must be closer to land than I thought."

"Where to, child?" Nigel asked, and the bat extended its wing to point the way.

"Due west by my calculations," said Mr. Grim, looking up at the stars. "Very well, then. Cleona, you return to your chambers and begin charging the panels."

"Yes, Uncle," she said, and sank at once through the roof.

"As for the rest of us," said Mr. Grim, "to the engine room!"

— FOURTEEN —

The Wasp Rider

y the time we arrived in the engine room, the wall sconces were burning bright again with blue animus. Everything else appeared to be normal too. The red fires in the ring of furnaces burned as before, and the crystal sphere still glowed yellow with fairy dust. Gwendolyn—her eyes heavy, her face smeared with chocolate—sat watching us from the front steps of her dollhouse.

"Is there something I can help you with, Pookie?" she asked.

Pookie?

"No thank you," said Mr. Grim, heading for the talkback. "You just enjoy the rest of your chocolate."

Gwendolyn smiled wide and popped another piece of chocolate in her mouth. I stood there gaping. Surely this was not the same Yellow Fairy I'd met before, what with her sunny disposition and pet names for Mr. Grim.

Noticing my surprise, Nigel whispered the word *chocolate* in my ear. I looked at him quizzically and he said, "How do you think Mr. Grim kept her from gobbling him up back there in the Black Forest?"

"Chomp, chomp," said the Yellow Fairy, and she began cooing—the same cooing I'd heard coming from Mr. Grim's coach just before we took flight over the countryside.

"Are you there, Uncle?" called Cleona from the talkback.

"Yes, love," replied Mr. Grim. "How are things progressing in your chambers?"

"Very well, I think. All the systems are up and running, and I've charged the wasp in comb number one."

Following Mr. Grim's gaze, I noticed for the first time that the engine room's ceiling resembled the inside of a wasp nest. All the combs were dark except for one, in which a pair of bulbous blue eyes shone brightly.

"And you've instructed the wasp what to look for?" asked Mr. Grim.

"Yes, Uncle," Cleona replied. "Its power should last you for quite some time—that is, unless you plan on trying another space jump."

"I plan on no such thing. Now, get some sleep before you charge the reserves."

"Pshaw. My strength is coming back just fine now."

"Never mind that. You do as I say."

"Oh, very well, then."

Mr. Grim flicked off the talkback and then hurried over to a large panel near the furnaces. The panel itself was made up of rows of numbered buttons, and as Mr. Grim looked up at the ceiling, he pressed the button labeled 1.

The eyes above us grew brighter, and then a giant insect crawled out from the comb and buzzed its wings—wings that, in the light from the crystal sphere below, flashed like plates of sparkling yellow glass.

"Great poppycock!" Lord Dreary exclaimed. "It really *is* a wasp!"

"A mechanical wasp," said Mr. Grim, "but a wasp none-theless."

As if on cue, the insect lifted off, buzzed around the engine room once, then slowly descended to the floor. Other than its large blue eyes, polished steel wings, and black metal frame, this wasp was identical to a real wasp—but it was also bigger than me.

"So that's how you built the Odditorium," Lord Dreary said in astonishment. "The screens and curtains outside—that was why no one ever saw any workers going in and out. You created these creatures to do the work for you!"

It was then that I spied the large hammer and chisel in

the wasp's front claws. And all at once I understood what I'd heard upon my arrival at the Odditorium. The loud black-smith's hammering had been Mr. Grim's wasps at work in the engine room.

"An excellent deduction, Lord Dreary," said Mr. Grim. "You see, old friend, one of the unique properties of the animus is that, as it is being transferred into a machine, one can instruct that machine to perform a specific task. And so this wasp and her deactivated sisters were charged with building the Odditorium."

"Incredible!" said Lord Dreary.

Mr. Grim squatted down and spoke directly to the wasp. "You understand your mission, Number One?"

The wasp nodded its round head and batted its antennae.

"Very well, then," said Mr. Grim, rising. "There is one problem, however."

"What's that?" asked Lord Dreary.

"The wasp is only a machine, unable to think for itself. Given the fact that Cleona, in her transference of the animus, instructed the wasp to find and remove the tracking mecha-nism, the wasp in turn will only be able to recognize those things that Cleona recognizes."

"The Siren's egg, you mean?"

"Or *eggs*, yes. However, if something else is out there— another type of tracking mechanism or perhaps something even more nefarious—the wasp won't be able to distinguish such objects from, say, the battle damage caused by Nightshade's minions."

"So what shall we do?" asked Lord Dreary.

"Well, I should think that the only way to be certain that the outside of the Odditorium is clean is to have a set of human eyes riding along with the wasp's."

"Great poppycock! You mean, you actually intend to ride that thing?"

"I would if I could. However, I am much too heavy for the wasp to stay airborne. The same goes for you and Nigel. No, in order to make an adequate sweep of the outside, we would need a much smaller rider."

Without thinking, I raised my hand and said, "I'll do it, sir."

Mr. Grim stiffened. "No. Not you, Master Grubb. It's much too dangerous."

"I agree with the boss," Nigel said. "Much, much too dangerous, Grubb."

"Please, sir," I said. "It's the least I can do, being your apprentice and all."

"Out of the question," said Mr. Grim. "We'll have to take our chances with just the wasp itself."

"I'm not afraid, sir. I'm quite accustomed to high places, and I'm very good at climbing and holding on tightly to things. Besides, if the wasp should need some help, I imagine that prying off a tracking mechanism couldn't be much different than scraping off soot from a chimney."

Mr. Grim studied me for a moment, and then, getting an idea, rushed over to the talkback. "Cleona, are you still awake?"

"I am now," she replied sleepily.

"Would you be so kind as to drop down into the engine room?"

"What for?"

"A matter of the utmost urgency."

"Has Gwendolyn had her chocolate?" Cleona asked. "I'm not in the mood for another quarrel."

"I assure you, Gwendolyn is quite amicable at present. Aren't you, Gwendolyn?"

The Yellow Fairy cooed.

"There, you see, Cleona?" said Mr. Grim. "You needn't worry about a repeat of your introduction this morning. She did the same thing to Nigel before we left London, and now the two of them are the best of friends. Isn't that right, Nigel?"

"If you say so, sir."

"Very well, then, Uncle. I'll be right down."

Mr. Grim flicked off the talkback and joined us again.

"But, Alistair," said Lord Dreary, "surely you don't intend to ask Cleona to ride that thing. You said that if she stays too long over the water she'll cease to exist."

"I am well aware of that. And even though Number One's

magic paint would most likely protect her, it would still be too much of a risk to send her out there. Which is why I intend on riding the wasp myself."

Nigel and I gasped.

"*You?*" cried Lord Dreary.

"Yes, old friend."

"But you just said that you're much too heavy."

"I am."

"But that means—"

"The wasp will not be able to hold me."

"Then you'll most certainly—"

"Fall into the ocean and drown, yes."

"But, Alistair—that's suicide!"

"Precisely!"

"But—"

"Quiet, Lord Dreary!" said Mr. Grim, gazing upward. "Here she comes."

Cleona floated feet first through the ceiling and down to the floor. "Here I am, Uncle."

"Thank you for coming, Cleona. I just wanted to inform you in person of my decision to ride Number One."

"What?"

"At this moment, I fully intend to get on Number One's back and fly around outside the Odditorium in search of more tracking mechanisms."

"No tricks?" Cleona asked, amazed.

"What does your instinct tell you?" replied Mr. Grim.

Cleona began to tremble, and her eyes streamed with tears. She clawed at her hair and stretched her lips apart in a ghastly O, and from deep within her throat came a deafening wail of *"AAAIIIEEEEEEEEEEEEAAAAAAAAAAHHHHH!"*

All of us, even Gwendolyn, pressed our hands to our ears, but it did little to block out the banshee's wailing—a wail that sounded like a cross between a cat screeching and a wolf howling at the moon.

"AAAIIIEEEEEEEEEEEEAAAAAAAAAAHHHHH!" Cleona cried again, and the entire Odditorium shook so violently that I was certain the engine room's ceiling would come crumbling down on us at any moment.

"I've changed my mind!" Mr. Grim shouted. "I will not ride the wasp but will allow Master Grubb to do so in my place!"

And just as quickly as she began, Cleona stopped her wailing. She blinked her eyes a couple of times, then wiped her cheeks with her sleeve and looked around as if nothing had happened.

"Good heavens!" cried Lord Dreary.

"Forgive the experiment," said Mr. Grim. "Are you all right, Cleona?"

"Oh yes, Uncle. Perfectly fine now, thank you."

"Experiment?" asked Lord Dreary.

"You see, as Cleona is a banshee who has attached herself to my family, based on my decision to ride the wasp, she foretold my doom. However, when I changed my mind and agreed to let Master Grubb ride the wasp, Cleona stopped wailing. But Master Grubb, you see, is now *also* part of our family. And so—well, do you see where I'm going with this, Lord Dreary?"

"You mean, the fact that she stopped wailing when you agreed to let Grubb ride the wasp indicates that the boy will be safe on his mission?"

"At this point in time, yes. However, as I just demonstrated, the future can be altered by even the most insignificant decisions made in the present. And so, Master Grubb, if for some reason Cleona should start wailing again, you must return inside at once. Do you understand, lad?"

"Yes, sir."

"You must also be very careful and precise in your instructions to Number One. For example," he said, leaning over the wasp. "Fly over to the sphere, Number One."

Immediately the wasp buzzed its wings and lifted off. It flew directly to the crystal sphere, but then just hovered there, as if awaiting further instructions.

"So you see, Master Grubb," said Mr. Grim, "if you wish Number One to land, you must tell it to do so."

Mr. Grim instructed the wasp to land on top of the sphere, and it obeyed.

"Now, Number One," he said, "until I tell you otherwise, you will follow only Master Grubb's instructions. Do you understand?"

From atop the sphere, the wasp nodded its head and batted its antennae.

"Number One," said Mr. Grim, "fly back to me and land at my feet."

The wasp did not move.

"Go ahead, then, Master Grubb. Tell it to fly back to you and land at your feet."

"Number One, fly back to me and land at my feet."

The wasp lifted off the sphere and did as I commanded.

"Very good," said Mr. Grim.

He crossed to a panel on the opposite wall and pulled a lever, whereupon a porthole opened in the floor, and a cool salt breeze flooded the engine room.

"Climb aboard," said Mr. Grim, and I mounted the wasp. "Hold on tight to that joint casing there," he added, indicating the raised rim running across the wasp's middle segment. "And be sure to keep your appendages clear of the wasp's wings."

"No need to worry, sir," I said. "I don't have any appendages, far as I can tell."

"Your *arms* and your *legs*, lad," said Mr. Grim, and I

swallowed hard and nodded. "Now," Mr. Grim continued, "despite the complexity of the Odditorium's inner workings, the outside is relatively simple. Number One should be able to spot the Sirens' eggs quite easily. However, if you should notice any other objects inconsistent with the rest of the exterior, direct Number One to fly toward it, and judge for yourself what belongs there and what doesn't. Understand?"

"I hope so, Mr. Grim."

"Very well, then, my young apprentice. Command Number One to fly you 'round the outside of the Odditorium. And good luck to you, lad."

"Right-o," Nigel said. "Good luck, Grubb."

"Good luck," said Lord Dreary and Cleona. Gwendolyn just cooed. And as I grabbed hold of the wasp's joint casing, I took a deep breath and said:

"Fly me 'round the outside of the Odditorium, Number One!"

The wasp batted its antennae and crawled forward, and then all of a sudden it seemed as if I had fallen into a cold black well. And had I not lost my breath, I most certainly would have screamed. The moon was full, the sky clear and bright with all its stars, and I could easily make out the silver rolling waves rushing toward me.

Only then did I realize that Number One and I had dropped through the porthole.

Up, up! I tried to shout, but I could not find my voice.

The wasp's polished steel wings began to buzz frantically at my sides—but still we kept dropping, the waves coming at me faster and faster. I closed my eyes, certain that at any moment we would crash. Then, at the last second it seemed, Number One veered sharply and we began to climb.

I opened my eyes, and in an ice-cold whoosh my voice returned.

"I'm flying!" I cried. "I'm flying!"

Number One leveled herself and picked up speed. The cold salt wind whipped at my cheeks, but my entire body felt on fire with excitement. And as I gazed out across the silver sea to the stars on the horizon, for a moment I forgot all about the tracking mechanisms.

Then Number One swerved unexpectedly to her left, jolting me so hard that I nearly slid off her back. I shrieked and grabbed hold of her antennae, and the wasp gently bucked and hitched me back into place.

"My apologies, Number One," I said, panting with fear. "I'll hang on tighter from now on."

The wasp nodded and batted her antennae, then banked into a steep climb. And as I tightened my grip on her joint casing, I caught sight of the Odditorium high above us.

Silhouetted against the stars, Mr. Grim's mechanical wonder resembled a great black cannonball with a flowing tail

of glistening yellow smoke. But as we drew closer, the out-line of the Odditorium's legs and toothy battlements turned the cannonball into a crowned spider with a single, glowing blue eye.

"Well done, Grubb!" Cleona called out, and I realized the spider's blue eye was in fact the light from the balcony. And there was Cleona, hovering just above Mr. Grim's pipe organ. "Tell Number One to locate the tracking mechanisms!" she shouted.

"You heard her," I said to Number One. "You locate the tracking mechanisms, and I'll keep a lookout for any-thing else!"

The wasp batted its antennae and leveled into our first pass. We hadn't far to travel before I caught sight of the Siren's egg flashing about ten feet below the battlements. Number One swooped in beside it, and in the blue light from her eyes we discovered a large black egg as big as my head.

"It must be attached with a clamp of some sort," I said, but the wasp just hovered there, her antennae waving back and forth as if examining it. Then the egg flashed and Number One began tapping away at it with her hammer and chisel. After a few moments the egg came loose and fell, flashing one more time just before it disappeared far below us with a splash.

"Well done, Number One," I said. "Now, let's see if there are any more of those tracking mechanisms flashing about."

And with that, Number One banked away from the Odditorium for another pass.

"Look!" I exclaimed as we came round the front again. "There's another one of those eggs lodged under the balcony!"

Without being told, Number One swooped in toward it.

"Were you able to remove the tracking mechanism?" asked Mr. Grim, rushing out onto the balcony. Nigel and Lord Dreary followed close behind.

"Yes, sir, but there's another one flashing just below your feet!"

"Good heavens!" cried Lord Dreary.

"Nice work, Grubb!" Nigel shouted, and then the wasp and I were under the balcony.

"You know what to do," I said, and Number One quickly went to work. This egg took some coaxing to come loose, but finally it fell and plunged into the sea, flashing one last time just beneath the surface in a brilliant circle of red.

"Another job well done," I said. "Now, Number One, rise up and hover before the balcony so I can speak to Mr. Grim."

The wasp pulled away from the Odditorium and did as I commanded.

"The egg is gone now, sir," I said.

"Are there others?" asked Mr. Grim.

"I didn't see any, sir. But I'd need another pass or two to be certain."

"A worthy apprentice, indeed," said Mr. Grim. "Very well, then, Master Grubb: another pass or two."

"Yes, sir, Mr. Grim!"

"And try not to look so pleased with yourself, will you?" he said, smiling.

"I will, sir. I mean, I won't, sir. I mean—another pass, Number One!"

And just like that we were off again.

"Be careful, Grubb!" Nigel called.

"And don't forget to look for other objects!" shouted Mr. Grim.

"I won't forget, sir!" I shouted back, and as Mr. Grim and the others disappeared around the side of the Odditorium, I leaned forward and said, "Would you please shine your eyes a little brighter, Number One?"

The wasp nodded her head and her eyes grew brighter.

"Very good, Number One. Turn your head toward the Odditorium and shine your light on the outside as we pass. I should think that if we travel from top to bottom and then from bottom to top, that would allow us to cover the most ground."

Number One nodded and quickly turned upward.

"Go slowly, Number One," I said. "Other than those Sirens' eggs, I'm not quite sure what I'm looking for."

Number One nodded and batted her antennae. And as we crested the battlements at the rear of the Odditorium and turned downward again, in the blue light from her eyes I noticed a Shadesman's battle-ax lodged in one of the Odditorium's massive leg joints.

"That doesn't belong there," I said. "Stop here, Number One, and see if you can't remove that battle-ax."

Number One pulled the battle-ax loose and let it drop.

"You're very strong, Number One. I certainly could have used a friend like you back home."

The wasp again batted her antennae and flew on. And when we reached the bottom of the Odditorium, I commanded Number One to circle the lower gunnery. Finding nothing unusual there, we turned upward again, careful to avoid the Odditorium's large rear-exhaust vent, out of which a trail of Gwendolyn's yellow energy fizzled and popped.

"As soon as the Odditorium is charged again," I said, "the blue animus will come out of here too. Mr. Grim said the Yellow Fairy dust makes it safe. The blue controls the steering mechanisms and the yellow makes the Odditorium fly. They work together to become something better. Just like you and me, right, Number One?"

The wasp nodded her head, and we continued on with our flight pattern—up and down, down and up, my eyes combing every inch of the Odditorium's exterior. I did not find anything else other than what appeared to be battle damage, and by the time Number One and I came round to the front again, I saw that Mrs. Pinch and Broom had joined the others on the balcony.

"All clear, Master Grubb?" asked Mr. Grim.

"Yes, sir," I replied, hovering before him. "I believe we're finished now."

"Well, it's about time," said Mrs. Pinch, squinting at me over the balustrade. "And blind me if I'm going to reheat your supper. Letting this boy fly around on wasps—your heads need oiling, the lot of you!"

Cleona giggled.

"You heard her," said Mr. Grim, smiling. "Let's clear off the balcony so Master Grubb can land Number One, after which we shall retire to the dining room—"

It was then that I heard a woman singing—soft and far away at first, but at the same time loud enough to drown out Mr. Grim and the buzzing from Number One's wings.

Who could be singing out here? I wondered, and as I turned in the song's direction, in the distance I saw a flowing black shape coming toward me against the stars.

The inside of my head grew heavy, and I felt a tingling behind my eyeballs. Then all at once the singing grew louder and I felt myself being pulled forward.

"The song," I said. "It's—it's—*beautiful*."

"What's wrong, Grubb?" Nigel called out from somewhere far behind me.

"What on earth?" said Lord Dreary. "Do you hear that singing, Alistair?"

The black shape drew closer, and I thought I heard myself tell Number One to fly toward it, but the voice upon my lips seemed not to be my own.

"The song," I said to myself. "The song . . ."

"Good heavens!" cried Mr. Grim. "Stop your ears! All of you! Don't—listen—it's—it's—*beautiful*!"

"Beautiful!" Nigel and Lord Dreary said together.

And then I heard Mrs. Pinch cry out in horror.

Wonder what all the fuss is about, I thought. No matter. Just listen to the song.

Yes, all that mattered now was the song, and the shape—no, not a shape, but a figure. Yes, that was it! A black figure of a bird flying toward me . . ."Snap out of it, Mr. Grim!" shouted Mrs. Pinch. "All of you, snap out of it!"

"It's too late!" said Cleona. "Look!"

Is it a bird? I wondered. Or is it a woman?

"Come back, Number One!" Mrs. Pinch called from somewhere behind me. "Oh, where did she fly off to? I can't see her!"

"She'll only obey Grubb!" cried Cleona. "Only Uncle can command her otherwise!"

Yes! I thought. It's a woman! But then the woman broke apart. "No," I heard myself say. "Not just one woman, but *five*!"

"Don't listen to them, Grubb!" shouted Mrs. Pinch, but her voice was far away. "Where is the boy? Can you see the boy, Cleona?"

"They've got him, too!" Cleona cried. "The samurai, Mrs. Pinch! Go get the samurai!"

In the blue light from Number One's eyes I could clearly see the women as they fanned out beside the leader—five *beautiful* women, with ivory skin and flowing black hair, flying toward me on the wings of angels.

"Angels," I whispered.

And their song . . . they were singing the most beautiful song I'd ever heard.

"Beautiful," was all I could say.

The women, one of whom carried a large black barrel, were closer now. Four of them flew past me toward the Odditorium while one remained behind—hovering there in midair with her arms extended only a few feet away from Number One's antennae.

"Are you an angel?" I asked.

"Come to me, child," she said, beckoning, but her singing continued in my head.

How can she speak and sing at the same time? I wondered.

It doesn't matter, I thought.

"Come to me, child," the angel said again, and only then did I realize I was standing on Number One's back.

"No, Cleona, you'll die!" cried Mrs. Pinch from somewhere, but again the voice in my head told me it didn't matter.

"That's it," said the angel. "Jump, my child. Jump!"

And so I jumped.

Time seemed to slow down, and as I floated in slow motion toward the angel, her face dissolved into a horrible mask of slimy blue scales. Her eyes glowed as red as two burning coals, and her lips parted wide to reveal a forked serpent's tongue slithering out between a pair of fangs.

"You're mine!" the angel hissed.

No, not an angel, I realized in horror, but a monster!

And then her claws reached out to catch me.

I tried to scream, but my throat would not allow it—when suddenly a blinding blue light flashed across my eyes.

"Noooooo!" Cleona cried, close beside me now, and the monster hissed and shielded her eyes.

"Cleona?" I whispered in a daze, and then there she was, looking down at me.

"Sirens," Cleona said, straining to speak. "Trying to— drown you—"

"Sirens?" I muttered, shaking my head. The singing had stopped. And I was vaguely aware of being carried—yes, that was it. Cleona had caught me and was now carrying me in her arms. But then everything—the stars, the sea, the Odditorium—began to swirl around me in a haze. I could see that I was heading back toward the balcony, but something was happening there. A brawl of some sort.

There were samurai everywhere, and Mr. Grim stood atop his pipe organ as if he meant to jump. Mrs. Pinch uttered a strange incantation, and then Broom flew of her own accord straight for one of the Sirens.

The Siren shrieked, and Broom began beating her in midair. Mrs. Pinch pulled Mr. Grim back onto the balcony, and the two of them fell out of sight behind the pipe organ. Nigel just stood there in a daze as the samurai slashed away at the Sirens. And Lord Dreary—incredibly, Lord Dreary was brawling with a samurai too.

"Unhand me!" he shouted as the warrior wrestled him back inside the library. "I want to go with them! I want to go!"

The Sirens darted this way and that, screeching and batting their claws, and then one of them grabbed hold of Broom and snapped her in half.

At the same time, a samurai warrior leaped atop Mr. Grim's pipe organ and cut the Siren down. The Siren shrieked and plummeted toward the sea—her great black barrel and the broken broomstick plummeting into the water after her with a splash.

"Water?" I said, my head beginning to clear. "What was that again about banshees and water?"

"Cleona!" cried Mrs. Pinch, popping her head over the balustrade. "Come back, Cleona!"

"Cleona?" I muttered, trying to remember what Mr. Grim had said. But when I saw the look of sorrow in Cleona's eyes, when I saw the pain in her face and her blue light begin to dim, in a rush my senses returned to me.

"No!" I cried. "You're not supposed to fly over water!"

But the tears flowing down her cheeks told me it was too late.

"I'm sorry," she said, her voice weak and raspy. "I don't even have the strength to wail for you."

"The banshee!" hissed one of the Sirens.

"The barrel!" hissed another. "Get the barrel before it sinks!"

Cleona's glow began to flicker and flash. I could see the stars behind her eyes. And then the two of us were falling.

"Cleona!" I cried again, reaching out, but my hands passed right through her!

The Sirens screeched and Mrs. Pinch cried out, but all I could see was Cleona, flickering and slipping away from me as we fell.

"Grab hold of me, Cleona!"

"I—I can't," she whispered, and without thinking I shouted:

"Catch us, Number One!"

Whereas time had seemed to slow down when I'd jumped toward the Siren, time now seemed to speed up. And as Cleona and I tumbled together toward the sea, she used the very last bit of her strength to solidify her hand and grab hold of my coat. But as she did so, the rest of her began to dissolve before my eyes.

"Hold on, Cleona!" I said. "Hold on!"

The silver waves rushed up at us with maddening speed—when finally, just as we were about to hit the water, Number One's claws clamped round my shoulders.

"Hurry, Number One!" I said as she whisked us away. "Throw us on your back and fly higher!"

"It's too late," Cleona moaned, her face now invisible beneath her hair. But then Number One flung us over her shoulders and we landed safely between her wings.

"Cleona!" I cried, grasping her hand. "Come back!"

"Grubb . . ." she croaked, and then all but her hand flickered out.

"Come back! You're safe now! Number One's magic paint will protect you!"

Cleona's hand flickered once inside my own, and then my fingers closed around the empty air.

"No!" I screamed, the tears beginning to flow. "You can't die, Cleona! You can't—"

Miraculously, Cleona's hand reappeared at my side.

"Cleona!" I cried with relief.

And with that the rest of her began to take shape—foggy and dim, but at the same time clear enough for me to see that she was sleeping with her head on my chest. I could not feel her body against my own, but I cradled her in my arms as if I could.

"That's it, Cleona," I said, her light growing brighter, her features more defined. "You're safe now. We'll get you back to the Odditorium so you can—"

"Grubb!" screamed Mrs. Pinch, but when I looked up from Cleona's sleeping face, instead of the Odditorium, I saw that we were surrounded by the Sirens.

I gasped.

And then the monsters swept Cleona and me up into their big black barrel.

— FIFTEEN —

Prisoners

Come on, lad," the man said. "Wake up, now."

"Coming, Mr. Smears," I said groggily, but a sinking feeling in my head told me I'd be much better off if I just stayed asleep.

"No, no, no," said the man, and he gently slapped my cheeks. "Come around, now, lad."

The sinking feeling at once turned to orange-colored waking. I blinked open my eyes and immediately gasped in horror when I saw the face staring down at me.

"Judge Hurst!" I cried. But as I tried to back away, my head bumped against something hard.

"That'll wake you," the judge chuckled. "Unless you knock yourself out again."

I rubbed my head and, gazing round, discovered that I was lying on the floor in a dark, windowless prison cell. The walls were black, like the Odditorium's, but the red glow streaming in through a porthole in the door told me I was someplace else.

And then there was the man sitting next to me—a man who Mr. Grim would never allow inside the Odditorium, a man who Mr. Grim suspected not only of murdering Abel Wortley, but also of being Prince Nightshade himself.

I began to panic.

"Where am I?" I cried. "What have you done with Cleona?"

"Cleona?" said Judge Hurst. "Who is Cleona?"

"Don't pretend! I know you know where she is!"

"I don't know what you're—"

"Cleona!"

"Quiet, lad!"

I tried to get up, but the judge pulled me back down.

"Do you want them to come back?" he hissed.

"Let go!" I said, struggling. "I know who you are! I know what you did to—"

Thankfully, the judge clamped his hand over my mouth before I said, *William Stout*. Yes, I thought, given his habit of hanging people, the less Judge Hurst knew about what Nigel had told me the better.

"Now, you listen to me," the judge said. "I don't know any Cleona, but I do know that if you don't pipe down, those armored skeletons will come back. And believe me, lad, you don't want them to come back."

The judge turned his face to show me his cheek. It was badly bruised, and I could see traces of dried blood in his beard. His hair stuck out from his head in dirty gray clumps, and his clothes were soiled and ragged.

"Now," he said, "if you wish to find this Cleona, you've got to keep your head. If you promise to keep your voice down, I'll let you go, all right?"

I nodded, and the judge removed his hand from my mouth.

"That's better," he said. "Now, first things first. As you seem to know who I am, would you mind telling me who you are?"

"My name is Grubb, sir," I said warily.

"Grubb?"

"That's right, sir. No first or last name, just Grubb with a double *b*."

"Ah yes. You're the boy from the Odditorium, aren't you? The one who caused all that fuss with the handbills?"

"Yes, sir, I'm afraid I am."

"I thought I recognized you when they dropped you off in here. Wish we could have met under different circumstances, but a pleasure to make your acquaintance, Mr. Grubb."

"Where are we, sir?"

Judge Hurst made a grand, sweeping gesture with his

hand. "Why, a castle dungeon in the clouds, of course," he said mockingly. "I've been a prisoner here since yesterday. Or has it been two days? I can't seem to remember. Ever since that winged monster whisked me away from London, I've had a hard go keeping track of the time."

"The Black Fairy."

"Come again?"

"The Black Fairy, sir. He's the one who brought you here."

"Fairy, did you say?" the judge asked, and I nodded. "Well, how about that. Not what I'd expect from a fairy. Although, he's a peach compared to those skeleton soldiers. Ill-mannered chaps, the lot of them, and certainly not ones for London Prize Ring rules."

Judge Hurst rubbed the bruise on his cheek. If the old man really was Prince Nightshade, what would he be doing all battered up in a dungeon?

"Why did the Black Fairy take you prisoner, sir?" I asked cautiously.

"I haven't the foggiest idea. But I must admit I was happy to see you come tumbling out of that barrel. Was afraid I'd go mad spending another night down here alone."

In my mind I saw myself again being surrounded by the Sirens. And although I couldn't remember anything that had happened after we were captured, I somehow knew that Cleona had gone inside the barrel with me, safe and sound.

But how could that be? I wondered. After all, there was no way Cleona could have survived over the ocean without the protection of Number One's magic paint.

Unless, of course, the barrel in question was no ordinary barrel.

"Cor," I gasped, the light finally dawning. "The barrel was painted black—just like Number One."

"What's all that about the barrel, lad?"

"Er, uh," I sputtered. Prince or no prince, I certainly wasn't about to tell Judge Hurst how magic paint could protect a spirit from water. "The Sirens, sir," I said quickly. "They used that barrel to capture Cleona and me."

"You mean to tell me those hideous women were Sirens?"

"I'm afraid so, sir. They work for Prince Nightshade."

"What's next?" said the judge, rubbing his forehead. "Evil fairies that spit black fire, Sirens with snake faces, and skeletons who like to take cheap shots. Any other fantastical delights of which I should be aware, Mr. Grubb?"

"I'm sure there are, sir. But begging your pardon, sir. You didn't happen to see anyone else come tumbling out of that barrel along with me?"

"I'm afraid not, lad. The Sirens only dropped you in here."

I frowned and looked at my shoes—I needed to find Cleona.

"And who is this Cleona, anyway?" asked the judge.

"Er, uh," I sputtered again, "Cleona is my friend, sir."

"Another resident of the Odditorium, I assume?" I nodded. "Ah well, I should have known something like this would happen. That Odditorium has been nothing but trouble since the start. But rest assured, if I ever get out of this dungeon alive, Alistair Grim is going to pay dearly for what he's done."

"Oh please, sir, don't blame Mr. Grim. It's partly my fault we're in this mess. In fact, had I not popped down the wrong chimney and stowed away in Mr. Grim's trunk, Prince Nightshade would never have known about the Odditorium in the first place."

"What on earth are you talking about, lad?"

I gave the judge a brief account of my life, including how I arrived at the Odditorium and the events leading up to my capture. Of course I dodged around the bits about the animus, the doom dogs, and anything having to do with Odditoria. But still, at the end of my tale the judge eyed me suspiciously and said:

"You're not telling me the whole story, are you? Particularly, why this Nightshade character would be interested in Alistair Grim's Odditorium to begin with."

My heart hammered—surely Judge Hurst would know if I tried to lie to him—but as I fumbled for a reply, he gently placed his hand on my shoulder and smiled.

"Let us speak plain, lad," he said. "Given my history with

Mr. Grim and the Stout brothers, I can understand why you'd be disinclined to trust me. However, as you and I are now pickles in the same jar, I should think that we'd have a better chance of getting out of here alive if we worked together. Wouldn't you agree?"

"Yes, sir," I said, but my mind was spinning. If Judge Hurst was shrewd enough to murder Abel Wortley and get away with it—or even worse, if he was Prince Nightshade himself—I would not be able to dodge his questions for much longer. At the same time, even if I was wrong, and the old judge was as blameless as a newborn babe, I still couldn't trust him—not to mention that I was Mr. Grim's apprentice and would never reveal to *anyone* the secrets of his Odditorium.

"Well, what do you say, Mr. Grubb?" asked the judge. "You have my word as a gentleman that this conversation shall remain confidential. And so I'll ask you again: why would a devil like Prince Nightshade want the Odditorium for himself? If you tell me its secrets, I might be able to bargain with him for our release."

I was just about to explain how I'd been sworn to secrecy, when a woman's voice cried out: "Hold your tongue, Grubb!"

"What the—?" said the judge, gazing around. "Did you hear that, Mr. Grubb?"

"Yes, I did, sir," I said, gazing around too.

"Hello?" the judge called. "Is there someone here? Who said that?"

"I did," said the woman. Her voice—gentle but firm, and marked by a strange accent—seemed to come from just outside our cell. Judge Hurst and I scrambled over to the door. The barred porthole was too high for me, but the judge peered out and said:

"There appears to be someone in the cell across the way." He pressed his face between the bars. "You, there, who are you?"

"Someone who knows better than to talk to judges."

"I beg your pardon!" Judge Hurst exclaimed. "What kind of talk is that?"

"Take care in whom you confide, Grubb," the woman said,

ignoring him. "Your secrets are your only advantage here."

Judge Hurst gasped. "Do you mean to tell me that you've been listening to our entire conversation?"

"Your secrets are your only advantage, Grubb," the woman repeated.

I stretched up onto my tippy-toes in an attempt to see out the porthole, but Judge Hurst elbowed me away from the door.

"Now see here, woman," he said. "I don't know who you are, but I assure you that I have nothing but this boy's best interests in mind."

"The Black Fairy was wise to take you hostage, eh, Judge?" the woman said. "A man like yourself who knows the Odditorium inside and out. Isn't that what you told him?"

My mouth dropped open in shock.

"What the—?" said Judge Hurst. "How did you hear that?"

"I also heard you bargaining with the prince," the woman said. "Heard you offer to help him find Alistair Grim in exchange for your life."

"What?" I exclaimed.

"Hold your tongue, woman!" the judge shouted, kicking the door. "You heard nothing of the sort!"

"You said you'd help destroy the Odditorium. Said you'd been inside and knew its secrets."

"That's a lie!" I cried, backing away. "Mr. Grim would never allow Judge Hurst inside the Odditorium!"

The judge whirled from the door. "You keep your mouth shut! You hear me, boy? Keep it shut!"

"You lied!" I shouted. "You knew all along why the Black Fairy took you here. He thought you belonged with us at the Odditorium!"

"I told you the truth! I had no idea why—"

"The best liars mix the truth with fiction," the woman called from across the passageway. "It'll serve you well to remember that, Grubb."

"Shut your trap!" the judge screamed through the porthole.

"That's why you wanted me to be quiet," I cried. "You were afraid I'd blow your cover!"

And with that the judge came for me, screaming at the top of his lungs and flailing his hands in the air. He knocked me down to the ground, straddled my belly, and was about to pummel me, but then the door swung open and a pair of Shadesmen rushed into the cell.

"Let go of me!" the judge cried, struggling, and the Shadesmen pulled him off me. "Tell them I'm Alistair Grim's friend! Tell them I've been inside the Odditorium!"

My mouth froze in terror, my heart in my throat.

"Tell them, Grubb!" the judge screamed as the Shadesmen

dragged him out. "Tell them I've been inside! Tell them I've been inside!"

The Shadesmen slammed the cell door and locked me in, the judge's screams trailing off as they dragged him down the passageway.

I ran to the door and listened. But then the slam from another door echoed loudly through the dungeon, then all was silent.

"Do not feel sad, Grubb," the woman said after a moment. "He would have betrayed you in the end. It'll do your conscience well to remember that."

I grabbed hold of the porthole's iron bars and pulled myself up. The porthole to the cell across the passageway was dark, but still I could make out the woman's eyes staring back at me. They were almond-shaped and sparkled with an almost feline intelligence.

"Your strength is impressive," the woman said. "Being a chimney sweep has made you stronger than you realize. Both inside and out."

"Who are you?"

"My name is Kiyoko, and I am a prisoner here like you."

"Do you know what's going to happen now to Judge Hurst?"

"I suspect the prince will keep him alive until the banshee's animus is extracted."

"You know about Cleona?" I asked, and Kiyoko nodded. "Where is she?"

"She is resting in another part of the castle. Doing fine, from what I gather."

"What about Mr. Grim and the others?"

"They were not brought here, but the banshee was very weak when she arrived. And so the prince must wait until she regains her strength before he can extract her animus. Do you know why he wants her animus, Grubb?"

"The prince wants to make purple-eyed Shadesmen. His army is limited right now to the ancient legions he's brought back from the dead with the Eye of Mars. But with the animus, he'll be able to mix it with the Eye's red energy to make as many purple-eyed Shadesmen as he desires. Red and blue make purple."

"This Mr. Grim has taught you well. I should like to meet him someday. If we ever get out of this dungeon alive."

"How did you get here?"

"The prince captured me the same as the others."

"Others?"

"The magical beings that serve him. Some, like the Black Fairy and the Sirens, do so willingly. While others, well . . . even the unwilling are forced to serve him in the end."

"Then are you a magical being, too, Miss Kiyoko?"

"No, I am human like you, Grubb, but a fierce warrior.

The prince brought me here to help him capture a spirit, but I refused. The prince needs animus from a spirit that is pure and uncorrupted by its own selfish intentions."

"A banshee—Cleona!"

"Yes. Banshees exist only to serve those to whom they are attached. Fortunately, the prince has been unsuccessful in capturing one—that is, until he found Cleona."

"We've got to rescue her!"

"I agree, Grubb. Now that Prince Nightshade has acquired a source for his animus, he won't have much use for you and me anymore."

"But how shall we escape?"

"I've been thinking about that for ages. The prince's fortress is impenetrable. The keys to the dungeon are kept in a room at the end of this passageway, but we have no way of fetching them."

Suddenly I felt a rumbling in my chummy coat.

"Mack!" I cried, and dropped to the floor.

"Mack? What is Mack?"

"Mr. Grim's pocket watch," I said, fishing him from my coat—when a bolt of terror shot through my body. If I opened him, Mack's animus, unprotected by Mr. Grim's magic paint, would surely summon the doom dogs.

"Hang on," I said, scanning the prison cell walls. They were painted black like the Odditorium's. Of course! If the prince planned on using the animus—and if, as Nigel said, the doom dogs work on their own and show allegiance to no one—then Nightshade would need to protect himself just like Mr. Grim.

"Is everything all right over there, Grubb?" Kiyoko called from her cell.

"Yes, miss," I said, and I took a deep breath and opened Mack.

"What time is it?" he cried.

"We need your help, Mack."

"What the—?" Mack said, spinning around in my hand. "Where are we, Grubb? This doesn't look like the Odditorium to me."

"We've been captured by Prince Nightshade. We're in his dungeon."

"Prince Nightshade?"

"There's no time to explain. We need you to get us out of here!"

"We? Who's we?"

"I've made a new friend in another cell. My plan is to slip you under the door so you can sneak down the passageway outside, fetch the keys, and set us free."

"Keys?" Mack said, chuckling. "Ya silly bam. Who needs keys when you've got ol' McClintock?"

"What do you mean?"

"Hold me closer to that keyhole, will ya, laddie?" I did as he requested. "A little more to the left and—ah yes, that's it. Just as I suspected."

And with that Mack shot a bolt of animus from his eyes into the keyhole.

The door unlocked at once.

"You did it, Mack!" I whispered—but then I saw his eyes had gone dark. "Mack," I said, tapping his XII, and he immediately crackled to life again.

"What the *buh duh-buh*," he moaned in a daze, his eyes fading in and out.

"Are you all right, Mack? You opened the door but then fizzled out again."

Mack wobbled his case and shook himself until his eyes glowed normally again.

"Ach," he said. "I forgot how much shootin' me animus knocks me for a loop."

"Do you think you've got one more in you?"

"Of course, laddie! I didn't get to be the chief of the Chronometrical Clan McClintock because of me looks!"

"All right, then," I said, cracking open the door. "But we've got to be quiet. When I hold you to the lock, you'll know what to do?"

Mack wobbled his case to say yes, and I slipped my head outside. Checking both ways down the dimly lit corridor, I spied a red burning sconce at each end, as well as more cells running along the sides of the passage.

"There's no one left down here except you and me," Kiyoko said. "Hurry, Grubb, before the guards return."

I tiptoed across the passageway and positioned Mack in front of Kiyoko's keyhole, whereupon he shot another bolt of animus from his eyes. The door unlocked and Mack's eyes went dark—when without warning Kiyoko burst forth from her cell.

In a streak of rushing black, she darted around behind me and clamped her hands over my mouth. I tried to scream, but Kiyoko dragged me backward into my cell, threw me to the floor, and quietly shut us inside.

Scrambling to my feet, I discovered a beautiful young woman listening intently by the door. She was dressed in a short black robe cinched at the waist and a pair of black trousers tucked into tight-fitting boots. Her hair was black, too, and rested in a thick braid upon her shoulder.

"Kiyoko?"

"Quiet, Grubb," she whispered, her finger to her mouth, and I noticed that her hands and ankles were in irons. "The guards are returning."

"But I don't hear—"

"The watch," Kiyoko said, shuffling toward me with her hands outstretched. "Use the watch again to unlock these shackles."

I hesitated.

"Do it!" she commanded, and I immediately tapped Mack on his XII.

"*Duh buh,*" Mack said groggily. But when he caught sight of Kiyoko, his senses quickly returned and he said, "Well, well, who might you be, lassie?"

"This is Kiyoko," I said. "My friend from the other cell. She needs you to free her from her shackles."

"Say no more, laddie."

Mack shot a bolt of animus into Kiyoko's shackles, and they instantly dropped to the floor. I squatted down at her feet and tapped Mack awake again, and he shot another of his bolts into Kiyoko's leg irons.

"That's some watch," Kiyoko said, eyeing Mack warily. "Is he all right?"

"Yes and no, miss. Mack runs on the animus. He fizzles out from time to time, but the upside is he never needs to be recharged. Even Mr. Grim can't figure out why."

A door clanged loudly from somewhere outside.

"Thank you," Kiyoko whispered. "Now turn around and face the wall, Grubb."

"The wall, miss?"

"Trust me; it's better if you don't see this."

I was about to protest, but Kiyoko motioned with her finger for me to turn around. I returned Mack to my pocket and faced the wall.

"Help!" Kiyoko called out through the cell's porthole. "I can't take it anymore! I want out, do you hear? Out, out!"

A moment later the Shadesmen were coming, the sound of their clanging armor growing louder as they approached from the passageway outside. The cell door opened and the Shadesmen entered, and Kiyoko let out a piercing cry of *"EEEEYYAA!"*

Startled, I shut my eyes as the scuffle broke out behind me—the clash of swords and the clanging of armor echoing through the chamber in a frenzied wall of sound. Then I heard a grunt and a growl and a loud *swish-clang-ping!* And all was quiet again.

"You may face me now, Grubb," Kiyoko said.

I turned around to find her with a sword in one hand and a Shadesman's helmeted skull in the other—its eyes blinking red, its jaw flapping open and shut as if silently jabbering. The rest of him and his companion lay in armor-clad pieces on the floor, the whole lot of them squirming about like a cluster of lively maggots.

My mouth fell open in amazement.

"Snap out of it, Grubb," Kiyoko said.

"But how did you—?"

"First things first," Kiyoko said, handing me the sword. She picked up the other Shadesman's head and moved to the door. The skulls stared back at me with their blinking red eyes and jabbering jaws—when suddenly I felt something grab my ankle.

A Shadesman's severed hand, arm and all, had crawled across the floor and latched on to me.

Gasping in terror, I kicked it away. I could hardly believe my eyes. The Shadesmen's body parts were beginning to join back together.

"Even I cannot destroy the armies of Romulus and

Remus," Kiyoko said as she hopped over the scattered body parts. "However, if we keep their bodies out of sight of their heads, they'll have a harder time regenerating."

Kiyoko dashed across to her cell, tossed the Shadesmen's heads inside, and closed the door. Then she took back her sword and motioned for me to follow.

"Are you coming?" she asked with a smile.

And without a word more the two of us fled from the dungeon.

SIXTEEN

There Be Dragons

W hat is it?" I asked.

Kiyoko motioned for me to be quiet and pressed her ear against the large iron door. By my count, this was the sixth iron door at which she had pressed her ear since we escaped the dungeon. Usually she listened only for a moment and then either entered or moved on. However, it was clear from her expression that this particular door had caught her interest.

"Is Cleona in there?" I whispered.

"No," Kiyoko said. "She is in the tower with the great machine."

"The great machine?"

"The one they will use to extract her animus."

"We've got to hurry!" I said, and Kiyoko again motioned for me to be silent.

I was growing impatient. We'd been traveling for quite some time—ever upward through a maze of narrow, red-lit passages that always ended in a flight of stairs or a door like this one. Many times we heard the clanging of armor echoing in the distance. And on one occasion, Kiyoko and I ducked into a small chamber just in time to avoid a regiment of Shadesmen marching past us.

That had been at least ten minutes ago. And since then we hadn't heard anything except our own footsteps and the moan of the wind through the passageways.

"Yes," Kiyoko said, running her hand along the door frame. "The wind is stronger here. On the other side of this door we shall find the Great Hall, at the end of which is the armory. I will need to stop there first and find my sword."

"But you already have the sword you took from the Shadesmen."

Kiyoko looked down at her blade and then narrowed her eyes at me.

"You call this clumsy piece of metal a sword?" she said. "When we get to the armory, I'll show you a real sword. I might even teach you how to use it someday. That is, if we ever get out of this castle alive."

Without a sound, Kiyoko opened the door just far enough for us to squeeze through into the Great Hall.

The cavernous black chamber was long and narrow, with great stone pillars that stretched up the walls and across the arched roof like a giant rib cage. High above us, shafts of red light cut downward through the gloom, and the massive hearth at the center of the hall blazed with a roaring red fire.

I'll wager all that red light is from the prince's Eye of Mars, I said to myself. *I'll also wager there are other Odditoria around here too—Odditoria from which the prince harnesses power just as Mr. Grim does.*

Gazing around, I discovered that we had entered the Great Hall through one of its many side doors. At one end of the chamber, a pair of wooden gates stood almost as tall as the ceiling itself; at the other end was a high, stepped dais, on top of which sat a great black throne. The prince's throne, I knew at once, and I shivered.

"We haven't much time, Grubb," Kiyoko said, moving quickly. "When the banshee's strength returns, the prince will begin to extract her animus."

"How do you know you're going the right way?" I asked, following closely.

"I have been a prisoner here for some time now. I studied the layout of the castle outside during the tournaments."

"Tournaments, miss?"

"Yes, Grubb. There were once others from my clan here powerful warriors like me who refused to help the prince. And so he made us fight his minions."

"His minions, miss?"

"The evil creatures that have joined forces with him here in his castle."

I swallowed hard upon the recollection of Mr. Grim's notebook—the trolls, the dragons, the goblins—and followed Kiyoko to a door at the far corner of the hall. Kiyoko listened for a moment, and then, without a word, the two of us slipped inside.

What I saw took my breath away.

The armory was packed from floor to ceiling with every sort of weapon imaginable. Racks of swords and spears and battle-axes stood in the center of the room, while stacks of helmets and shields and other bits of armor rose up in great piles against the walls.

Kiyoko and I immediately began zigzagging our way through a maze of even more weapons—crossbows and long bows and maces and flails—as well as high stacks of crates labeled with words and symbols I did not understand.

"Where are you, Ikari?" Kiyoko whispered, darting this way and that.

"Who are you talking to, miss?"

"My sword. The prince stole Ikari from me when he captured my clan. She is in here somewhere. I can feel it."

I was growing impatient. We needed to find Cleona, and here we were looking for a scraper in a mound of soot.

"Begging your pardon, miss," I said, "but what's so special about this sword? I should think you could have your pick of the litter in this place."

"A shinobi warrior trains with one sword her entire life, and so Ikari is an extension of my spirit."

"Shinobi, did you say?"

"Some call us ninja, but names mean nothing in combat. My people are known as the fiercest warriors in Japan."

"The same Japan from where the samurai hail?"

Kiyoko stopped and turned to me. "How does a chimney sweep know about samurai?" she asked suspiciously.

"Mr. Grim uses them to guard the Odditorium. Their armor is powered by the animus."

Kiyoko nodded approvingly. "I would indeed like to meet this Mr. Grim."

"Mr. Grim says the samurai are the fiercest warriors in the world, but I'm certain he'd change his mind if he met you. Which makes me wonder, how on earth did the prince manage to capture you, miss?"

"The prince and the Black Fairy surprised my clan in our secret mountain fortress. We were no match for their magic. The Red Dragons, you see, led them straight to us."

"Red Dragons?"

"A clan of winged serpents that have allied themselves with the prince. They were men once, long ago, but so evil that the ancient gods saw fit to turn them into half-human, half-demon monsters. They have plagued the shinobi for centuries, but we have had our revenge on them in the tournaments."

"You mean, the prince made you fight these dragons?"

"Dragons and other monsters. I am the last of my clan to survive. There are many such beasts in this castle, but I have no intention of introducing you to them."

"That's fine by me, miss."

Kiyoko gazed round the room with her hands on her hips. I followed suit, and through a tiny space in a stand of long rifles, I spied a rack of swords in the next aisle.

"Mr. Grim's samurai use swords like those," I said, pointing. "Perhaps yours is among them."

Kiyoko dropped her Shadesman's sword and, in a flash, leaped over the rifles and landed on the other side. Dashing after her, I joined Kiyoko just as she was unsheathing a sword from its scabbard. It was much plainer than all the other swords nearby—and for a moment I thought the shinobi would go on searching—but then she closed her eyes, dropped to her knees, and cradled the sword to her breast.

"Avenge me, Ikari," Kiyoko whispered, and then quickly sheathed the sword and tied the scabbard to her back. "You are full of surprises, Grubb. If not for you, I might never have found Ikari."

"Your sword, it isn't much to look at when compared to the fancier swords here. But Mr. Grim says the most powerful Odditoria are usually those things that, on the surface at least, appear ordinary."

"You are wise beyond your years, Grubb," Kiyoko said, rising. "And so I shall be forever in your debt for helping me find Ikari."

Kiyoko bowed her head in gratitude, and I felt my cheeks go hot. Then she began removing other objects from the rack —black darts and knives and spikes and strange-looking star-shaped disks that she inserted into hidden sleeves throughout her garment.

"Begging your pardon, miss," I said. "But are Ikari and all those other weapons magical?"

"No," Kiyoko said as she slipped on a pair of black open-fingered gloves. "But in the hands of a shinobi, such weapons are the next best thing."

From inside her robe, Kiyoko produced a black stocking and slipped it over her head. Then she donned her hood and tied it off under her chin. She was now covered completely from head to toe in black, save for a narrow opening through which her piercing eyes gleamed back at me.

"How do I look?" she asked.

"I wouldn't want to fight you, that's for certain. Which reminds me, miss: shouldn't I have a sword too?"

"Have you ever used one?"

"I'm afraid not, miss."

"Then the answer is no."

"But miss, what if we run into more of Nightshade's minions?"

"Then you stay close to me or keep running. You'll know what to do when it's time. Either way, you'll fare better by using your wits instead of a sword."

"Yes, but—"

"The first weapon a shinobi learns to use is the mind," Kiyoko said with a hand on my shoulder. "Master that first, Grubb, and you have my word that someday I'll teach you how to use a sword."

Kiyoko winked, and despite my disappointment, I smiled back.

And with that we were off, the two of us dashing back through the maze of weapons the way we had come. Upon reaching the armory door, Kiyoko cracked it open ever so slightly and listened.

"There is movement," she said after a moment. "Breathing in the castle's old receiving chamber just outside the Great Hall gates."

"But that's on the other side of the hall, miss," I said, listening too. "How could you possibly hear anything that far away?"

"The second weapon a shinobi learns to use is the senses," Kiyoko said, her eyes smiling, and then we slipped through the door and dashed across the Great Hall to its tall wooden gates.

"Breathing, yes," Kiyoko whispered with her ear upon the gates. "They're still sleeping, but we'll have to be quiet as mice to make it past them."

"Who are you talking about, miss?"

"The Red Dragons," Kiyoko said, and I gasped. "Remember, stay close, Grubb. But if you feel the need to run, then by all means do so and don't look back."

Kiyoko cracked open the gates, reached back over her shoulder and gripped her sword, and slipped into the next room. She just stood there listening for a moment and then motioned for me to follow. With my heart hammering, I obeyed.

The receiving chamber was not nearly as large as the Great Hall, but just as high. And in the red light from the ceiling grates, I could see the sleeping dragons hanging by their tails from the rafters—their scaly wings wrapped tightly around their bodies, giving them the appearance of a cluster of crimson caterpillar cocoons.

Without a sound, Kiyoko headed for the doors at the far end of the chamber. I followed close behind, shadowing her every step—when suddenly I felt a rumbling in my chummy coat.

"Not now, Mack!" I whispered.

"*Ssh!*" Kiyoko said with a finger to her lips, but Mack would not cease shaking. Indeed, he was shaking so violently that I thought at any moment he might leap from my coat and fall on the floor.

Without thinking, I quickly snatched him from my pocket and tapped him on his XII before he had time to speak. Sighing with relief, I was about to slip him back inside my coat when, much to my surprise, Mack began to shake again!

"No!" I cried, bobbling him between my hands.

Mack tumbled to the floor with a loud, echoing *clack!*

"What time is it?" he cried as his case sprang open.

I scooped him up immediately, tapped him on his XII, and thrust him back inside my pocket. The receiving chamber was painted black like the rest of Nightshade's castle, so I wasn't worried about the doom dogs. However, when I saw the look in Kiyoko's eyes as she gazed up at the rafters, I knew that something just as terrifying was about to come for us.

"The doors!" Kiyoko cried, unsheathing Ikari. "Run for the doors!"

But I just stood there gazing upward, my legs frozen in terror, as one of the dragons unfurled its monstrous wings to reveal a hideous serpent's snout and pair of glowing red eyes.

"Shinobi!" the dragon hissed. The creature arched its long

neck and growled, and then the other dragons spread open their wings and began growling too—their forked tongues lashing out like whips from between their sharp teeth.

"Run, Grubb!" Kiyoko shouted, and thankfully this time my legs obeyed.

The dragons took flight from the rafters. And as I ran for the door, the chamber became a bedlam of howling and rushing wind from the creatures' wings. Certain that one of the dragons would swoop down upon me at any moment, I glanced over my shoulder just in time to see Kiyoko jump up into the air.

"EEEEYYAAA!" she cried, her sword flashing like lightning, and two of the dragons exploded in a burst of blinding red light, their bodies instantly vaporized.

Kiyoko flipped over and landed on her feet, but immediately another dragon was upon her. She slashed at it with Ikari, but the creature dodged her and, with a swipe of its great tail, sent her flying across the room.

"Kiyoko!" I cried, and she scrambled to her feet.

"Run, Grubb! I can handle them!"

I whirled around. The doors were only a few yards away from me now—yes, I was almost there—but then a dragon landed in front of me and blocked my path.

The monster hissed and gnashed its teeth, and it was then

that I got my first good look at the beast. True to Kiyoko's tale, the Red Dragons retained some of their human characteristics. They had the upper body of a man and two muscular arms, at the ends of which was a pair of three-toed talons that the creatures used to drag along their fronded serpent's tails.

"Where do you think you're going?" the dragon hissed.

I spun on my heels and made to run in the other direction, but another dragon swooped down and blocked my path too. It swiped at me with its talons, missing my face by inches, and then Kiyoko leaped between us.

"*EEEEYYAA!*" she cried, and before the two dragons even realized she was there, the shinobi vaporized them in a whirl of flashing steel.

"Thank you, miss!" I said.

Kiyoko's eyes met mine for an instant, when another dragon swooped down from the rafters and tackled her.

In one moment I saw Ikari go skidding across the floor; in the next, I saw the dragon wrap its tail around Kiyoko's neck—her legs kicking helplessly as the creature lifted her into the air.

"No!" I cried, and before I could think twice about it, I picked up Kiyoko's sword and buried the blade deep within the dragon's side.

The creature yelped in pain and swiped at me with its talons, but I jumped back, and the monster caught the side of my coat, shredding it to bits. The dragon swiped at me again, but this time I dove forward, slicing Kiyoko's sword entirely by accident along the monster's foreleg as I tumbled past.

The Red Dragon flung Kiyoko across the room like a rag doll and made to charge me—when I felt the fiery hot breath of another dragon swooping down and snatching me up in its talons.

For a brief moment I could see Kiyoko scrambling on the floor below. But then the dragon knocked Ikari from my hand, tossed me up toward the rafters, and, catching me by the collar, spun me around to face its snarling muzzle.

"Bottoms up!" the dragon growled, its forked serpent's tongue lashing at my face. There was something familiar in its expression—relishing and cruel, like how Mr. Smears often looked when he knocked me down. I cried out in horror, but just as the dragon opened its jaws to eat me, Ikari sailed through the air and pierced the creature's head.

The dragon exploded instantly in a burst of brilliant red light.

And then I was falling.

I closed my eyes, bracing myself for the impact on the hard stone floor. But just before I hit, Kiyoko caught me in her arms.

"Thank you again, miss," I said, sighing with relief However, as Kiyoko set me down, I spied the dragon I'd

wounded opening the gates to the Great Hall. I could also see a blue light flashing between its talons.

"Look!" I cried. "The dragon's escaping!"

Kiyoko snatched up Ikari from the floor and hurled it across the room. But the dragon was already too far gone, and just as the monster slipped inside the Great Hall, Kiyoko's sword buried itself in the wooden gates behind it.

"Come on!" I said. "We can't let it get away!"

"There's no time. We're already too late."

"What do you mean?"

Kiyoko pointed at my chummy coat. One of my pockets had been completely torn away. Instinctively I reached inside the other, but when I found it empty, I knew at once what had happened.

The blue light I'd seen flashing in the dragon's talons—the monster had somehow snatched Mack from my pocket!

"Mack!" I cried.

"It's no use, Grubb. The dragon must have stolen him during the battle."

Kiyoko freed her sword from the gate and slipped it back inside the scabbard on her back.

"But we've got to find him!" I cried.

"The Black Fairy will be here any minute. There is only one chance for us now, but you have to trust me."

My head was spinning—Cleona, Mack—what was I going to do?

"Grubb!" Kiyoko hissed. "It's now or never!"

And then Kiyoko and I were running for the doors.

As we slipped out into the castle's inner yard, I spied the outline of a tall tower against the early morning sky. Cleona was in there. I just knew it. But instead of heading for the tower, Kiyoko made a beeline for a large, red-lit archway at the opposite side of the yard.

"But Cleona is over there!" I cried.

"There's no time to explain!"

I followed Kiyoko through the archway and gasped when I realized where she'd led me. We were in the prince's stables, and there in the stalls were the massive, red-eyed steeds that had drawn the prince's chariot when he attacked the Odditorium.

"What are you doing?" I asked. "These are the prince's horses!"

"Would you rather ride one of those skeleton steeds instead?"

Kiyoko snatched a bridle from its hook and leaped up onto one of the stalls. The horse inside whinnied and shot smoke from its nostrils. There were four horses in all, each with its name emblazoned above its stall. The steed Kiyoko had chosen was called Phantom.

"You're going to steal one of the prince's horses?" I asked in amazement.

Ignoring me, Kiyoko jumped onto Phantom's back. The beast reared and shot fire from his mouth. I ducked for cover behind a post, but Kiyoko remained calm and quickly slipped the bridle onto the horse's great black head.

"There, there, Phantom," Kiyoko said soothingly. "You remember me, don't you? We've ridden together many times in the tournaments."

And with that the horse settled down.

"But what about Cleona and Mack?" I asked. "Shouldn't we find them first?"

"My fighting skills are useless against the Black Fairy," Kiyoko said. She drew Ikari and with it deftly unlatched the door to Phantom's stall. "We need to flee before he comes after us."

Phantom reared up on his hind legs and shot fire from his mouth. The door to his stall flew open, and the steed quickly trotted out under Kiyoko's command.

"You mean you intend to leave without Mack and Cleona?"

"We have no choice, Grubb."

"No!" I cried, backing away.

"Mack is powered by the animus, is he not?"

"Yes, but—"

"And you said he does not need to be recharged?"

"Yes, but—no, I—"

"Don't you see, Grubb?" Kiyoko said, trotting toward me. "Now that Nightshade has the pocket watch, he has his source of animus. He won't need Cleona anymore to make his army of purple-eyed Shadesmen."

"But I can't leave Mack and Cleona behind!"

"Climb up, Grubb," Kiyoko said, holding out her hand. "If we don't leave now, the prince will kill us both!"

"No!" I cried. I ran for the stable door. Cleona! I had to rescue Cleona! But as soon as I stepped out into the yard, I spied a pair of empty white eyes staring down at me in the dark.

"The Black Fairy!" I gasped, stopping dead in my tracks, and then there appeared the jagged, black-and-white crescent of the demon's smile.

"Run, Grubb!" Kiyoko called from somewhere behind me, but my legs would not budge. And as the Black Fairy stood up to his full height and spread his wings, I lost all sight of the tower's silhouette behind him.

"*Shinobi!*" the Black Fairy hissed, turning his eyes toward the stables, and then he arched back his head in preparation to spit.

"Leave her alone!" I cried. And I ran straight for him.

"No, Grubb!" Kiyoko screamed, but I was already swinging for the Black Fairy's legs. My knuckles exploded with pain as if I'd punched an oak tree, but the Black Fairy only laughed and swatted me away like a beetle, sending me tumbling head over heels in the dirt until I came to a stop on my bottom.

Suddenly Kiyoko shot out of the stables and galloped past him.

The Black Fairy screeched and spit his black fire, striking the ground and causing a spray of rubble only inches from Phantom's forelegs. The great steed reared and whinnied, but Kiyoko quickly gained control of him and sped off across the courtyard in the opposite direction.

Now the Shadesmen were coming—their armor clanging, their glowing red eyes bobbing to and fro in the shadows as they poured out of the barracks.

I scrambled to my feet, searching for Kiyoko amidst the gloom, and caught sight of her galloping away on the far side of the yard.

The Black Fairy arched his head back and spit another bolt of black fire straight for her—but at the last moment Phantom flew up into the air and carried Kiyoko over the castle walls. I saw them outlined briefly against the early morning sky, and then the Black Fairy's fire slammed into the battlements in an explosion of smoke and stone.

"No!" I cried—but as the dust quickly began to settle, Kiyoko and Phantom were nowhere to be found.

Did they make it over the wall in time? I wondered in horror.

The Black Fairy arched back his head, spread his wings, and screeched up at the sky in frustration. Then he whirled his empty eyes on me and bared his teeth.

"Take him to the prince!" he hissed. *"The shinobi is mine!"*

And with that the Black Fairy took flight and disappeared over the castle walls.

"Fly, Phantom!" I screamed. "Carry Kiyoko away as fast as you can!"

But then a host of bony hands clamped down upon me, and I was dragged away kicking and screaming, amidst a sea of glowing red eyes.

SEVENTEEN

In the Court of Nightshade

For a long time afterward I was made to kneel before the prince's throne with my nose pressed against the Great Hall's cold stone floor. If I dared so much as breathe, it seemed, the Shadesmen would poke me in the ribs with their ax handles and growl at me to stay down.

But that didn't stop me from hearing.

The first thing that caught my attention was the distant toll of a church bell, followed by the sounds of the castle coming to life outside. Doors slammed and footsteps echoed all around. There was a swelling sense of everything drawing closer, and then all at once the Great Hall was filled with the din of an angry mob.

Hooting and jeering came at me from every direction, along with grunts and growls and words I didn't understand. The chamber took on a putrid stench of livestock and rotting trash, making me sick to my stomach. I raised my head, seeking relief. There was no poke from the Shadesmen this time, and as I gazed about the Great Hall, I understood why.

I was surrounded by a horde of horrible monsters, all of them pushing and shoving to get a look at me. The Shadesmen had formed a line to keep them at bay, but through their ranks I spied a group of short, fat creatures scuffling for position at the fore. I recognized their enormous heads and wide slobbering lips from the drawings in Mr. Grim's notebook. Trolls. And upon their shoulders? Dozens of green, yellow-eyed fiends with toadlike mouths and snapping tongues. I recognized them, too. Goblins.

The sickness in my stomach was promptly replaced with ice-cold terror. Scores of other creatures had gathered around me too, but before I could take them all in, I was startled by the loud clang of an iron door. The crowd fell silent, and a dozen more of the troll creatures spilled out onto the dais. Each carried a large, animal skin–covered drum, and as they lined up on either side of the throne, they began a slow, steady beat like a death march.

The drums echoed low and ominous throughout the chamber, and whereas before the only fear I had felt in the Great Hall had been my own, I became aware of a growing apprehension amongst the crowd.

A loud cranking began overhead, and I gazed upward to

find one of the massive iron grates sliding open in the ceiling. The entire hall seemed to grow darker, the air thick with fear, and then a black-armored figure in a billowy black cape emerged from between the rafters.

My whole body froze in terror. It was Prince Nightshade.

Like an enormous spider on an invisible thread, the prince descended slowly from above. And when his boots lighted on the dais, the trolls stopped their drumming, and a pair of goblin attendants caught the corners of his cape. The Great Hall was deathly silent, the fear pounding in my ears as Prince Nightshade's burning red eyes stared down at me from beneath his spike-crowned helmet.

"Welcome," said the prince, sitting down on his throne. The red gash that was his mouth broke apart in jagged strands as he spoke, and his voice was deep, at once both near and far away as it echoed forth from the empty black pit of his face.

"You may rise, young Grubb," said the prince—but I was too frightened to move. "Go ahead, lad. You have nothing to fear. *Yet.*"

The monsters snickered and snarled behind me.

Slowly—knees aching, my legs like jelly—I rose to my feet.

"How old are you, boy?" asked the prince.

"Twelve or thereabouts, sir."

"Impressive. A boy of twelve or thereabouts who at once proves himself more useful than any of my subjects here."

The monsters grumbled crossly, but the prince raised a hand to silence them.

"Turn around, Grubb," he said. "Turn around so your admirers can look at you." I obeyed, and the prince shouted: "Behold the bringer of the animus!"

The monsters gasped and looked at each other in amazement. Then the lot of them drew closer, teeth bared, their eyes bulging with hatred behind the line of Shadesmen that held them at bay.

Prince Nightshade chuckled—a guttural, menacing chuckle that sent a chill down my spine. "That will do, Grubb," he said. "You may turn around again."

I obeyed, and the prince leaned forward on his throne.

"Tell me, lad," he said, "does Alistair Grim know why I want the animus?"

"Yes, sir—"

"Yes, *sire*," said the prince, gently correcting me, and I gulped.

"Yes, sire," I said. "Mr. Grim says you want to mix the blue animus with your red Eye of Mars energy to make an army of purple-eyed Shadesmen."

"Your candor is much appreciated," said the prince with a smile. "And so I will assume that Alistair Grim also knows about our archaeological rivalry these last ten years—a rivalry of which I had been entirely unaware until the unexpected discovery of the animus in London. Alistair Grim has you to thank for that little mishap, does he not?"

I looked down guiltily at my shoes.

"How deliciously ironic," said the prince. "Alistair Grim covers the walls of his Odditorium with magic paint, just as I have done my castle, then has me gadding about the world chasing doom dogs—all the while the animus was right there under my nose!"

The prince chuckled loudly, and the monsters mumbled and grumbled behind me.

"And as if that wasn't enough," the prince went on, "who would've thought Alistair Grim a collector of *magicalia*, too? He never gave the slightest indication that he was interested in such things. Then again, knowing Alistair Grim, I'm certain he would never use an ordinary word like *magicalia*."

I swallowed hard and shifted uncomfortably. But despite my terror, the prince's comments about "knowing Alistair Grim" were not lost on me.

Nigel was right, I thought. Whoever this Prince Nightshade was, not only had he murdered Abel Wortley ten years ago, but he must also have been one of Mr. Grim's society friends from London!

"Magicalia," the Prince muttered to himself. "No, no, no, Alistair Grim would think a word like that too ordinary,

indeed. And given the name of his establishment, let's see . . . how about *Odditoria*? That seems like something Alistair Grim might say."

I gazed up at him in disbelief.

"Ah yes," said the prince. "The answer is in your eyes, young Grubb. Odditoria it is then. Has a pleasant ring to it, I must admit. Odd-ih-*tor*-ee-ahhh . . ."

The prince's eyes dimmed slightly, as if he was lost in thought. A heavy silence fell over the hall, and then one of his goblin attendants whispered something in his ear.

"But of course," said the prince. "You see, Grubb, since for over a decade now I have been unsuccessful in acquiring a spirit that would give me its animus, I am thus forever in your debt for bringing me something much, much better."

The prince reached into his belt and pulled out McClintock.

"Mack!" I cried, rushing forward, but the Shadesmen immediately restrained me. "Give him back!" I shouted, struggling. "He belongs to Mr. Grim!"

"Not anymore," said the prince. He opened Mack and tapped him on his XII.

"What time is it?" Mack cried, and the prince held him up for all his subjects to see. A chorus of gasps exploded behind me.

"What the—?" Mack sputtered when he saw me with the Shadesmen. "What are you bone bags doing to Grubb?"

"Behold the *animus*!" shouted the prince, and the monsters oohed and aahed.

Mack spun around in the prince's hand. "Not you again!" he cried upon seeing who held him. "Run, Grubb, run! He'll turn you into a purple-eyed Shadesman!"

Prince Nightshade chuckled and tapped Mack out on his XII.

"Extraordinary," said the prince. "I suspected something like this when the doom dogs led me to the street urchins. But a pocket watch that radiates an unlimited supply of animus? Even I dared not dream of such a device!"

"Don't you touch him!" I cried, struggling against the Shadesmen's grip. But the prince just ignored me, and upon returning McClintock to his belt, he shouted up at the ceiling:

"Bring him!"

Something roared and hissed above my head, and then a Red Dragon emerged from the opening between the rafters. It appeared to be carrying something—or *someone*, I realized as it swooped down toward the dais. The trolls made room for the beast, and as it landed with its quarry beside the prince's throne, I gasped with horror.

The dragon was carrying Judge Hurst!

"Oh no," I moaned, my heart sinking. The judge's face was deathly white, his lips curled in a bloodred snarl. And his eyes, ringed with black circles, glowed a devilish purple.

Judge Mortimer Hurst had been turned into a Shadesman!

"A fitting end for the old judge," the prince announced to his subjects. "In life, he made a career of turning people into corpses. Now in death he shall do the same!"

The prince and the monsters howled with laughter—cheering and clapping as Judge Hurst, oblivious to it all, just stood there staring vacantly ahead.

"So you see, young Grubb," said the prince, silencing the crowd, "this dragon and I owe you much gratitude. By bringing along Alistair Grim's pocket watch, you have not only guaranteed me my army of purple-eyed Shadesmen, but you have also secured this dragon here a promotion to general."

The dragon lowered its head and growled at me.

"In addition," the prince said, "you have saved me the arduous task of extracting the banshee's animus by force. And for that I am most grateful."

"Where is she?" I cried, rushing for the steps. "What have you done with Cleona, you devil!"

The Shadesmen pulled me back and forced me to my knees.

"Watch your tongue," said the prince. "Remember to whom you're speaking."

Judge Hurst hissed at me and lurched forward, but the Red Dragon batted him aside and said, "Let me kill him for this impudence, Your Highness. He helped the shinobi slaughter my brothers!"

"*Kill* him?" said the prince. "Is that how you treat a fellow soldier in our army?"

"Fellow soldier?" the dragon gasped.

"But of course. After all, the boy brought the animus, did he not? Therefore, you and Grubb shall serve your prince together."

"Serve with my brothers' murderer?" the Red Dragon snarled. "Never!"

"As you wish," said the prince, and in a flash he flew straight for the dragon. The beast gasped with terror, but before it had time to escape, the prince drew a sword from his belt and cut the creature down.

"MINE!" the prince roared, and the dragon was reduced to a shimmering explosion of bright red light.

But then something strange happened. The explosion immediately appeared to reverse itself. The light contracted, getting smaller and smaller in front of the prince's face as if he was inhaling what was left of the Red Dragon into his mouth.

Mr. Grim was right, I realized with horror. Prince Nightshade is absorbing the dragon's magic!

And with that the last of the red light disappeared between the jagged edges of the prince's mouth. His eyes brightened,

and then Prince Nightshade let out a long, satisfied *"Buuurrrp!"*

"That takes care of that," he said, sheathing his sword, and he sat back down on his throne. The Great Hall was silent as a tomb, and the monsters, even the most fearsome of them, cast their eyes down at the floor.

"Very well, then, Grubb," said the prince. "Looks like you shall serve in our army without the dragon."

"I'll never serve you," I said, bracing myself for an attack. But Prince Nightshade only nodded his head and smiled wide.

"So there you have it!" he shouted, addressing his court. "By refusing to serve in our army, young Grubb has proven himself a traitor and is thus sentenced to fight in the tournament!"

The crowd of monsters hooted and cheered. The Shadesmen released me, and I staggered to my feet, confused.

"Don't look so bewildered, lad," said the prince, silencing his court. "Since your pocket watch radiates its animus perpetually, I no longer have need of the banshee. And thus, as you might expect, I shall consume her magic as I did the dragon's. *Publicly.*"

"Cleona," I whispered, my heart in my throat.

"Your death in the tournament shall be our main event," the prince said. "And of course, the banshee shall provide your funeral dirge."

The crowd of monsters laughed.

"I wonder if Alistair Grim will mourn the loss of you as

he did Elizabeth," the prince said thoughtfully. "A bit of a sentimental fool, he always was."

I gazed up at the prince in shock. Did he just say *Elizabeth*?

"Sentimental and selfish," the prince went on, more to himself. "All that time and effort spent to get her back, when all poor Elizabeth wanted was to get away from him."

My mind was spinning with confusion, but my tongue got the best of me. "You take that back," I said. "Mr. Grim is not selfish. He gave me a home. He—"

Prince Nightshade chuckled. "Your loyalty to your master is charming, young Grubb, but naive nonetheless. Alistair Grim would never have given you a home if he didn't think he could get something in return for it. Same with the banshee and everything else at the Odditorium." The prince sighed remorsefully. "All of it for Elizabeth."

I just stood there, fumbling for a reply.

"How delicious," said the prince, noticing my confusion. "Alistair Grim didn't tell you—did he—the reason why he acquired the banshee in the first place?" I shook my head. "Well, I must confess, I had no idea myself until I learned that the Odditorium was actually a ship that could transport him to the Land of the Dead."

"The Land of the Dead?" I gasped.

"But of course, lad. That nasty little hole in the sky through which you escaped. Why else would Alistair Grim invent an interdimensional Sky Ripper if not to travel to the Land of the Dead?"

I did not know how to answer.

"You mean, Alistair Grim didn't tell you about all that, either?"

I said nothing, but at the same time remembered Mr. Grim exclaiming, *I'm here!* during our space jump. And hadn't he whispered, *I was there, Elizabeth,* upon our return to Earth?

Who was this Elizabeth?

"Nevertheless," said the prince, "given that the Land of the Dead is merely another dimension that occasionally intersects with this one, it's quite obvious that Alistair Grim should use the banshee's animus to create a bridge between the two. And why else would he want to go there if not to bring back Elizabeth's spirit and keep her in the Odditorium, safe from the doom dogs and protected by his magic paint?"

"But who is Elizabeth?" I asked.

"Why, Elizabeth O'Grady, of course. The woman Alistair Grim was to marry."

I gasped. Mr. Grim was to be married? Could Elizabeth O'Grady be the Lady in Black, the woman from the portrait in the parlor?

"Then again," said the prince, "in order to put the pieces

together, one would have to have known the circumstances surrounding Elizabeth's disappearance in the North Country twelve years ago."

"The North Country?" I asked.

"Of course," said the prince. "That is where Elizabeth's family settled when they came from Ireland. So, naturally, that is where her family's banshee settled too."

I could only stare back at him dumbfounded.

"A tragic story," the prince went on, sighing. "Then again, all the best love stories are. A broken engagement, a scandalous affair, and a terrible misunderstanding that sent Elizabeth fleeing London in despair. Rumor had it she was already heavy with Alistair Grim's child, and for months he searched for her in the North Country, until one day word came that her body had washed up on a beach near Blackpool. Drowned, they said. The child, if there ever was one, was never found."

"Poor Mr. Grim," I whispered, my heart breaking.

"Something must have happened during Alistair's search in the North Country," said the prince. "Something that compelled the banshee to join him back in London. Sly devil, that Alistair Grim. Always was."

The prince chuckled malevolently, and I clenched my fists, the anger burning in my stomach at his making light of Mr. Grim's tragedy.

Presently, the Great Hall gates swung open and a loud

screech echoed through the chamber. It was the Black Fairy, the wind from his wings caressing my cheeks as he flew overhead and lighted on the dais beside Prince Nightshade.

Then I saw what he was carrying.

"No!" I gasped, for there in the demon's inky black claws was Kiyoko's sword, Ikari, its naked blade flashing red in the light shining down from above.

My heart sank and the tears welled in my eyes. Kiyoko would never give up Ikari unless she was dead. And as if reading my mind, the Black Fairy smiled at me and handed Ikari to the prince.

"If you're as sentimental as Alistair Grim," said the prince, "you might want to use the shinobi's sword in the tournament. There'd be a certain poignancy in that, don't you think?"

The prince tossed Ikari at my feet.

"Besides," he added dryly, "she won't have much use for it now."

The entire court once again erupted with laughter, but I just swallowed back my tears and picked up Kiyoko's sword.

"Why not just finish me here?" I said. "Why go through all the trouble of a tournament when I surely won't be able to give you much of a fight?"

"Because I'm sentimental too," said the prince. "Chalk it up to the *old gladiator* in me!"

The prince for some reason thought this comical, and he

and the Black Fairy again laughed heartily. The other monsters joined in, but I sensed they didn't understand what they were laughing at any more than I did.

"But seriously," said the prince, regaining his composure. "This will be the last tournament for quite some time, for now that I have the animus, my subjects and I are going to be quite busy gathering up our army and preparing for war—the first step of which, I assure you, will be the destruction of Alistair Grim's Odditorium."

An icy chill whipped through my body. "You'll have to find someone for your tournament elsewhere," I said defiantly. "I won't fight."

"Oh, but you *will*," said the prince. "If you are victorious, your life shall be spared and you are free to leave this castle. However, the victor also has the choice to free someone else in his place."

"Cor," I said, suspicious. "You expect me to believe that if I win, you'll spare Cleona and set her free?"

"If that's your wish. You have my word on that."

I looked down at Kiyoko's sword, thinking.

"You see, Grubb," said the prince, "as it was during the gladiatorial contests of ancient Rome, a man fights hard for his own life, but he fights even harder for the life of someone he loves. The shinobi understood this, which is why they refused to fight each other but fought so valiantly when given the chance to free one of their own. Kiyoko was the only one ever successful. As for the others . . ."

The prince chuckled, and his court joined him.

"How do I know you'll keep your word?" I asked. "How do I know that you won't absorb Cleona's magic if I win?"

"You don't," said the prince. "But you know for certain that I will absorb her magic if you lose."

I swallowed hard and clenched Ikari to my breast. "Very well then, sire," I said after a moment. "I'll fight."

"Then it is decided!" the prince announced, rising. "Young Grubb shall give us our tournament!"

The crowd cheered, and then a loud wailing rang out above the din. The entire court turned at once in its direction.

"*AAAIIIEEEEEEEEEEEEAAAAAAAAAAHHHHH!*" Cleona wailed in the distance.

But rather than feel frightened at her foretelling my doom, a wave of relief washed over me. Cleona was all right.

"*AAAIIIEEEEEEEEEEEEAAAAAAAAAAHHHHH!*" she wailed again, and Prince Nightshade cupped his hand to his ear as if he was straining to hear.

"Do you hear that, lad?" he said. "Your funeral dirge has begun."

EIGHTEEN

The Tournament

Fortunately, the tournament began at once. I say
fortunately because there was no time for me to
be frightened as the court prepared for the fes-
tivities.

Prince Nightshade gave the order, and the trolls again
commenced their slow, steady drumming. The monsters
joined in with chants of "Fight! Fight! Fight!" all the while
clapping their hands and stomping their feet to keep the time.

I could no longer hear Cleona above the din, nor could I
hear what Prince Nightshade said to the Black Fairy before
the prince flew up and vanished back into the ceiling whence
he came. The Black Fairy gave a deafening screech, and then
took off like a shot across the Great Hall and out into the
yard. Sirens and other winged creatures set off after him, and
then the monsters began moving in a single mass before me.

"Fight! Fight! Fight!" they chanted, pushing and shoving

one another as they led me from the hall—the Shadesmen in a protective circle around me, the trolls bringing up the rear with their low, steady death march.

Judge Hurst and the prince's attendants were behind me too, and as the crowd of monsters spilled out from the castle, on the far side of the yard I spied a massive drawbridge closing into the castle walls. The prince's crows were perched atop the tower, and a group of goblins was already in position on the nearby battlements. Each goblin held a long, skinny horn, and upon seeing me, they raised them to their slobbering lips and blew a drawn-out, groaning *buhwaaahmp!*

The drums beat on, and the monsters continued to chant "Fight! Fight! Fight!" as they formed a wide, open circle in the middle of the yard. The Shadesmen escorted me to its center, and then left me there alone with Kiyoko's sword.

Buhwaaahmp! groaned the horns again, and the chanting crowd broke into cheers. I followed the monsters' gaze and discovered Prince Nightshade standing on the balcony above the castle doors.

"Fight! Fight! Fight!" cried the prince, pumping his fist, and his subjects immediately took up the chant again.

The drummer-trolls now flanked the entrance to the stables, out of which emerged the prince's chariot, drawn by four black steeds. My heart sank. Phantom was among them—the

Black Fairy must have brought him back to the castle after he killed Kiyoko.

Buhwaaahmp! groaned the horns. Phantom and the other steeds reared, and a goblin attendant rushed over to settle them. A wave of panic rippled through me, and I gripped Ikari tightly with both hands.

I might be Mr. Grim's apprentice, I thought, but when it comes right down to it, I am still just a humble chummy. What chance could a lad like me possibly have against these monsters?

The first weapon a shinobi learns to use is her mind, I heard Kiyoko say in my head. She was right. If I was going to save Cleona, I stood a much better chance using my wits than a sword.

The prince raised his hand, the drumming stopped, and the crowd of monsters immediately fell silent. Indeed, *everything* was silent, except for the wind in the battlements.

That's odd, I thought. If I were going to die, wouldn't I hear Cleona wailing?

As if reading my thoughts, the prince shouted, *"Bring me the banshee!"*

Everyone turned their eyes toward the tower as a loud cranking noise began overhead. Near the top of the tower, an entire section of the wall split apart and a small platform extended out over the yard. On top of the platform was a large conductor sphere like the one in the Odditorium's engine room. But instead of glowing yellow, this sphere flashed and crackled with red and purple light.

"Cleona," I gasped. I could see the vague outline of her form inside, but I could not see how she was faring, nor could I hear her wailing.

No matter, I thought. I am still going to die. I just can't hear her wailing because she's stuck in that sphere.

But maybe something has changed, I answered back in my head. *Like when Mr. Grim changed his mind about riding the wasp. The future can be altered by even the most insignificant decisions made in the present, he said.*

But the only decision I made was to use my wits instead of Ikari.

"The banshee!" the Black Fairy hissed, and he stepped out onto the platform beside the sphere. The crowd cheered, and the Black Fairy spread his wings and took off across the yard. All eyes followed him as he circled the battlements—but something else had caught my attention.

Neither the ground nor the castle's outer walls were covered in magic paint. The sun was still low in the sky, so the majority of the yard was engulfed in shadow. And the stench—I would not have though it possible, but the stench out here seemed even worse than in the Great Hall.

"Mack," I muttered, glancing over at the prince. I could see that the pocket watch was still tucked in his belt. And just like that I knew what I had to do.

The Black Fairy swooped down into the yard, snatched up Judge Hurst, and landed with him on the prince's balcony. A handful of goblin attendants stepped out beside them, and then Prince Nightshade, leaning over the balustrade, addressed the crowd below.

"Today dawn's a new age," he began. "An age in which the old kingdoms shall be destroyed, and the new kingdom, *our kingdom*, shall rise up to rule both the land of the living and the Land of the Dead!"

The crowd of monsters cheered.

"And so, to celebrate this auspicious occasion, I give you a very special tournament. A tournament that shall mark the beginning of the *Age of Animus*!"

Buhwaaahmp! groaned the horns, and the crowd cheered. The prince nodded proudly and let them go on for a bit, then he raised his hand and all was silent.

"And now, I have the great honor of introducing our three eligible combatants. First, one of our fiercest competitors of all time, this giant of gore comes to us from the fjords of Norway with an impressive record of seventeen kills. That's right, the most terrible troll of them all, *Borg Gorallup*!"

The monsters cheered, and a squat, pear-headed troll with

an eye patch and a pronounced underbite stepped forward from the crowd. His shoulders were as broad as Nigel Stout was tall, his legs and arms as thick as tree trunks. And he was naked, save for an animal skin around his waist and a pair of spiked leather bands around his massive forearms. In one hand he carried a large mallet; in the other, a studded wooden shield.

"Gorallup!" the troll croaked, and he pounded his mallet in the dirt. The earth shook and the crowd cheered, and then the prince raised his hand and all was silent.

"Our next combatant," he announced, "comes to us from deep within the caves of Lascaux, France. Boasting an unparalleled record of twenty kills even, and known in these parts as 'the Scourge of the Shinobi,' your favorite goblin and mine, *Moosh-Moosh*!"

The crowd went wild, and one of the larger, toad-faced goblins leaped over the heads of the other monsters and landed next to Borg Gorallup. His green, sinewy frame stood only as high as the troll's waist, but his yellow eyes glowed fiercely, and between his pointy ears stretched a mouth littered with fangs. The goblin carried no weapons, but given the long, sharp claws on his hands and feet, I could understand why he didn't need them.

"And finally," said the prince, silencing the crowd, "I give you one of the newest additions to our menacing menagerie.

An up-and-comer who has already racked up an impressive nine kills, each in less than a minute!" The crowd murmured excitedly. "Here he is, that mysterious, entomological nightmare from the Americas—*Moth Man*!"

The monsters cheered as Moth Man spread his enormous insect wings and lifted off the battlements. From where I was standing I could see that the black-eyed creature was carrying a spear, but when he landed next to Moosh-Moosh I noticed that—well, with a name like Moth Man, perhaps no further description is necessary.

"There you are, then, Grubb," said the prince. "Choose your opponent and give us our tournament."

"I choose none of them," I said, and the crowd grumbled with confusion.

"None of them?" asked the prince. "But surely you know what will happen to the banshee if you choose not to fight."

"I do, sire," I said. "Which is why I choose to fight *you*."

The monsters gasped.

"*Me?*" asked the prince, amazed. "You choose to fight *me*?"

"Yes, sire."

"But don't you know who I am, lad? Don't you know that there is not a creature on this planet, magical or otherwise, who has ever proven a match for me?"

"Perhaps, sire. But if it's all the same to you, I'd like to take my chances. Unless, of course, you're a coward."

The monsters gasped and the prince stiffened. The air hung tensely for a moment—but then the prince threw back his head and laughed heartily. The Black Fairy and the rest of the crowd joined him, and for a moment I thought the whole castle might come crashing down from all their belly shaking.

"Very well," said the prince, regaining his composure, and his subjects immediately grew silent. "How can I resist such insolence?" Then he leaned over the balustrade and whispered: "Besides, it will make snuffing out Alistair Grim all the more enjoyable when I tell him it was I who broke your neck for you."

The prince smiled widely and then jumped down from the balcony.

The Black Fairy screeched, the monsters cheered, and Gorallup, Moosh-Moosh, and Moth Man scattered back into the crowd.

The prince landed in the yard, and a cloud of dust billowed up around him—his bright red eyes shining through like a pair of lanterns in the fog. Prince Nightshade lowered the visor on his helmet, and as the dust began to settle, he drew his fiery-tipped whip.

A bolt of terror shot through me, and with my heart in my throat, I raised Ikari as I had seen Kiyoko do against the dragons. As if in reply, the prince raised his whip and cracked it over his head. Lightning flashed and thunder rumbled, and then the goblins gave the signal for the tournament to begin.

Buhwaaahmp!

"Fight! Fight! Fight!" cheered the crowd.

I held the blade out in front of me in expectation of the prince's attack. But instead of advancing, Prince Nightshade fell to his knees, stretched his arms out wide, and said: "Go ahead, boy! Strike me anywhere you wish."

I hesitated, unsure of what to do.

"No need to be afraid," said the prince. "You have my word as a gentleman. I give you the honor of first strike as a reward for your courage."

This had to be a trick, I thought, and held my ground.

"Does everyone here distrust me so?" the prince asked with mock offense, and the monsters laughed. "Very well, then, Grubb. I shall allow another to strike first in your place." The prince surveyed his subjects and shouted, *"Gorallup!"*

The troll stepped forward from the crowd.

"Oh, Borg, dear," said the prince. "Would you be so kind as to show young Grubb that my word is still that of a gentleman?"

"Gorallup!" croaked the troll, and without hesitation, he lumbered over to the prince, raised his enormous mallet, and brought it down hard upon the prince's head!

I gasped, unable to believe what I was seeing, but as soon the troll's mallet struck the prince's helmet, it snapped back, lifting the troll off his feet and sending him flying backward into the crowd.

The monsters laughed and applauded, and then the prince stood up as if nothing had happened.

"Thank you, Borg," he said. "Consider the first blow yours, young Grubb. And so, without further ado, it is my turn."

Instinctively I backed away, and then the prince came rushing toward me. He looked as if he was about to leap into the air, but at the last moment he skidded to a halt in the dirt, cocked his whip, and let it fly.

I dove out of the way just in time, and the fiery tip exploded somewhere behind me. Lightning flashed and thunder cracked, and the air was sucked from my lungs as I landed face-first in the dirt.

Coughing, I quickly rose to my feet and turned around. The prince was upon me at once, swiping his black-armored fist straight for my head.

I ducked and rolled away as fast as I could. And before I even had time to regain my footing, the prince's whip came for me again.

Somehow I scrambled out of the way, and Prince Night-shade's whip cracked near my bottom and sent me tumbling head over heels. Finally I landed on my feet, and the monsters burst into raucous applause. Even the prince himself let out a howl of laughter upon seeing me standing there on guard with Ikari.

"Splendid!" he said. "This is proving to be quite entertaining after all!"

Then the prince raised his whip again, and just as its tip crested above his head, in a split second I decided that it was time to make my move.

I tossed aside Ikari and took off like a shot. The crowd cheered—and I heard the whip come cracking down—but I dove between the prince's legs and sprang to my feet behind him. Hidden beneath his cape, I grabbed hold of his sword belt and pulled myself up to his waist.

Prince Nightshade whirled around and gasped at seeing me gone. But then the monsters began to laugh and point at him, and he understood where I was. The prince twisted and turned and batted blindly at his back, but his chunky black armor made it impossible for him to reach me. Still, he cackled heartily and, to please the crowd, shook his bottom as if dancing a jig. The monsters nearly fell over with laughter, but I quickly slipped my hand around his waist and snatched Mack from his belt.

Then, without warning, Prince Nightshade fell backward in an attempt to squash me, but I let go of him just in time and tumbled away in the dirt. The prince landed square on his bottom, shaking the ground, and as the crowd was distracted by his antics, I opened Mack and tapped him on his XII.

"What time is it?" he cried, crackling to life.

"No time to explain, old friend," I said. "Just stick to the shadows for as long as you can and try not to fizzle out."

"What the—?" Mack said, spinning round. "Where are we, Grubb?"

I promise I'll get you back," I said.

The monsters began pointing and shouting, "Animus! The boy has the animus!" Confused, Prince Nightshade rose to his feet and groped at his belt, but upon catching sight of me with Mack, he let out a deafening roar of, "MINE!"

"My apologies, Mack," I said.

And with that I promptly hurled Mack into the crowd.

"McClintock!" he cried as he sailed through the air. The monsters gaped and gasped, and then one of the goblins reached up and caught Mack in its claws.

"Give me back the animus!" the prince screamed, but the monsters ignored him and began fighting with one another for possession of Mack.

"Let go of me, ya ugly neep!" Mack shouted, his blue light illuminating the monsters' faces as they tossed him about. And then old McClintock was swallowed up into the crowd.

"MINE!" cried the prince, pushing his way amongst

them, and the Black Fairy swooped down from the balcony and joined the fray too.

It's now or never, I thought, and I retrieved Ikari and raced across the yard. It sounded as if total bedlam had broken out behind me, but I dared not look back, and quickly dashed over to the prince's chariot. I climbed up onto Phantom's back, and when the stallion reared, I grabbed hold of the stable roof and pulled myself up. From there, I somehow managed to hoist myself up onto the battlements, sword and all.

It was then that I saw the first of the doom dogs take shape in a darkened corner of the yard below. I'd remembered from our previous encounter that it took nearly a minute for them to appear after Mack was opened. And as if on cue, another of the hounds materialized in the shadows nearby. And then another. And another—their burning red eyes brightening as they picked up on the animus and set off toward the crowd of scuffling monsters.

A chill shot through my body—I was counting on those smelly monsters to throw the doom dogs off my scent. After all, if the doom dogs tracked people who touched the animus, wouldn't they track monsters, too? That was my hope, anyway.

I dashed across the battlements as fast as I could, and just as I reached the corner of the castle wall, a cry of anguish from the yard told me my plan was working.

"Get it off me!" a monster screamed. "Get it off me!"

Gazing down from the battlements, I saw Moosh-Moosh come tumbling out from the crowd. He landed in a sunny portion of the yard, screaming and thrashing about in an all-out brawl with his shadow—which, to my horror, had taken on the shape of a large, black hound. Nigel's warning from the marketplace echoed through my mind.

Sunlight or no sunlight, once a doom dog latches on to you, you're as good as done for.

More monsters began tumbling out into the sunlight, each screaming and wrestling with a doom dog. But the prince and the Black Fairy ignored them, and just batted the others out of the way as they searched for Mack amidst the crowd. My heart squeezed with worry for my mate, but my plan demanded that I rescue Cleona first.

Besides, I thought, it'll take more than a gang of monsters to scrap old Mack.

I took off again across the battlements. The horn-blowing goblins had also joined the ruckus, so I had a clear shot across to the tower—but then something in the yard again caught my attention, and I stopped dead in my tracks.

Prince Nightshade seized McClintock from the crowd and punched one of the trolls in the face. The troll went flying backward, taking out at least a dozen or so of his mates along the way as the doom dogs dragged more monsters into the sunlight. I counted seven of the hounds in all—their victims screaming and writhing in agony as the other creatures backed away in terror.

The prince, on the other hand, seemed unafraid. He stormed over to Moosh-Moosh and, lifting the visor on his helmet, shot the goblin with a bolt of red lightning from his eyes. For a brief moment Moosh-Moosh was engulfed in a shower of shimmering sparkles, but then the light dissolved, and with it, the goblin's doom dog too.

"Rise," said the prince, and Moosh-Moosh stood up and stared vacantly ahead. His eyes were no longer yellow, but glowed with the evil of a purple-eyed Shadesman.

I gasped in amazement. So that's how the prince uses the animus to make his Shadesmen. He shoots his magic at them just before the doom dogs take their souls!

Then a voice in my head told me it was no time for gawking.

My legs sprang into action, and as I climbed up onto a parapet, I was aware of the prince shooting more of his red lighting in the yard below. My heart sank at the idea of him making more purple-eyed Shadesmen, but still, my thoughts had room for only the tower. The jump from the battlements to the platform that held Cleona's sphere was much farther than it had appeared from the ground.

"I'll never make it," I said to myself, and then the Black Fairy landed on the battlements beside me. My blood froze.

"THE BANSHEE!" roared the prince, and I glanced down into the yard to find Nightshade and his entire court of monsters staring up at me.

The Black Fairy screeched and reared back his head to spit.

Jump! I told myself. And before I could think twice about it, I did.

The Black Fairy spewed his bolt of thick black fire—I could feel its heat through the soles of my shoes—but thankfully I had jumped just in time and the bolt blew apart a section of the battlements instead.

As I feared, however, my landing came up short, and I hit the platform with my lower half dangling over the side.

"No!" the prince shouted at the Black Fairy from below. "You'll hit the banshee!"

I grabbed one of the sphere's conductor pipes and pulled myself up onto the platform. I took in the whole of the contraption at once. Unlike the sphere in the Odditorium's engine room, its polished steel pipes twisted back into the sphere itself. And there was Cleona inside, staring back at me amidst the crackling red and purple light. My heart soared. She was all right!

"Thank goodness you're safe," I said. Cleona pounded her

fists against the inside of the sphere. I could see that she was trying to tell me something, but I couldn't hear her through the red and purple flashing glass.

"Don't worry, Cleona," I said. "I'll get you out!"

But then, in the reflection of the polished steel pipes, I saw the figure of the Black Fairy rise up behind me.

Without thinking, I struck the sphere as hard as I could with Ikari—but the blade merely bounced off, the force of it spinning me round. At the same time, the Black Fairy swung his fist for my head. Happily, I still had enough wits about me to duck, and the demon smashed one of the conductor pipes instead, tearing it free.

A freezing blast of air hit my cheek. The Black Fairy screeched and raised his fist to pound me. But then, in a streak of bright blue light, Cleona shot out from the ruptured pipe like a cannonball.

"AAAIIIEEEEEEEEEEEEAAAAAAAAAAHHHHH!" she cried, and slammed headfirst into the Black Fairy's chest. The creature screamed, his arms and legs pinwheeling as he fell backward off the platform and out of sight onto the battlements below.

"Behind you, Grubb!" Cleona cried, zooming back in my direction, and I spun round to find Prince Nightshade standing above me atop the sphere. In one hand he held McClintock; in the other, his fiery-tipped whip.

"MINE!" roared the prince, readying to strike, but then Cleona whizzed past me and slammed smack-dab into his face. Nightshade howled with surprise, and as he tumbled off the sphere and into the yard below, Mack went flying from his hands.

"Mack!" I cried. And in a blur of streaking blue, Cleona darted upward and snatched him from the air.

"Quick, Grubb, we've got to get out of here!" she said, and she traded me Mack for Ikari. I slipped Mack into my remaining pocket, and Cleona stood with her back to me. "Wrap your arms about my neck," she said. I obeyed, and in a flash Cleona took flight, soaring up and over the yard with me hanging on behind her.

"*After them!*" Prince Nightshade shouted. He leaped into the air and cracked his whip, but Cleona had already flown us much too high for him to reach, and the prince tumbled back to earth with a roar of frustration.

"*Bring me the animus!*" he cried, dashing for his chariot. Scores of Shadesmen mounted their skeleton steeds, while other monsters scrambled for weapons and shouted for the drawbridge to be lowered.

Higher and higher we climbed. And as Cleona flew us out beyond the battlements, I could see that the castle moat was completely empty. Farther off, all around the moat was a rocky cliff that dropped off abruptly into a sea of dark clouds, giving one the impression that Prince Nightshade's fortress had been ripped from the earth, ground and all.

The sound of a tolling church bell drew my attention back to the castle. The heavy wooden drawbridge was being lowered over the moat.

"They're coming!" I cried.

"I am well aware of that, thank you," Cleona said.

As we dove toward the clouds, I looked behind me just in time to see the first wave of Shadesmen galloping out of the castle, and then everything went dark. I held my breath for what felt like hours, certain that at any moment the Shadesmen's arrows would tear into the clouds after us, until finally Cleona and I burst out into a clear blue sky.

"Look!" I shouted. Far below us rolled a land unlike any I had ever seen—rugged hills covered with thick forests and crystal-blue streams that zigzagged toward the horizon in every direction. "Where are we?" I asked.

"I don't know," Cleona said. "But I can't carry you on my back like this forever!"

Thunder and lightning crashed behind me, and I glanced over my shoulder to see Prince Nightshade's chariot burst forth from the clouds—the steeds galloping hard and spitting fire. The Black Fairy and Moth Man emerged close behind, followed by the Sirens and then the Shadesmen on their horses—all of them gaining on us quickly as the prince led the charge.

"Hurry, Cleona!" I cried. The prince cracked his whip. And with a crash of thunder and lightning, the Black Fairy and Moth Man pulled ahead of him.

"The trees," Cleona said. "Maybe we can lose them in the forests below!"

"We'll never make it," I said, gazing down. "We're still too high, and they're coming too fast."

"It's our only hope."

"I'm slowing you down," I cried. "Take Mack and let me go!"

"Pshaw," Cleona said, and she fell into a steep dive.

The Black Fairy screeched, and I peered behind me to discover that both he and Moth Man were diving straight for us. The Black Fairy arched back his head to spit, and Moth Man readied to throw his spear.

"Look out, Cleona!" I screamed. But then a shimmering ball of yellow light streaked across the sky and smacked the Black Fairy square in the chest.

"*Aaaggghhhh!*" he screeched, tumbling upward into the clouds—his wings useless in the glowing yellow bubble.

Moth Man looked around in confusion, and then out of nowhere a giant black hawk swooped down from the sky and snatched him up in its beak.

"NOOOOO!" roared the prince in the distance.

And with that the great black bird gobbled up Moth Man whole.

"Gwendolyn!" I cried.

Yes, there was the Yellow Fairy, tucked snugly in the feathery nape of the giant hawk's neck. She waved at me and then hurled another ball of fairy dust at the prince.

The prince, however, smacked it with his whip, and in a flash of thunder and lightning Gwendolyn's ball exploded in a shower of sparkles.

"Look!" Cleona cried.

I turned round and could hardly believe my eyes.

An entire flock of the enormous birds was coming straight for us. And at the head of the charge was Mr. Grim, mounted upon the lead hawk's back.

"Climb aboard!" he shouted, swooping in beside us. Cleona grabbed hold of his outstretched hand and Mr. Grim swung us up onto the bird behind him.

As we climbed higher and pulled away from the prince, I saw there were about a dozen more of the great black birds following us. On some rode the samurai, but on one of the birds in particular rode—but that was impossible!

"Kiyoko!" I cried.

"You look as if you've seen a ghost," she said, steering her bird alongside Mr. Grim's. Her hood and mask were gone, and her long braid thrashed about wildly in the wind.

"But the Black Fairy said you were dead!"

"He thought I was," Kiyoko said. "He clipped me with his fire and sent me falling into the clouds. Luckily Gwendolyn had gone looking for you, and she caught me in one of her big yellow bubbles."

"I believe this is yours, miss," Cleona said, and she handed Kiyoko her sword. "The prince gave it to Grubb to use in the tournament."

"Once again I am in your debt, Grubb," Kiyoko said with a bow of her head.

Mr. Grim must have thought we were talking about our birds, for he nodded his head and with a smile shouted, "That's right! They're called Thunderbirds! A species of Odditoria indigenous to the Americas!" He pointed at Gwendolyn's bird. "They just love to eat moths!"

Gwendolyn swung her bird beside us, and the other Thunderbirds screeched.

"The Americas?" I asked, amazed. "You mean, down there is—?"

"We were close to the shore when the Sirens attacked!" shouted Mr. Grim. "The reserves and Number One got us inland, and then I sent Gwendolyn and the bats out looking for you! They found Miss Kiyoko instead."

"But how did you—"

"You needn't worry about the others!" said Mr. Grim, interrupting me. "Lord Dreary and Mrs. Pinch are holding down the fort!"

"Why are you shouting, Mr. Grim?"

"I can't hear you!" he hollered back, pointing to his ears. "Beeswax! A precaution against the Sirens!"

"That reminds me," I said to Cleona. "Why weren't you and Mrs. Pinch—"

"Silly, Grubb," she said. "Only men are enchanted by the Sirens' song. Everyone knows that."

"But how did Mr. Grim get the Thunderbirds?"

"Beats me," Cleona said. "But I should think if he could convince the Yellow Fairy to join him, a flock of big black birds would be child's play for Alistair Grim."

Cleona giggled, and as we sped through the air, I gazed back over my shoulder to discover Prince Nightshade and his army gaining on us. Mr. Grim saw it too.

"Samurai!" he shouted. "You take the Shadesmen! Shinobi, you take the Sirens!"

"With pleasure!" Kiyoko replied, and then she and the samurai flew off on their Thunderbirds toward Nightshade's minions.

"Gwendolyn!" shouted Mr. Grim. "You know what to do!"

"Get to gobbling," she shouted back. "Chomp, chomp!"

"No!" Cleona cried. "Prince Nightshade will absorb your magic if you try that!"

"Shut your gob, banshee! I'm not afraid of him!"

"Be sure to aim for the horses, Gwendolyn!" shouted Mr. Grim, oblivious to their bickering. "Your fairy dust will have no effect on the prince!"

"I know what I'm doing, twig!" Gwendolyn shouted, and she quickly banked her Thunderbird away from us. Mr. Grim just nodded and smiled, unable to hear her.

"He's gaining on us!" I cried.

Kiyoko and the samurai had already split off into two groups, and were now approaching the Shadesmen at their flanks. The prince pulled ahead with the Sirens, and the armies crashed into each other behind them—the sound of clanging metal and screeching Thunderbirds echoing across the skies. For a moment I lost sight of Kiyoko amidst the fray, but then the first of the Shadesmen and their skeleton steeds began falling toward the forest below.

"*EEEEYYAA!*" Kiyoko cried victoriously, and she emerged from the mass of clashing soldiers with Ikari held high above her head.

The battle raged on with frightening speed, the samurai slashing the Shadesmen into smoke with their animus-infused swords as Kiyoko banked her Thunderbird in pursuit of the Sirens. She came upon them quickly and cut down two of the monsters at once, their bodies exploding against the clear blue sky in a flash of brilliant red light.

The remaining two Sirens screamed in terror and began their retreat toward the clouds. But before Kiyoko could pursue them, Gwendolyn swooped past the shinobi on her Thunderbird and leveled a ball of fairy dust at the prince.

"Aim for the horses!" shouted Mr. Grim, pulling out the wads of beeswax from his ears. "Don't get too close!"

But Gwendolyn ignored him. "Eat this, you blighter!" she shouted, and hurled her sparkling dust ball straight for the prince. The prince, however, easily destroyed it with his whip, and in a flash of thunder and lighting, caught Gwendolyn with its fiery tip.

"Gwendolyn!" cried Mr. Grim.

But the Yellow Fairy and her Thunderbird were already falling.

"MINE!" roared the Prince, and he steered his chariot into a steep dive after them.

Mr. Grim swung his Thunderbird around and dove after them too—when without warning, Cleona left us and went streaking through the air.

"Cleona!" I cried as she raced downward.

The prince's horses closed in fast on Gwendolyn, who was gently spiraling toward the earth along with the feathers from her fallen Thunderbird. Prince Nightshade raised his whip and snapped it down—but at the last moment Cleona snatched Gwendolyn out of the way, and the tip exploded against the empty air.

Prince Nightshade howled with frustration as Cleona flew skyward with Gwendolyn in her arms. Pulling hard on his reins, the prince swung his chariot around and gave chase. He was upon them almost at once, but before he could raise his whip, out of nowhere Kiyoko leaped from her Thunderbird and landed beside him on his chariot.

The shinobi slashed Ikari in vain against the prince's armor, and in return Nightshade let go of his reins and swung his fist for her head. Kiyoko ducked and scrambled to the front of the chariot. And with a single swipe of her sword, she cut loose the prince's team of horses, and the chariot began falling from the sky.

At the same time, Cleona lighted on our Thunderbird with Gwendolyn.

"Don't look, Grubb," Cleona said, but I could not turn away. And as the prince's horses flew back toward his castle in the clouds, Nightshade knocked Kiyoko's sword from her hand, grabbed her by the neck, and then leaped from his chariot with the shinobi in his arms.

"Kiyoko!" I gasped in horror. But Kiyoko fought on, fiercely punching and kicking the prince all the while she

plummeted with him toward the ground. The chariot crashed and disappeared into the forest canopy below, and then Kiyoko and Prince Nightshade, still in their violent embrace, were swallowed up into the trees too.

"We've got to save her!" I cried.

"A human could not survive that fall," said Mr. Grim, steering our Thunderbird skyward. "Prince Nightshade, on the other hand, *could*."

"But, Mr. Grim—"

"I'm sorry, lad, but she's gone."

I swallowed hard, the tears welling in my eyes.

"Besides," said Mr. Grim, "if we're going to have a chance of saving Gwendolyn, we need to get back to the Odditorium now."

Cleona cradled the Yellow Fairy in the crook of her elbow. Gwendolyn's eyes were closed, and her skin, as well as the once-bright halo of yellow light surrounding her, now glowed a sickly white.

"Fall back!" Mr. Grim called out to the samurai, and in the distance I saw the Shadesmen retreating into the clouds with the samurai and their Thunderbirds close on their tails. Indeed, it seemed to me that now that Prince Nightshade and the Black Fairy were gone, the Shadesmen no longer wished to fight at all. Their numbers had dwindled considerably, but unfortunately our boys had lost a warrior or two from their ranks as well.

"Fall back!" Mr. Grim called again, and the samurai dropped their pursuit of the Shadesmen and fell in line with the Thunderbirds behind us.

"Shouldn't the samurai go after them, Uncle?" Cleona asked. "If they attack the castle, perhaps they can defeat Nightshade's minions once and for all."

"That's exactly what the Shadesmen want," said Mr. Grim. "The shinobi told us that Nightshade's castle is fortified with lightning cannons that I suspect are powered by his Eye of Mars. Add to that his archers and an entire army of evil creatures—no, the samurai wouldn't stand a chance, even with the Thunderbirds and Gwendolyn at full strength."

"But we've got them on the run!"

"We've lost the element of surprise, making a siege on Nightshade's castle at this point impossible. Besides, if my suspicions are correct, the prince's armor will have enabled him to survive that fall. Thus, once his forces regroup and rescue him, he should prove even more impenetrable than his castle."

"Yes, but—"

"I'm sorry, Cleona. I simply don't have the weapons to defeat him. Not yet, anyway."

Cleona sighed, unconvinced, and Gwendolyn's eyes fluttered open.

"Chomp, chomp," she whispered. "Stand and fight, you lily-livers."

"Ssh," Cleona said. "Save your strength, Gwendolyn."

"Shut—your—gob," she replied weakly.

And then the Yellow Fairy slipped away again into sleep.

— N I N E T E E N —

The Mirror

Losing Kiyoko once was hard enough, but losing her a second time left me feeling as if half my heart had fallen with her from the sky. She had saved us from Prince Nightshade, and Mr. Grim said the best way to show our gratitude was to make certain that her death had not been in vain.

"We haven't seen the last of Prince Nightshade," he said. "Therefore, we mustn't cheapen the shinobi's sacrifice by giving him time to catch up with us."

Mr. Grim's words, however, did little to ease my sorrow. And as the Thunderbirds flew us farther and farther into the wilderness, it was all I could do to keep from weeping. Finally, we came to a high, rocky cliff pockmarked with caves. At the base of the cliff, hidden amongst the trees in a small grove, was the Odditorium.

The samurai leaped from their birds and took up position on the roof, while our Thunderbird dropped us off on the balcony. Cleona handed Gwendolyn to Mr. Grim and immediately flew up to her chamber to begin charging the Odditorium's systems.

Just then I felt a rumbling in my chummy coat.

"Begging your pardon, Mr. Grim," I said, handing him McClintock. "But please don't scrap old Mack, sir. We couldn't have escaped Prince Nightshade's castle if it wasn't for him."

"Oh, nonsense," said Mr. Grim, and he opened the pocket watch.

"What time is it?" Mack exclaimed, but then he saw who was looking down at him. "Ach! You're not going to scrap me now, are you, sir?"

"On the contrary, old friend. You shall be rewarded for your bravery."

"Rewarded for me bravery?" Mack asked, amazed.

"No time for particulars," said Mr. Grim, tapping Mack on his XII. Then he slipped him into his waistcoat, and we rushed Gwendolyn into the library. Mrs. Pinch and Lord Dreary were already waiting for us.

"Blind me!" Mrs. Pinch said, squinting. "Is that Gwendolyn?"

"She ran into the wrong end of a whip," said Mr. Grim.

"Good heavens!" cried Lord Dreary.

The Yellow Fairy's color had gone nearly white, and she

was shivering and mumbling incoherently. Mr. Grim prepared a makeshift bed for her on one of the armchairs and then instructed Mrs. Pinch to fix her something from the kitchen.

"I know just the thing," said Mrs. Pinch, and she was gone.

"You stay with her, Master Grubb," said Mr. Grim. "She's fond of you, and your presence will undoubtedly do her good."

Mr. Grim hurried back out onto the balcony, and Lord Dreary followed him, waving his arms frantically.

"Great poppycock, man!" he cried. "Aren't you going to tell me what happened?"

As the gentlemen exchanged heated words outside, I knelt down and took Gwendolyn's tiny hand in my own. Her breathing was shallow and her skin ice-cold.

"Chin up, Gwendolyn," I whispered. "If anyone can take a crack from the prince's whip, it's you."

"Chomp, chomp . . ." she muttered.

A moment later, Lord Dreary returned.

"How does Alistair do it?" he said to himself, sitting down at Mr. Grim's desk.

"Begging your pardon, sir?"

"He's out there right now with the leader of the Thunderbirds. Asked me to excuse him, he did, so they could speak in private. And then there's the banshee and the Yellow Fairy. How does he find them? How does he convince them to help him?"

Other than what Nigel told me about Mr. Grim giving Gwendolyn some chocolate, I really had no idea. Come to think of it, where *was* Nigel?

"It boggles the mind, I tell you," Lord Dreary went on, more to himself. "He uses star charts to calculate our position off the coast of the Americas, lands the Odditorium in its present position, then sets off up that cliff with a mirror and comes back an hour later with a flock of Thunderbirds!"

"A mirror, sir, did you say?"

Mr. Grim entered from the balcony. "We're not out of the woods yet," he said, but upon seeing Lord Dreary sitting at his desk, he cleared his throat with an irritated, *"Ahem!"*

Lord Dreary rolled his eyes and moved away to the bookshelf. And as the old man was busy wiping his head with his handkerchief, Mr. Grim quickly slipped the Lady in Black's mirror from inside his coat to its case upon the desk.

"Now, then," said Mr. Grim, sitting down, "despite the loss of their friend, the Thunderbirds have agreed to assist us if we're unable to get the Odditorium flying again."

"I'm not going to bother asking again how you secured their services," said Lord Dreary. "However, I do think I am owed an explanation as to how you rescued the boy and the banshee!"

"Everything shall be explained in good time. But there are more pressing matters at hand—the first being the unfortunate task of deciding what Odditoria to take with us in the event Gwendolyn does not recover."

"You mean, you're planning on abandoning the Odditorium?"

"Yes and no. It's only a matter of time before Prince Nightshade discovers the location of the Thunderbirds' caves for himself. And if he should find the Odditorium abandoned here, in addition to pillaging its contents, he would also learn its many secrets. And that is something I simply cannot allow to happen."

"But that means you'd have to —"

"Yes, Lord Dreary. If Gwendolyn does not recover, the Odditorium will be unable to fly. And therefore I will have to destroy it."

I gasped, and Lord Dreary cried, "Great poppycock!"

"It's my own fault," said Mr. Grim, rubbing his forehead. "If only I hadn't been so preoccupied with things here, I might have discovered Prince Nightshade's identity. Consequently, I might've been able to stop him in his tracks years ago."

"So then," Lord Dreary said, approaching the desk, "the story you told me during our journey here—you're saying you've found proof to support your theory that Abel Wortley's murderer and Prince Nightshade are the same person?"

"Proof?" said Mr. Grim. "What I wouldn't give for an ounce of proof. Nothing but hypotheses and supposition at this point, never mind the fact that Judge Hurst is still missing."

"Begging your pardon, sir," I said tentatively. "But Judge Hurst can't be Prince Nightshade. We were prisoners together in the prince's dungeon. The judge ran afoul of him, and Prince Nightshade turned him into a purple-eyed Shadesman."

"Good heavens!" cried Lord Dreary. "Are you certain, lad?"

"I'm afraid I am, sir."

"Well there you have it, then," said Mr. Grim. "After all these years, my prime suspect in the murder of Abel Wortley has been proved innocent."

"But at what cost?" said Lord Dreary, wiping his brow. "Judge Mortimer Hurst a Shadesman? I wouldn't wish that fate on anyone."

"Tell me, Master Grubb," said Mr. Grim. "Did you learn anything else during your imprisonment at Nightshade's castle?"

My throat tightened and my stomach sank. Given everything Prince Nightshade had told me about Elizabeth O'Grady, I felt ashamed for knowing things about Mr. Grim's past that I shouldn't—not to mention that I didn't want to hurt his feelings or embarrass him in front of Lord Dreary. At the same time, however, I knew that I had to tell him what Prince Nightshade had said—or at the very least, the nub of it.

"Well, sir," I began. "The prince went on a bit about knowing you—about your past and such. Said he never guessed you for a collector of magical objects, since you never showed much interest in such things."

"Is that so?" said Mr. Grim, leaning forward intently. "And what else did the prince say he knew about me?"

My heart began to hammer, and my eyes flitted to Lord Dreary. Hadn't *he* spoken of Elizabeth O'Grady to Mr. Grim yesterday, in this very room?

"You can speak plain in front of Lord Dreary, lad," said Mr. Grim, reading my thoughts. "I trust him with my life."

It was clear there was no avoiding it now, but how could I tell Mr. Grim everything without causing him grief? I didn't think it possible, but after sputtering about nervously for a moment, it all came tumbling out anyway.

"Begging your pardon, sir," I said. "But Prince Nightshade made light of your loss, sir."

"My loss?"

"Of Elizabeth O'Grady, sir."

Lord Dreary stiffened and looked anxiously at Mr. Grim. I expected at least the same reaction I'd witnessed in secret the day before, but much to my surprise, Mr. Grim appeared unmoved.

"I see," was all he said, and he sat back in his chair, thinking.

"Alistair, I—" Lord Dreary began uncomfortably, but Mr. Grim held up his hand, and the old man was silent.

"All that was common knowledge twelve years ago," said Mr. Grim. "Still is, apparently. Nevertheless, a job well done, my young apprentice."

I swallowed guiltily and looked at my shoes. Despite Mr. Grim's approval, it didn't feel like a job well done at all. A heavy silence hung about the room as Lord Dreary searched for something to say. But then Mr. Grim hopped up from his desk and crossed to a bookshelf.

"Well, no use getting all gobby eyed about it," he said with a smile. "We're on an adventure, after all, and thus haven't the time for such things."

"But, Alistair," said Lord Dreary, "given what this lad just told us, it appears as if your theory about Nightshade being one of our old antiquities associates is true."

"I'd wager my life on it," said Mr. Grim, scanning his books. "And yet, even if we knew for sure the prince's identity, it wouldn't do us much good unless we could pry him out of that armor."

"Yes," said Lord Dreary. "It appears to be impenetrable."

"Nothing is impenetrable, old friend. Not even the secrets of the universe. You just need the right tools."

Mr. Grim pointed to his head and winked. And then, with a low humming sound, the library's lamps and wall sconces came alive with blue animus.

"Ah," said Mr. Grim. "Looks as if Cleona is doing her part; now all we need to worry about is Gwendolyn."

"Chomp, chomp . . ." she muttered deliriously. And as if on cue, Mrs. Pinch entered with a bowl of steaming brown soup and a tiny spoon.

"Here we are, then," she said. "This should get her going again."

Mr. Grim and Lord Dreary came over to the armchair, and Mrs. Pinch took my place next to Gwendolyn. She set down the bowl on the end table and, gently propping up the Yellow Fairy's head, spooned some of the soup into her mouth.

"Mmm," Gwendolyn said at once. "Chomp, chomp."

"It's seems to be working," said Mr. Grim, relieved.

"Well, of course it is," said Mrs. Pinch. "What kind of witch would I be if I didn't know how to cure a fairy?"

"You mean—" I sputtered in amazement. "You mean Mack wasn't just calling you names? You really are a witch, Mrs. Pinch?"

"But of course! Who else but a witch could run Alistair Grim's Odditorium?"

"Cor blimey!" I gasped. "Then that makes you—"

"Yes, Master Grubb," said Mr. Grim. "Mrs. Pinch is Odditoria, too."

"Great poppycock!" said Lord Dreary.

"I think Master Grubb agrees with you, old friend."

"Her color is coming back now," said Mrs. Pinch. And as the old woman fed her some more soup, Gwendolyn's glow turned yellow again and she blinked open her eyes.

"Where am I?" Gwendolyn asked.

"Back where you belong," said Mr. Grim. "You gave us quite a scare there, going head-to-head with the prince like that."

"A big bully he is," said the Yellow Fairy. "But the boy is all right?"

"Yes, miss," I said, stepping forward. "Thanks to you."

Gwendolyn smiled and tried to sit up. "Right, then, let's get on with round two."

"There, there," said Mrs. Pinch. "You need to eat and regain your strength."

"Yes," Gwendolyn said, shaking her head. "I'm afraid I still feel a bit loopy."

Mrs. Pinch gave her another spoonful of soup. Gwendolyn's eyes grew heavy and a look of peace came over her face.

"What's in that soup?" asked Lord Dreary.

"Most of it's secret," said Mrs. Pinch. "Except for the chocolate. Never met a fairy who didn't like chocolate. Never met a boy who didn't like chocolate either."

And with that Mrs. Pinch produced a normal-size spoon from her apron and gestured for me to take it.

"For me?" I asked.

"Of course," said Mrs. Pinch. "Fairies will eat anything made of chocolate. But since this old witch had to make her brew without her spectacles, I need a taster to tell me if I got the recipe right."

Mrs. Pinch winked and I took the spoon.

"Oh, thank you, ma'am!" I said, and served myself a mouthful.

"Well?" she asked. "Is it good?"

"It's delightful, ma'am. I haven't had chocolate since before Mrs. Smears died. And never in my life have I had chocolate soup!"

"Mrs. Smears, did you say?" asked the Yellow Fairy.

"That's right, miss. The wife of my former master. She died when I was six or thereabouts, and Mr. Smears wouldn't allow me sweets for fear I might grow too fat for the chimneys."

"I thought I recognized you!" Gwendolyn said.

"Miss?"

"You're the lad I left on the Smearses' doorstep twelve years ago!"

"You mean," I sputtered, astonished, "you mean Mrs. Smears was telling the truth about where I came from?"

"Well, of course," said Gwendolyn. "A woman like Mrs. Smears wouldn't lie. And after all, she'd been coming into the Black Forest for years asking me for a child."

"Well, blind me!" said Mrs. Pinch.

"Great poppycock!" cried Lord Dreary.

"An intriguing turn of events!" said Mr. Grim.

"But how," I stammered, "who—"

"You were given to me by your mother," Gwendolyn said. "The hooded sorceress, I called her."

"Hooded sorceress, miss?"

"I never saw her face, you see. And I don't know if she really was a sorceress, but she knew how to summon me in the language of the ancients."

"Who was she?" I asked.

"Beats me," Gwendolyn said. "But she told me she was dying and asked me to find you a good home."

A wave of sorrow gripped my heart. "Then my real mother is dead?" I asked.

"I would think so, lad," Gwendolyn said gently. "But had I known that Mrs. Smears was dead too, and had I known that her bully husband had treated you so unkindly, well, I would've snatched you back and chomped him up right quick!"

The adults laughed, but all I could do was gaze round at them, wide-eyed and gaping. I felt sad at learning about my mother, but then Nigel appeared with Broom in the parlor doorway, and my heart filled with joy.

"Nigel!" I exclaimed, running to hug him. "And Broom! You're all right too!"

Broom, whose stick had been mended with a bandage, gave a quick curtsy and set about tidying up the library.

"Number One fetched her from the water," Nigel said, scooping me up in his big arms. "And sorry I couldn't join the fight, Grubb, but I used the last of my animus to charge up the bats."

"You mean—"

"That's right, Grubb. I only had enough left to send them off before I fizzled out. Cleona just finished recharging me, in fact. So I should be right as rain for a while now."

"Yes," said Lord Dreary. "It's good to have you back, William—er, uh—"

"Nigel, sir," the big man said, smiling. "Less confusing that way, isn't it?"

"Well, well," said Mrs. Pinch, rising with Gwendolyn in her arms. "Given the day so far, I should think that all of us could use an early lunch."

"Come to think of it," said Lord Dreary, "I *am* a bit hungry."

"Me too," Nigel said.

"Chomp, chomp!" Gwendolyn said, and she began to coo.

"All of us downstairs to the kitchen," said Mrs. Pinch, squinting as she carried the Yellow Fairy to the door. "Master Grubb, you take along Gwendolyn's soup."

"Yes, ma'am," I said, hopping from Nigel's arms.

"Oh dear," Nigel said. "I almost forgot. Cleona asked to see you, Grubb."

"Me?"

"That's right. Her chamber is upstairs, two doors down from Mr. Grim's. You think you can find your way up and back down again to the kitchen without my help?"

"Yes, Nigel. One landing up the spiral staircase, through the secret panel next to the lift, and then two doors down from Mr. Grim's chamber."

"Right-o," Nigel said. He took from me the bowl of chocolate soup, and all of us made for the parlor except Mr. Grim.

"I'll be down in a moment," he said, moving to his desk. He looked as if he was thinking very hard about something.

"Everything all right, sir?" Nigel asked.

"Oh yes, Nigel," said Mr. Grim, smiling thinly. "We've got quite an adventure ahead of us once we get the Odditorium up and flying again. I just want to make sure everything is in order."

"Humph," said Mrs. Pinch, annoyed. "Well, blind me if I'm going to keep your lunch hot for you!"

And so we left Mr. Grim in his library. The others traveled down in the lift to the kitchen, while I dashed up the spiral staircase and slipped through the secret panel. The portraits that lined the upstairs gallery had yet to be cleaned of Cleona's chalk mustaches and nasty comments, but still I found no humor in them. On the contrary, a wave of sadness rippled through me as I passed by the portrait of Mr. Grim as a child.

Kiyoko, I said to myself. *She had wanted so badly to meet him.*

I took a deep breath and swallowed back my tears—no time to get gobby eyed when on an adventure, Mr. Grim had said. I hurried down to the end of the hallway, counted backward two doors from Mr. Grim's chamber, and knocked.

"Come in," Cleona said, and I opened the door.

The first thing I saw in the wall opposite me was a large porthole cover with a wheel at its center. Hanging from a mechanical arm above it was a strange machine that looked like a giant silver egg that had been sawed in half lengthwise. Pipes zigzagged from it and into the ceiling in every direction, and sticking out from the egg's belly was a wide, stubby cannon. The rest of the room, including the floor, was covered with hundreds of paneled mirrors. And as I closed the door behind me, it looked as if a thousand other Grubbs closed the door behind them too.

"Over here, Grubb," Cleona said.

I discovered her lying on her back, closer to the floor in another one of the strange egg machines. A mechanical arm connected it to the wall on one side, while a dozen or so pipes connected it to the wall on the other.

"Cor blimey, miss. Is this where you charge the Odditorium?"

"Yes. The mirrors store my animus, and that machine over there with the cannon is Uncle's Sky Ripper."

"That's what Prince Nightshade called it too. A Sky Ripper."

"Speaking of Prince Nightshade, I never got a chance to thank you for rescuing me from that sphere of his. The energy surrounding it prevented me from escaping. So, thank you, Grubb."

"You're welcome, miss, but I should be the one thanking you. You saved me from Nightshade's Sirens, and then you saved me again back there at the castle."

"Pshaw. That's what family's for, and you're part of our family now, aren't you?"

I looked down at my shoes.

"What is it, Grubb?"

"Begging your pardon, miss, but it's not my place to talk to you about it."

"Why not? If you can't tell your family things, to whom can you tell them?"

"I suppose you're right, miss."

"Well, then?"

"Well, miss. While you were stuck in that sphere, Prince Nightshade told me about Mr. Grim and Elizabeth O'Grady."

"Oh," Cleona said, looking away. "I see."

"Then it's true what the prince said? Mr. Grim built the Odditorium to travel to the Land of the Dead and bring back her spirit?"

"Yes," Cleona said quietly. "I'm afraid it is."

"And you agreed to help him, miss?"

"Well, of course. After all, he helped me, didn't he?"

"Helped *you*, miss?"

"Yes, Grubb. Although we banshees can foretell the death of a person to whom we're attached, we cannot tell exactly how or when it will happen. And even if we could, supernatural law dictates that we are not allowed to interfere. If we do, we are doomed to walk the earth in anguish for eternity, and without a family to whom we may attach ourselves. Have you ever heard the wind wail on a dark and stormy night?"

"Yes, I have."

"Those are the cries of banshees who have broken our sacred law of noninterference."

"Good heavens," I said, swallowing hard. "So—if I'm following you correctly, miss—are you saying you tried to interfere with the death of Elizabeth O'Grady?"

"I tried, yes. I was still a novice back then, and had only recently been attached to her family. And when I started wailing, I didn't even know which of the O'Gradys it was for until I saw Elizabeth standing atop that cliff. It was impetuous of me, I know, but before I could think twice about it, I dove into the water after her."

"You mean, she threw herself from the cliff?"

"Threw herself from the cliff and drowned."

"But the sea—you can't fly over water."

"Not for long, no. And struggle as I did, I could not save her before I had to go back to land. But, you see, even though I failed, the fact that I tried to save Elizabeth from drowning was enough for the banshee elders to cast me out. And so there I was, roaming the earth in anguish, until Alistair Grim saved me."

"How did he save you?"

"He found my silver comb."

"Your comb?"

"All banshees have hair like mine, and so they always carry a silver comb tucked in their robes. I lost my comb when I tried to save Elizabeth, and Uncle later discovered it snagged in her petticoats. Most people would have thought it just a silver comb, but not Alistair Grim. He knew the legend of the O'Grady banshees, and concluded that the comb must belong to one of them."

"But how did Mr. Grim save you from your banishment?"

Cleona smiling knowingly. "Alistair Grim: inventor, fortune hunter . . . and some say, mad sorcerer."

"You mean he used his magic, don't you."

"That's right, Grubb. He used my comb and a magical spell to draw me out of banishment and attach me to his family. You see, back then, there was no Odditorium. But still, I thought the least I could do was help him bring back Elizabeth."

"From the Land of the Dead, you mean?"

"It didn't start out that way," Cleona said. "About ten years ago, Uncle originally built a machine to transfer my spirit energy into a dead body—Nigel was his first successful experiment with that. But Elizabeth O'Grady had been dead for two years at that point. And when Uncle realized she wouldn't come back to him as she was in life, he built the Odditorium so that her spirit could live with him here."

"The magic paint. If he took Elizabeth someplace that wasn't protected, the doom dogs would snatch her spirit back to the Land of the Dead."

"That's right, Grubb."

"But why did Elizabeth run away from Mr. Grim in the first place?"

"I don't know. Uncle never told me. However, everything he has done here at the Odditorium has been out of love for her. After all, love is the most powerful Odditoria of them all, is it not?"

"I suppose it is, miss."

"Grubb?" Nigel called from somewhere. "Are you still there, Grubb?"

I gazed round, and Cleona pointed to the talkback beside the door.

"Yes, Nigel," I said, flicking the switch. "I'm here."

"On your way down, would you mind seeing what's keeping the boss? He won't answer on the talkback, and Mrs. Pinch is growing impatient."

"Yes, Nigel. I'm on my way now."

I flicked off the talkback and turned back to Cleona. "Thank you for telling me all this, miss."

"You're welcome, Grubb. As far as I'm concerned, there shall be no secrets between us. Agreed?"

"Agreed, miss."

"However," Cleona said, smiling, "I can't promise there shall be no tricks."

"Neither can I, miss," I said, smiling back. "Which is why, being Mr. Grim's apprentice, I think it best not to tell you where your comb is at present."

"You mean, you know where Uncle hid it?" Cleona asked, amazed.

"Maybe I do and maybe I don't. Either way, I should think the trick's on *you*, miss."

"Why, you little—!" Cleona cried, but I didn't hang around to hear the rest. I dashed laughing from the room and down the hall, bounded down the spiral staircase and through the parlor, and came to a stop in the library doorway.

The wall behind Mr. Grim's desk was still open, so I had a clear view of him out on the balcony. He stood with his back to me, shoulders hunched, his head tilted down as if he were looking at something on his pipe organ.

"Mr. Grim?" I called tentatively.

But he did not respond.

As I approached him, all the questions that I'd never dare ask flooded my head at once. However, as I stepped out onto the balcony, I became aware of a bright light flashing up at Mr. Grim's face.

"Mr. Grim?" I called again.

He stiffened and lifted his head. And as he slowly turned,

I spied the Lady in Black's mirror in his hand. The glass was no longer dark, but fizzled and popped in a kaleidoscope of swirling colors.

My eyes grew wide and my mouth fell open—when suddenly the mirror crackled and flashed, and in its glass I saw my own face staring back at me.

"What an odd mirror," my reflection said, my voice hollow and distorted. "I should think the Lady in Black would have a hard time seeing herself."

I heard Cleona giggle and saw myself spin around, and all at once I understood what I was witnessing. The mirror was somehow playing back the moment when I first discovered it in the library. And just as I saw myself setting the mirror down on its box, the scene dissolved and the glass grew dark again.

I gazed up at Mr. Grim in disbelief, and imagine my surprise to find him weeping.

"It is you," was all he said. "It is you."

— TWENTY —

One Last Bit

The odd was the ordinary at Alistair Grim's. And so, I suppose it's only natural that a lowly chimney sweep like yours truly should wind up being the secret son of a distinguished inventor, fortune hunter, and purveyor of antiquities—not to mention a master sorcerer.

Indeed, Mr. Grim—begging your pardon, *my father*—welcomed me as his son with open arms. We had a lot of catching up to do, he said, but as is so often the case when on an adventure, there was little time to get all gobby eyed about it.

Yes, I'm afraid there were many more secrets to be revealed in the days to come, not the least of which had to do with the Lady in Black's mirror, the return of an old friend, and the quest for more Odditoria.

And yet, if the word *Odditoria*, at once both singular and plural, is used to classify any object living, inanimate, or otherwise that is believed to possess magical powers, perhaps the greatest secret I learned back then is that love truly is the most powerful Odditoria of them all.

You'll have to take my word on that for now.

And who am I that you should do so?

Why I'm Grubb Grim, of course. Spelled like a worm that's unhappy, but with a double *b*. However, as I'm sure you've guessed, I was anything *but* unhappy back then. Come to think of it, I wouldn't have traded my new life at the Odditorium for all the gold in the Lady of the Lake's castle.

Good heavens! There I go getting ahead of myself again.

My apologies, but I'm afraid you'll have to take my word on all that Lady of the Lake business too. At least for now. Father is calling. Time for my organ lesson, you see.

After all, if one is going to inherit the Odditorium, one must learn to fly it.

An intriguing turn of events, wouldn't you agree?

Character List

Some folks in the North Country

Grubb: Name spelled like the worm but with a double *b*, Grubb is twelve years old or thereabouts and the narrator of our story. A chimney sweep by trade, he can also read a bit and count higher than his fingers and toes.

Mr. Smears: Grubb's brutal master, his favorite pastimes include drinking beer and knocking down Grubb for no reason in particular.

Mrs. Smears: Gentle and kind, she died when Grubb was six or thereabouts.

Mr. Crumbsby: A swindler and the proprietor of the Lamb's Inn, he is fat, has red whiskers, and spoils his twin sons rotten.

Tom & Terrance Crumbsby: Fat, redheaded devils like their father, the Crumbsby twins eat loads of jam and enjoy beating up Grubb when they catch him.

The Crumbsby Women: Mrs. Crumbsby and her two daughters, Anne and Emily. They are very fond of Grubb and sneak him food when the others are not around.

Old Joe: A donkey that sometimes shares its stable with Grubb.

A number of relevant persons in and around London

Alistair Grim: Fortune hunter, purveyor of antiquities, and, some say, mad sorcerer. He is the inventor of the Odditorium, a house of mechanical wonders, and thus the chap after whom our story is named.

Prince Nightshade: Mr. Grim's nemesis and antiquities rival, the self-proclaimed prince is an evil necromancer capable of absorbing magical power.

Nigel Stout: Alistair Grim's coachman and all-around right-hand man, he is big and bald and wears a pair of thick black goggles.

Mrs. Pinch: Mr. Grim's nearsighted housekeeper and cook.

Lord Dreary: Mr. Grim's business partner and longtime friend.

Kiyoko: A fierce shinobi warrior and prisoner in Nightshade's castle.

Judge Mortimer Hurst: An enemy of Mr. Grim's, he sentenced Nigel's brother to hang a decade earlier.

Noah the Pickpocket: A dapper thief about Grubb's age.

Frog Eyes & Flat Nose: His not-so-dapper mates.

And, of course, a few who are either dead or just talked about

Abel Wortley: An elderly philanthropist, purveyor of antiquities, and dear friend of Alistair Grim's, Mr. Wortley and his housekeeper were murdered in London ten years before our story begins.

William Stout: Nigel's twin brother, who was hanged for the crime.

Maggie Stout: William's daughter, Maggie, was sent to live in the country after her father was hanged.

Elizabeth O'Grady: Mr. Grim's long-lost love, she died under mysterious circumstances twelve years ago. Grubb often refers to her as the Lady in Black.

Glossary of Odditoria

Not to be confused with Mr. Grim's Odditorium (which ends with an "um"), loosely defined, the word *Odditoria*, at once both singular and plural, is used to classify any object living, inanimate, or otherwise that is believed to possess magical powers.

Some relevant Odditoria at Mr. Grim's

Dougal "Mack" McClintock: Chief of the Chronometrical Clan McClintock, Mack is a Scottish pocket watch who likes a good brawl now and then.

Gwendolyn, the Yellow Fairy: A wood nymph who is very fond of chocolate and gobbling up nasty grown-ups.

Cleona: A mischievous banshee prone to wailing and playing tricks on people.

Animus: The mysterious blue energy that powers the Odditorium's mechanics.

Broom: The Odditorium's maid, she is just that, a broom.

Samurai: Legendary Japanese warriors; Mr. Grim uses their magic-infused armor to guard his Odditorium.

Doom dogs: A pack of vicious shadow hounds charged with fetching escaped spirits back to the Land of the Dead.

The Eyes of Mars: A pair of magical orbs that the Roman god of war gave to his twin sons, Romulus and Remus. Alistair Grim has one Eye, and Prince Nightshade has the other.

The Lady in Black's Mirror: A silver-handled mirror with dark glass that Mr. Grim keeps on his desk.

Number One: A large mechanical wasp.

Thunderbirds: An even larger species of bird indigenous to North America.

Some relevant Odditoria at Prince Nightshade's

The Black Fairy: An evil winged demon and Nightshade's second in command, he excels at blowing up things by spitting bolts of nasty black fire.

Shadesmen: The long-dead armies of Romulus and Remus resurrected by Prince Nightshade.

Sirens: Beautiful but dangerous sea witches whose songs lured ancient sailors to their deaths.

Red Dragons: A clan of half-human serpents that are enemies of the shinobi.

Phantom: One of Prince Nightshade's horses, he can fly and shoot fire from his mouth.

Borg Gorallup: A large Norwegian troll and oft-featured gladiator in Prince Nightshade's tournaments, he holds an impressive record of seventeen kills.

Moth Man: This newcomer from the Americas boasts a record of nine kills, each in less than a minute.

Moosh-Moosh: A pint-sized goblin that tops off the prince's fighting roster with an unparalleled record of twenty kills even.

Various other monsters: Including more goblins and trolls that have allied themselves with the prince.

Acknowledgments

First and foremost, I must thank my superhuman agent Bill Contardi at Brandt & Hochman Literary Agents, as well as my brilliant editors Emily Mcchan, Laura Schreiber, and Elizabeth Law. Words cannot possibly express my gratitude for their enthusiasm and guidance throughout this process, and I am truly honored and humbled to have worked with them. A mountain of thanks must also be heaped upon the magical team at Disney-Hyperion who helped bring this book to life: the amazing Whitney Manger, Su Blackwell, and Colin Crisford for their stunning cover, my keen-eyed copy editor Brian Luster, and the remarkably talented Vivienne To, whose illustrations ended up exceeding my wildest expectations.

As always, I am eternally grateful to my wife, Angela, and my family for their unwavering love and support. Further appreciation goes out to Jessica Purdy and her son, Jack Schneider, whose obsession with Grubb and his adventures made me believe again. Loads of thanks to my colleagues John

Shearin, Jill Matarelli-Carlson, Patch Clark, Natalie Stewart, and Robert Caprio for always taking the time out of their busy lives to read my work, as well as to my former students Malcolm Armwood, Jason Brown, Victoria Kite, Bobby Cassell, McKenna Cox, Andrew Britt, Grayson Sandford, Devan Mitchell, Nick Iyoob, Tyler McAuley, and John Barnick—all of whom unwittingly helped me develop Grubb's voice as I read to them in class. Thanks also to Jim McCarthy at Dystel & Goderich, my old mentor John C. Edwards for turning me on to all things Dickens, and my dear friend Michael Combs, whose insight and collaborative spirit never cease to amaze me.

And last but not least, a long overdue thank-you must go out to my ninth grade English teacher, Mrs. LaFauci. You planted the seed all those years ago; my sincerest apologies that it took so long to bear fruit.

Don't miss Grubb's next adventure!

Turn the page now for a sneak peek.

The Sorcerer's Apprentice

o ahead," Father said, and he passed me the Black Mirror.

The handle was warm to the touch, and I could barely make out my reflection in the mirror's polished black glass. My eyes narrowed and my lips pressed together tightly. This was not the first time I'd gazed upon this strange black mirror. But unlike on previous occasions, I now knew what to say.

"There's nothing to fear," Father said. "All you have to do is ask."

I swallowed hard. "Show me my mother," I said, and the glass burst to life in a swirl of sparkling colors. I gaped in disbelief, my heart hammering as the colors began to churn faster and faster. The mirror flashed, and in its glass appeared the face of a woman weeping. I recognized her from the portrait in the parlor.

Elizabeth O'Grady, the Lady in Black.

"I'm sorry, my love," she said, her voice hollow and distorted. She turned as if something caught her attention, and then her image dissolved and the glass went dark again. A heavy silence hung about the room.

"There, you see?" Father said finally. "Among other things, the Black Mirror is capable of holding the last reflection of anyone who gazes into it, words and all."

"So that's how you knew," I said in amazement. "Because I'd looked into the mirror before, you saw my reflection when you asked to see your son."

"An excellent deduction, my young apprentice." Father took the mirror and slipped it into a wooden case upon the desk. It was nighttime, and yet, in the soft blue glow of the library's lamplight, I could see his eyes had grown misty.

"Begging your pardon, Mr. Grim—"

"Father," he said gently. It had been nearly a month since I learned that the man sitting across the desk from me was my father. But still, I hadn't gotten used to saying it out loud.

"Begging your pardon—Father—but how did you come by this mirror?"

"It was a gift from Elizabeth O'Grady upon our engagement. Legend has it one of her ancestors stole the Black Mirror from a sorceress, after which it was handed down in her family for generations. What you saw was your mother's last message to me before she died."

A long silence passed between us. "I wish I'd known her," I said finally.

"I wish you had too," Father said.

I stared down at my shoes. There were still so many questions I wanted to ask, but Father was not the sort to talk about such things. Besides, we were on an adventure. And when one is on an adventure, there is little time to get gobby-eyed about the past.

"Now, on to more pressing matters," Father said, "the

first of which is preparing you to inherit the Odditorium." He pointed to the notebook of spells on the desk before me. "Let's hear it, then."

"Sumer . . . te . . . sulumor," I read aloud, slowly, and Father snapped his fingers.

"The correct pronunciation is *suh-meer teh suh-loo-mahr*. It's 'Romulus et Remus' in Latin, spelled backward."

"Of course!" I exclaimed, the light dawning, and I uttered the spell again, this time properly.

Father nodded, then crossed to the hearth and pressed a secret button on the mantel. Above it, a large lion's head with glowing red eyes swung open to reveal a hidden compartment in the wall. At the center of the compartment was a small crystal conductor sphere with a tangle of pipes branching out from it in every direction. And inside the sphere floated the light source for the lion's eyes: a fiery glass ball called the Eye of Mars.

Standing on his tippy toes, Father opened the conductor sphere's porthole and removed the Eye.

"There are essentially two types of magical objects in this world," he said. "Ones that are activated by simple physical actions or verbal commands, such as the Black Mirror; and ones that can be activated only by the precise utterance of a magic spell, such as the Eye of Mars."

Father waved his hand over the glowing red ball. "Sumer

te sulumor," he said, and the light went out. I'd seen him do this dozens of times, and yet the simple act of turning the Eye of Mars on and off never ceased to amaze me.

"Go ahead, lad," Father said, passing it to me. I swallowed hard and waved my hand over the Eye.

"Sumer . . . te . . . sulumor," I said—but nothing happened.

"Try it again. A magical spell is only as strong as the belief of the person who utters it."

I took a deep breath. "Sumer te sulumor," I said with conviction, and the Eye of Mars ignited, its red glow warm in my hands.

"I done it, sir!" I cried, and Father mussed my hair.

"That you *did*. Now do it a hundred times more and we'll move on."

"Cor blimey, sir! A hundred times?"

"Consistency is everything in sorcery. Whining is not. Thus, if you wish to inherit the Odditorium someday, I suggest you carry on with your lesson."

Father winked and, raking his fingers back through his long black hair, stepped out through the library's wide-open archway and onto the balcony.

"Sumer te sulumor," I said with a wave of my hand. And as the Eye of Mars went dim again, Father sat down at his pipe organ and began to play. I could barely see him out there in the dark—his long, slender back just a smudge of shadow against the starless sky. And yet the tune he played—"Ode to Joy," I believe it was called—was so festive and cheerful, I could tell how proud of me he was just the same.

My heart swelled, and I tried to carry on with my lesson as best I could, but as Father shifted into a series of expertly fingered flourishes, my eyes began to wander about the library's fantastic contents.

Not much had changed since my arrival at the Odditorium, and yet I could hardly believe that someday it would all be mine. The countless books and clocks and mechanicals. The priceless antiquities. The suits of samurai armor and the lion's head above the hearth—not to mention the Eye of Mars and all the other magical objects about the place.

And yet, for all the wonders I'd encountered, none was nearly so wondrous as the tall, dark man playing the organ out on the balcony.

I suppose every lad thinks his father special—save, of course, for the poor wretch with a father prone to drink and beating him now and then. My father was prone to neither, thank you very much, but to me he was much more than special. In fact, I'd wager there wasn't another father like mine in the whole wide world.

Since when did you *become an expert on fathers?* you might be asking. And for those of you who know me, I must say I can't blame you. After all, when last we left each other, I'd only known my father a short while—not to mention that I caused him quite a bit of trouble back then. However, for those of you joining me on this adventure for the first time, I suppose a bit of catching up is in order.

You might say that it began with a pocket watch and ended with a prince. And somewhere in the middle, a run-away chimney sweep learned that he was the secret son of an inventor, fortune hunter, and sorcerer all rolled into one. That son, of course, was me, and my name is Grubb. That's right, Grubb. Spelled like the worm but with a double *h*, in case you plan on writing it down. And my father was none other than Alistair Grim.

I say "none other" because, had you lived in London at the time, you no doubt would have heard of Alistair Grim. Had you lived in some other place, you might have heard of him there too. Or at least caught a glimpse of him flying about in his Odditorium—a house of mechanical wonders that looked like a big black spider with a tail of sparkling green smoke.

If you didn't see the Odditorium flying about, you most certainly would have heard it. *Where's that organ music coming from?* you might have remarked, upon which (had I been on the ground with you) I'd have replied, *The Odditorium, of course.* You see, that's how Alistair Grim used to fly his house of mechanical wonders: by playing its pipe organ.

The organ sat upon the Odditorium's balcony and faced

outward so that its massive pipes twisted up and down the front of the building like dozens of hollow-steel tree roots. I must confess, I found it very difficult to play the organ properly at first, but eventually I learned how to make the Odditorium go where I wanted it to—except when traveling underwater.

Good heavens! There I go getting ahead of myself. I suppose if I'm going to tell you about all that underwater business, I best back up and tell you how we got there in the first place. Come to think of it, for those of you unfamiliar with my tale, I best back up to the beginning. Otherwise you might get confused and abandon this adventure altogether.

All right, then: the beginning.

Twelve years before I arrived at the Odditorium, Alistair Grim's bride-to-be, Elizabeth O'Grady, fled London under mysterious circumstances and drowned in the North Country. Before she died, however, Elizabeth gave birth to a son and entrusted him in the care of Gwendolyn, the Yellow Fairy. That son was yours truly, and the Yellow Fairy dropped me off on the doorstep of a kind childless woman by the name of Smears. Unfortunately, she passed away when I was six or thereabouts, and for the next half of my life I had the miserable lot of being apprenticed to her nasty chimney sweep husband, Mr. Smears.

Unbeknownst to me at the time, while I was busy

collecting soot for Mr. Smears, my father, Alistair Grim, was busy gadding about the world collecting Odditoria. Not to be confused with his mechanical marvel the Odditorium (which, as you can see, ends with an *um*), the word *Odditoria*, at once both singular and plural, is used to classify any object—living, inanimate, or otherwise—that's believed to possess magical powers.

In other words, the Odditori*um* is the place, and Odditori*a* are the magical things *inside* the place.

Out of all the Odditoria Alistair Grim collected over the years, there are only three from which he harnesses magical energy to power his Odditorium. The first is none other than the Yellow Fairy herself, whose magic yellow dust enables the Odditorium to fly. The second is the red Eye of Mars, which powers the Odditorium's lightning cannons. The third is a mischievous banshee by the name of Cleona, who provides the Odditorium with a blue spirit energy called animus.

Cleona's animus is by far the most important of Alistair Grim's colored energies; for it's the blue animus that gives life to the Odditorium's various mechanical functions.

However, there was *someone else* gadding about the world collecting Odditoria too: a wicked necromancer by the name of Prince Nightshade. And not only did this Nightshade bloke harness power from his magical objects just as Alistair Grim did, but he'd also gathered about himself an army of nearly every evil creature imaginable: dragons, trolls, goblins, and, most terrifying of all, the Black Fairy.

But for all the prince's success at collecting Odditoria, there remained one magical object that continued to elude him: a source of the animus from which he could create an army of the walking dead.

I suppose that's where I come in. I got into some trouble while sweeping chimneys at an inn with Mr. Smears and, fearing for my life, hid myself in a trunk belonging to one of the guests. That guest turned out to be Alistair Grim, who whisked me away on a flying coach and took me on as his apprentice. My entire life had changed in an instant—not to mention that I made loads of new friends, including Father's right-hand man, Nigel, and an animus-powered pocket watch named Mack (short for McClintock). An odd one, that Mack is, for not only does he never run out of animus, he also stops ticking now and then for no apparent reason.

In fact, it was Mack who kicked off this entire adventure. My first day on the job, I accidentally brought him outside the Odditorium, whereupon Prince Nightshade picked up on his animus and came after us with his army of skeleton Shadesmen. However, Nightshade didn't have many of those bone bags left, so he wanted the animus to turn flesh-and-blood people into Shadesmen too. I'd seen him do it myself—to Judge Hurst, Father's old enemy from London—and let me tell you it was not a pretty sight.

So that's the nub of it, and right about where you found me during my lesson. Cleona and I had narrowly escaped captivity in Nightshade's castle a few weeks earlier, and Father had since come up with a plan to defeat him. The only catch? He wouldn't tell anyone except Nigel what he was up to. The fewer people who knew about his plan the better, in case the prince caught up to us before we arrived at our final destination.

Our final destination. I hadn't a clue where it was, but I got the sense that if we didn't get there quickly, Father's secret plan to defeat Prince Nightshade would fail. After all, the evil prince was still out there, plotting his next move to steal Mack's animus and create his army of purple-eyed Shadesmen.

Coincidentally, as I was gazing around the library thinking about Mack's animus, the old pocket watch began shaking in my waistcoat. I'd since traded my raggedy old clothes for an entire wardrobe that Mr. Grim—er, my *father*—had lying about since he was a child. If only my mates back in the North Country could see me now, I thought, they'd think me on my way to being a right proper gentleman.

I slipped Mack from my pocket and opened his red-and-gold-checkered case.

"What time is it?" he cried. His mechanical eyes flashed blue, and his thick, curved hands twirled to VIII and IV so they formed a mustache atop his smiling mouth.

"Quiet, Mack," I whispered. "I'm in the midst of my lesson."

"Sorry to disturb ya, laddie," he said. "But if ya wouldn't mind setting me next to me chronometrical cousin there, I'll shut me gob so's ya can carry on."

I glanced over at Father. He was still playing up a storm out on the balcony, so I placed Mack beside the clock on his desk.

"Ten past eight!" Mack exclaimed, and he twirled his hands to the proper time. "I tell ya, Grubb, now that I always know what time it is, I feel like a lad of yer age. Why, I remember when I was—"

"You best quit your jabbering, or Father might ban you from the library again."

"But passing the time with me clock cousins is me reward for helping ya escape Nightshade's castle. Mr. Grim said so himself!"

"I don't mean he'd ban for you good, Mack. Just until my lesson's over. I've got to do this a hundred times, he says."

Waving my hand over the Eye, I spoke the magic spell and the glass ball ignited.

"Well done, laddie," Mack said. "Tell ya what. You do that ninety-nine more times and I'll keep count for ya. After all, what good's the chief of the Chronometrical Clan McClintock if he can't help his best friend become a sorcerer?"

"Why, that's a splendid idea, Mack. I should think it much easier to concentrate on what I'm doing if I don't have to keep track of how many times I'm doing it."

"All right, then, laddie. Off ya go!"

"Sumer te sulumor," I said, waving my hand, and the Eye of Mars went out.

"That's two," Mack said. "Now try again."

"Sumer te sulumor," I repeated—but as the Eye caught fire, it floated out of my hand and hovered in the air just above my head!

"Aye, yer getting good at this sorcery business, laddie," Mack said. "I didn't know you could make things fly."

"But I'm not doing that!" I cried. I rose to my feet and tried to snatch back the Eye, but it darted away from me and began floating toward the hearth—slowly now, as if daring me to follow.

"Father!" I called out in panic. Father ceased his playing at once and came in from the balcony.

"Done already?" he asked, when the sight of the Eye of Mars hovering near the mantel stopped him dead in his tracks. Father's face grew dark and his fists clenched. A long, tense moment of only clock ticking hung about the library, and then Alistair Grim crossed fearlessly to the center of the room.

"Show yourself," he commanded.

And to my horror, someone actually *did*.